THE TOMORROW SERIES #5
BURNING
FOR
REVENGE

THE TOMORROW SERIES

Tomorrow, When the War Began

The Dead of Night

A Killing Frost

Darkness Be My Friend

Burning for Revenge

The Night Is for Hunting

The Other Side of Dawn

THE TOMORROW SERIES #5

BURNING FOR REVENGE

JOHN MARSDEN

SCHOLASTIC INC.
New York Toronto London Auckland
Sydney Mexico City New Delhi Hong Kong

 Published by Scholastic Inc., 557 Broadway, New York, NY 10012, by arrangement with Houghton Mifflin Company. Originally published in Australia in 1997 by Pan Macmillan Australia Pty Ltd.

ISBN 978-0-439-85803-8

12 11 10 9 8 7 6 5 13 14 15/0

Printed in the U.S.A. 40
First paperback edition, December 2006

ACKNOWLEDGMENTS

Many thanks to Charlotte and Rick Lindsay, Rachel Angus, Mary Edmonston ("Miss Ed"), Paul Kenny, Catherine Proctor, and Helen Kent.

To my sister Louise Marsden, with much love

AN AUSSIE GLOSSARY

abattoir: slaughterhouse

Aga: wood stove

(**on the**) **backfoot:** in a defensive position

batts: insulation material

biro: ballpoint pen

bitumen: asphalt, tar

blowie: blowfly

bugger: something difficult or unpleasant

bush: uncleared Australian countryside

CBD: Central Business District

cactus: doomed

Cazaly: an Australian footballer famous for his high leaps

chewy: gum

chipping burrs: cutting out prickly weeds

chook: chicken

cockies: farmers

crack onto: to make a sexual advance toward someone

crash hot: pretty good

dags: wool around a sheep's anus

daks: trousers

dogleg: a bend in the shape of a dog's leg

dubbin: leather preservative

dunny: toilet

echidna: small Australian mammal

Esky: insulated container, cooler

Fergie: brand of tractor

fibro: type of building material

footy: Australian rules football

fortnight: two-week period

gantry: crane

goss: conversation

graziers: farmers who have sheep or cattle

(**on our**) **hammer:** close behind

hectare: an area equaling 100 acres

hessian: coarse material

Humphreys: dolls named after Australian TV character

jemmy-shaped: curved at each end

jumper: sweater

k: kilometre

Kiwis: New Zealanders

(rate of) knots: going very fast

milkbar: small corner store, mini-mart

Mortein: fly spray

one-tonner: small tray-top truck

Panadol: brand of pain reliever

pile driver: machine that rams posts into the ground

posies: positions

pull-throughs: cords for cleaning rifles

queue: line

rabbiting: gabbing

rack (off): "go away" (said with anger)

rapt: delighted

removalist: mover

rissoles: meat patties

rocket: greens used in salad

scroggin: nuts and cereal mixture, gorp

shires: counties

slab: case of beer

slag: spit

sledgie: sledgehammer

synchromesh: system which facilitates gear-changing in vehicles

Tassie: Tasmanian

tip: dump

torch: flashlight

uni: university

ute: utility vehicle

wasted: not appreciated

whingeing: whining

willy-willy: dust storm

wombat: small Australian mammal

wrigglers: mosquitoes at their larval stage

yabbying: fishing for crayfish

1

The summer storms are the wildest. Maybe that's because they're so unexpected. But they can really rip a place apart. It's like the sky saves it all up, then lets it go in one huge blast. The air shakes. There's nothing soft or gentle about the rain: it pours down, a huge heavy torrent that wets you to the skin in half a minute. The thunder's so close and loud you feel it all around you, like a landslide or an avalanche. And sometimes there's hail.

Before the war, I found summer storms exciting. I enjoyed the noise and the violence and the out-of-control wildness, even though I knew there'd be problems afterwards. Trees blown down or struck by lightning, fresh-shorn sheep getting dangerously cold, creeks flooding.

Occasionally the problems came during the storms. One time I had to go out in a massive rain to move a small mob of ewes, because a falling tree brought down their fence and the rams were getting horny. I started moving the mob but Millie, the dog, got a bit excited and when one sheep went the wrong way she chased it straight into the creek. The creek was running at a million k's an hour, about to break its banks. The water was just beginning to lap over on both sides. The ewe and the dog, both paddling like mad, got swept away. I ran along the bank, trying to find a spot where I could jump in and pull them out. To be honest, I didn't think they had much hope. But a kilometre down the paddock they were washed up on a gravel spit. The ewe staggered out, half-drowned.

Millie staggered out, half-drowned too. She didn't hesitate. She went straight after that sheep again, chasing it back to the mob.

Poor sheep. There are times when I feel quite sorry for sheep.

Another time we were out at the Mackenzies' when a big storm hit. We got home to find a sheet of galvanised iron had come loose on the shearing shed. It was flapping in the wind with a sound I've never forgotten. Like it wanted to beat itself to death — a frantic, desperate, wild noise. When I got up on the ladder, I could see the iron tearing centimetre by centimetre: solid indestructible metal being ripped apart by the wind. It was quite scary trying to hammer down this crazed, thrashing thing in the dark.

Here, in this place I've learned to call home, a summer storm is dramatic. In the Bible it says Hell is a place of heat and fire. This is officially called Hell — that's the name on the maps — and it does get hot in summer. But when a storm drops on top of us, it's hypothermia country and the temperature can fall fifteen degrees in half an hour.

Of course if life had gone the way it was meant I wouldn't be sitting in a little tent in Hell, watching the fabric stretch and pull, watching the rain chuck a tantrum against the fly, listening to the screech of another branch ripping and falling, and trying to keep writing this record of our lives.

I would have been sitting in our snug cabin in New Zealand, eating pizza and reading *Pride and Prejudice* or *The Horse's Mouth* for the fourth time. Better still, I would have been back at my real home, checking the water troughs in the paddocks or yabbying in a dam or cutting the poor breeders out of a mob of cattle, to send to market.

Well none of those things would happen for a while yet. They might never happen again. I just had to accept that, but it didn't stop me playing the old useless game of "if only."

If only our country hadn't been invaded.

If only we could have carried on the way we used to, watching other people's wars on television.

If only we'd been better prepared, and thought more about this stuff.

Then later, when we'd got ourselves out of the battle zone, if only we hadn't agreed to come back and continue the fight, to help the Kiwi soldiers in their failed attempt at the airbase.

Well, we didn't really have much choice about coming back — Colonel Finley put so much pressure on us.

And we put pressure on ourselves.

That was another "if only." I suppose we would have felt guilty if we hadn't come back. Besides, we had such high hopes of meeting up with our parents again. If only we could have all been as lucky as Fi. She at least got to see her parents for half an hour.

I was still burning about Colonel Finley. The helicopter he was meant to send. The helicopter he'd promised us. The way he more or less abandoned us after his Kiwi troops went missing. The way that when we called up and asked for the chopper, suddenly they were too busy. For a dozen crack New Zealand troops we knew there'd have been no problem. But for us, there was a major problem.

The joke was that we'd achieved more with our

rough-and-ready tactics, our homemade bombs and make-it-up-as-you-go approach than just about any professional soldiers could have done. We thought so anyway, and when we were in New Zealand enough people were ready to tell us that. Only now that we were back here, trapped in lonely wild Hell, they seemed happy to forget us.

If only the chopper had turned up and whisked us back to safety. I wanted it to be like a taxi: just dial the number. Where are you going? How many passengers? What name? We'll have it there in no time, love, no worries.

It was hard not to be bitter. We felt like Colonel Finley had dumped us. We talked about it nonstop for a week, till we got sick of it as a topic for conversation, and agreed not to talk about it anymore. That was the only way we could stop it poisoning us.

After we'd finished our week or so of sulking we started getting restless. Lee was the worst. Since he found out about the death of his parents he was burning for action. When I say action I don't necessarily mean revenge, although he sure was keen on that. But I think he could have been distracted from thoughts of revenge if there'd been other things to think about, other things to do.

There was nothing. We'd built a few odds and ends in Hell — the chook shed mainly — but we couldn't build anything else because it was too dangerous. There was such a risk of being seen from the air or even from the top of Tailor's Stitch, the ridge that wound far above us, the west wall of our hideout. Lee didn't seem interested in reading the few books we'd brought, he didn't have his precious music with him and he wasn't in the mood for talking. All he had were his thoughts. He sat alone for hours every day and wouldn't even tell me what he was thinking.

Homer and Kevin weren't any better. One afternoon they spent four hours trying to hit a tree trunk with pebbles. They sat on the bank of the creek and chucked stones at the tree until they ran out of ammo, then they went over and picked up the pebbles and started again. By the end of the afternoon Homer had hit it six times and Kevin three. Fair enough, it was fifty metres away, but I thought they could have done better. I thought I could have done better. That wasn't what bothered me though. It was their mood. They seemed so flat, so uninterested. I nearly suggested going out and attacking the enemy again, just to get them motivated.

As it happened I didn't need to suggest that. Almost at the same moment as I thought it — well, less than half an hour later — Lee suddenly turned to me and said: "I'm leaving here, going to Wirrawee or somewhere. Cobbler's Bay maybe. Stratton even. I'm not going to spend the rest of the war sitting around waiting to be rescued. I want to do as much damage as I can."

My breath went. I knew I couldn't stop him. In some ways I didn't want to stop him. In other ways I did. I was deeply in like with Lee. Maybe even love. I wasn't sure about that. Sometimes it definitely felt like love. Other times I didn't want anything to do with him. When it came to Lee, I felt the full range of emotions, from wild passion to revulsion. On the average I think I was in like with him.

But it wasn't just Lee that I wasn't sure about; it was everything. Maybe it's just a teenage thing, not being sure about stuff. I wasn't sure if there was a God, if there was life after death. I wasn't sure if I'd ever see my parents again, if Lee and I should have made love, if we'd been acting the right way since the invasion, if the sun would rise in the morning or set at night. I wasn't sure if I liked eggs hard-boiled or soft.

So Lee saying calmly and strongly that he was going out to continue the fight — how could I tell him he was doing the wrong thing? I was less sure about that than I was about the sun rising.

We were sitting quite a way up the track, on the last flat bit, at the point where it started to climb to Wombegonoo. For a long time neither of us spoke. I knew what a big statement he'd made. I knew we were approaching the end of our short rest. We both knew we might be approaching the end of our short lives. Death might be sneaking up on both of us right now. Because I knew, of course, that I couldn't let Lee go out there on his own.

I think we both felt that none of us, none of our group of five, would let Lee go alone. In a way I should have resented him putting us under this kind of pressure, not giving me or the others a real choice. He'd done it to us before and I hadn't liked it. I didn't like anyone putting me under pressure, telling me what to do, making decisions for me. I remember going off my head when Homer announced we were coming back from New Zealand in the first place. If it was different this time, perhaps it was because I knew things were getting too desperate; the war was at such a critical stage and our help was needed like never before. We simply couldn't lounge around having long rests between gigs.

When we talked to the others I found things were a bit more complicated than I'd expected. Homer and Fi reacted like I thought they would — pretty much the same as me. But Kevin . . . well. I hadn't let myself think that any of us might go off like he did.

How could I? If I did, I might have to think about my own fears. Those fears had sent me into panic when Colonel Finley said he wanted us to come back from New Zealand. Those fears had taken control of me completely when the enemy soldier walked towards me in the streets of Wirrawee. Those fears caused a scream to come ripping out of my throat, when silence was the only option. For all I knew, my scream might have caused the capture or death of the twelve New Zealand guerillas.

So I couldn't think about Kevin not being as brave as me. I couldn't condemn him for lacking a bit of guts sometimes.

It happened while we were at the fireplace, eating a lunch that was mainly rice, like a lot of our meals these days. Lee started making his big announcement, but he'd hardly finished his first sentence before Homer burst out: "We might as well go and do something. This is hopeless, sitting around here. Even if we do some tiny little thing, it'd be better than this."

"Danger's a drug," I thought, as I sat there watching him. "And you're hooked on it, Homer."

"I don't mind doing little things," Fi said. "I just hope you guys can stop at little things. But you never seem satisfied with that. You always want to go for the big blast."

Kevin said nothing for a minute. Then, with his voice shaking, he said: "I don't think we should do any more. The way Finley's dumped us here . . . it sucks. Why should we do anything for him? He's sold us right down the creek."

No one seemed to know how to answer that. I mean, I

think we did know; it's just that no one wanted to be the one to do it. We weren't too keen on flowery patriotic speeches.

For some stupid reason I opened my mouth though. I had no right to, but I did.

"Kevin, this isn't anything to do with Colonel Finley. We've all said about a thousand times what we think of him not sending the chopper. That's not the issue. The main thing is that we're in a position to do something to help and no one else can. I don't think we've got much choice."

Then I said the stupid thing, the unforgivable thing. "I know we're all scared Kevin, but we've just got to go out there and do it."

There were some things we never said to each other and the word "scared" was one of them. Oh, maybe at night in our sleeping bags when we were being honest and we couldn't see each other's faces, but this wasn't one of those times.

Kevin went red and even Fi, sitting beside me, drew away a little.

"At least I don't scream when I see a soldier," Kevin said.

He got up and walked off. I sat there burning with shame and fury. I knew why he'd said it: even in my rage I knew why he'd said it, but I didn't know if I could ever forgive him. I had enough trouble forgiving myself.

Homer said, "That wasn't very smart Ellie."

"Oh leave her alone," Fi said.

Lee didn't say anything. That hurt too. I thought he would have stuck up for me, especially against Kevin, who he didn't like much.

So that was why I was lying in my tent listening to the

summer storm smashing into the bush, watching the thrashing and threshing of the tent, crying out in fear as a small branch landed on the nylon fly. The thunder boomed and blasted, the rain had never fallen more heavily, and I never felt more alone in my life.

2

We were all paralysed by the tension between Kevin and me. I thought it would blow over in an hour or two, like most of our arguments, like the summer storms. But Kevin wouldn't talk to me and no matter how keen the others were to get out of Hell they didn't seem able to make a move while this coldness went on. I tried to apologise to Kevin, but he wouldn't listen. That made me feel I was definitely in the right now, which didn't help settle things, as it made me less interested in trying again.

On the third day though Lee settled it, in a kind of way, by saying suddenly and aggressively: "Look, I said to Ellie the other day that I was going, whether anyone else came or not. I should have gone then, when I said I was. So the hell with the lot of you, I'm going now."

"I'll come," Homer said, straightaway.

"So will I," Fi said.

"I will if you want me," I said.

"Of course I bloody want you," Lee said, looking irritated.

No one looked at Kevin, who was trying to clean a fry-pan that had some burnt rice stuck to it. I don't know what recipe he'd used for his fried rice, but it hadn't worked too well. His face was red, but probably not from the sweat he put into his scrubbing. He didn't say anything for so long that we gave up and assumed he wasn't going to speak at all. Instead we started talking about what we needed to take with us. Suddenly Kevin interrupted. "You could at least include me in this," he grumbled.

We looked at each other. This time I wasn't going to be the one to say something. No one else seemed in a hurry either. Finally Fi, the peacemaker, said: "Well, we weren't sure if you wanted to come."

"Of course I'm coming," Kevin snapped. "What, did you think I was going to stay here on my own? I'm not that stupid. You saw what happened to Chris."

There was another pause, then we kept going with our plans, with Kevin making the occasional comment, usually negative. For once though we didn't have many plans. I didn't like that. Normally we gave a lot of thought to what we were doing. The longer the war lasted, the more we seemed to make things up as we went along. It made me feel insecure.

There was only one thing I wanted, and that was to go in the direction of Holloway, to look for my mother. The others had no particular objection to that. Homer's parents were thought to be somewhere near Stratton, and we didn't want to go that way. The country there was too built up, too closely settled. It seemed too dangerous for us. We didn't have much clue where Kevin's family was — somewhere to the north apparently. All we knew was that his mother was in the Showground, like my father. We had no hope of getting into the Showground. Anyway, we weren't keen on going towards Wirrawee or Cobbler's Bay for a while. We'd made things a bit hot for ourselves in these places. If we went the long way towards Holloway — via the Wirrawee-Holloway road instead of taking the shortcut through the mountains — we would then have a choice of going to Goonardoo or Holloway. Goonardoo was on the main north-south railway line, so we might be able to do a bit of damage there, and they were both big towns.

That was as far as our actual plans went. The rest of the time we just threw ideas at each other. Lots of sentences beginning with "Maybe we could . . . " or "What about if we. . ." It was like playing "if only" with the future, instead of the past.

Fi wanted to call Colonel Finley, to tell him we were leaving Hell. There was no particular objection to that either. That was the trouble. No one particularly objected to anything, except Kevin, who objected to everything. All we had was this strong feeling that we should get back out there and be useful.

I don't know about the others but I'd started blocking out fears about danger and death. Seeing so many people die, including some of my own friends, had made me feel weird about my own life. I'd moved gradually into a different state of thinking, where I didn't dream much about the future. Maybe that had happened to all of us and that's why we didn't do a lot of planning.

I think I'd started to believe I wouldn't survive the war. One of the slogans people chucked around a lot in peacetime was "Live for the day." It's like in sport, "Take it one match at a time." Unconsciously we'd started doing that now. I'd never lived that way before the war; I hadn't liked the idea at all. It wasn't a good way to farm. "Live as though you'll die tomorrow, but farm as though you'll live forever." Everything you planted, everything you built, had to be for the long term. No good sticking up a fence that would fall down in a year or two. We'd dig a hole a metre deep for a corner post but that wouldn't suit Dad. "Better go down another foot. Be on the safe side."

"You mean thirty centimetres," I'd tease him.

We'd never hold back from planting an oak tree just because it wouldn't come to maturity for fifty years. "I won't live to see this full-grown," Dad would say. Then he'd plant it anyway. He grumbled at the way the nurseries advertised everything as "rapid growth," "quick growing," "instant." He thought that was a bad approach to life.

Now I had to face the possibility that I wouldn't live to see those oak trees full-grown either. I was living the way we never had, the way I'd been taught from the cradle not to live, the way every instinct in my body told me not to live. But it was hard to stick to my parents' ideas in the face of the deaths of Robyn and Corrie and Chris. Their deaths, the deaths of all the other people I'd seen or heard about, and the disappearance of the twelve New Zealand soldiers had been working on me slowly and steadily. Eating away like a creek at a gully. Like footrot in sheep. Like cancer.

So I left Hell with the others, feeling pessimistic, wondering if I'd ever see it again. And with no real plans. If I could find Mum, I'd be happy. I didn't think beyond that. I didn't know if I'd live beyond that. But at the same time I knew we had to keep fighting. We were well past the point where we sat around debating if it was morally OK to fight and kill. We'd gone so far down that road, there was no turning back. We had to go on to the end, no matter what it might be, trusting it would work out OK. Some of our earlier talks about fighting seemed naive to me now.

On and up we climbed. The storm had come through here with a vengeance. Fallen trees cut the track in three separate places. I had this little game with myself, that the three trees represented Robyn and Corrie and Chris, and that if we found any more it would mean some of us would die.

Well, we didn't cross any more on the track out of Hell, but on the way up to Wombegonoo we came to two others. As I climbed over the splintered limbs, the broken branches and the crushed leaves — the trees were very close to each other — I couldn't help wondering if they meant anything. Were they symbolic, or was I just being stupid? In English we'd done so much stuff on symbols. We'd given Ms Jenkins such a tough time about them. "Oh come on Miss," we'd say, "don't tell us the author meant it that way! I bet if he were here he'd say, 'I don't know what you're talking about. I was just writing a story.'"

There was a bit in *To Kill a Mockingbird* where Jem stops Scout from killing a roly-poly, whatever that is, and Ms Jenkins said the roly-poly was a symbol of Tom Robinson, but I don't know, it seemed a bit far-fetched to me.

On the top of Wombegonoo a strong fresh wind was blowing. It had chased away the clouds, and left a sky that glowed. The temperature was cool but not cold. We'd had a lot of rain lately, quite a few storms. They leave the air so clean and clear. They wash the dust away and let the stars shine. But I don't think I've ever seen it as bright as it was that night.

If I were looking for symbols, maybe that was another one. The stars were so many different colours. Mostly shades of white of course, but some tinged with blue, some with red, some with yellow or gold. And others, a few, burning a strong red. When the Slaters had their Japanese friend visit a few years back she told me they were lucky to see a dozen stars at night in Tokyo. Well, I don't know how many we saw that evening. In places they were so bright they became one shining stream of light.

Radio reception was good at first too. Colonel Finley sounded more relaxed. I guess the war must have been going a bit better. I don't know, maybe he'd just had a second helping of dessert. Maybe he'd been promoted. Maybe he was happy to hear our friendly voices. He'd probably been sitting around the office saying "Gee, can't wait to hear from my little buddies again. I miss them, you know. Might send a helicopter to pick them up."

We had to be careful what we said of course. When we were back in New Zealand Colonel Finley told us to assume the enemy was listening whenever we used the radio. He told us to be "brief and circumspect." Col and Ursula said the same thing. I've never figured out exactly what circumspect means but it wasn't hard to guess.

Homer did the talking. He just said we were going out into enemy territory, but not specifically to look for the "Dirty Dozen" — which is what we'd nicknamed the missing New Zealand soldiers. We had no real hope of seeing them again, unless it was by luck. If they were still alive we were sure they wouldn't be in this area. Stratton maybe, but not around Wirrawee or Holloway. The best we could hope for was that they were prisoners, and of course they'd be in a maximum security prison, not Wirrawee Showground.

The nearest maximum security prison was Stratton, as we well knew, and it mightn't be open for business anymore. It took a hell of a pounding during at least one Kiwi air raid that we'd experienced. The air raids might have meant the end of Stratton as a place to lock up dangerous criminals, like us, or the Kiwi soldiers.

So we told the Colonel we were heading in a different direction, to do whatever damage we could. He didn't sound quite so relaxed when we told him that. In his usual dry formal way he said: "Anything you do will be appreciated. If they have to move one soldier to your district in response to your activities, then that's one soldier less to fight in the critical areas. Is there anything we can do for you?"

It was a pretty illogical question, as there wasn't much he could do from way back in Wellington. But Homer grabbed the chance. "A lift out of here would be nice."

Colonel Finley actually sounded a bit guilty when he answered. "Don't get the wrong idea. We haven't abandoned you. We will get you out, but we just can't do it right at this moment. Don't give up on us though."

I think we all cheered up a bit when we heard that. But a moment later the reception went crazy: static and whistles and chainsaw noises. Homer started trying to call the Colonel back but I stopped him. The sudden loss of the signal and the weird noises on such a clear night scared me. It made me think that maybe one of our fears was justified: maybe they were monitoring us. I got him to turn the radio off. There wasn't any point anyway. It was good to hear a friendly adult voice — nice and comfortable — but there was nothing else we could say to him. Not much else he could say to us, either.

We left pretty soon after that. We'd done our packing. Lee took the radio, wrapping it in plastic in the little emergency pack that he carried around his waist. I watched him, half smiling. He was so organised, so thorough. Sometimes it annoyed me, maybe because I knew I wasn't like that myself. This time I couldn't help making a comment. "You're like a girl, you're so neat," I said.

Lee shrugged. He didn't seem upset. "You might thank me one day," was all he said. I knew he was right, and I knew my comment had been unusually dumb — even for me — so I shut up.

We threaded our way along Tailor's Stitch. Oh, "threaded our way" — I think I just made a joke. Well, it's what we did. I mean I exaggerate a bit when I write about Tailor's Stitch. It's not like a razor blade, where if one of the boys fell with a leg on either side he'd have a nasty accident. For most of the way you can walk quite easily, sometimes even two people side by side. At other points though it really is narrow and you have to be a bit careful. I mean if you did fall you wouldn't plunge a thousand metres to your death. You'd just roll down the slope a way. If you fell awkwardly you might break a leg, but you can do that anywhere of course.

There is a track, worn by the boots of bushwalkers over the years. It's always been quite a popular area for bushwalking. Some weeks we'd get a dozen people coming through our place on their way up to Tailor's Stitch. Other times, especially in winter, we'd go a couple of months without seeing anybody.

The track wasn't just made by humans. I was leading, followed by Homer, then Fi, then Lee, with Kevin quite a way back — surprise, surprise. But I had to slow down when I found myself behind the fat backside of a wombat, waddling along at his own pace. Wombats are a law unto themselves. When I was little, I had a friend out from town for the weekend: Annie Abrahams. She'd never been on a farm before, and the first night, just after dark, we were coming back from putting the chooks away — a little later than we should have — and she saw a wombat. Before I could say anything Annie ran up and gave it a hug. I guess she thought it was some kind of cute cuddly bear. Well, the wombat didn't hesitate. He turned around and buried his teeth in Annie's leg. She screeched like a cockatoo at twilight. I tried to pull the wombat off, but it was impossible. They're so strong. I was screaming for Dad, and Annie was screaming nonstop and the wombat was grunting louder than a bulldozer on a slope. It was scary. I didn't know how much damage it might do to Annie. I thought her leg might be mangled to pieces. Eventually Dad came running out. He tried to pull the wombat off too and failed, and finally he gave it a hell of a kick in the guts. The wombat let go and staggered away into the darkness. Then I didn't know whether to be more upset about the health of the wombat or the state of Annie's leg. But her leg wasn't too bad. Although it was bruised, the skin wasn't broken — I think it was more the shock and fear that had her screaming her head off.

I never found out what happened to the wombat.

Another time a wombat got trapped in a small toilet at the end of the shearing shed. I don't know how it got in and I sure as hell don't know why it got in. Looking for food maybe. Maybe it wanted to use the toilet. Anyway no one found it till morning. I wasn't there when they got it out, but I know it took forever. I saw what damage it did though. Unbelievable. If you'd gone in with a sledgie and spent the night swinging it round at full strength you couldn't have done more damage. It was a wooden dunny lined with fibro, but there was no fibro left intact. It was in fragments all over the floor. The only bits still on the walls were the little pieces nailed to the timber. But much of the timber had been splintered and broken. It was like the wombat spent the whole night headbutting the place. I guess that's exactly what he had done.

So, when I realised we were following this wombat's big bum I slowed down. There wasn't much room on the track, and I wasn't looking for a fight just yet.

"Oh look," said Fi, from behind me, "a wombat. Isn't it cute."

I had an immediate fear that this would be a repeat of the Annie Abrahams story.

"Yeah, real cute," I said. "Just keep a safe distance."

Fi paused and we watched the wombat as it waddled on ahead. We were getting close to the turnoff where the four-wheel-drive track went down the mountain to the farm, and the wombat started to veer to the left. I thought I'd grab the chance to show Fi a party trick that I'd never tried myself but had heard Dad talk about. With no knowledge of whether it would work, and not much confidence, I said to Fi: "Did you know that they'll follow a torchlight?"

Fi had been teased by us so often, been the victim of so many practical jokes, that she wouldn't believe me this time. "Oh sure," she said doubtfully.

"No, really, I promise."

I swung my pack down and opened the side pocket, pulling out my torch. Leaving the pack, I went forward ten metres and flicked on the torch. We were down below the tree line, so there was no danger from enemy soldiers. I focused the beam of light on the ground in front of the wombat and then moved it away to his side. To my surprise he turned as soon as I did it, and followed the light obediently. Of course I didn't let the others know I was surprised. I just acted cool, like this was exactly what I'd expected.

I took the wombat for a little walk by moving the light around. I felt like a choreographer. The others were all cracking up. "Oh my God," Fi kept saying, in her light little voice that sounded sometimes as if it'd float away, "that's amazing."

There still wasn't much room around me, because Tailor's Stitch was just behind and we were surrounded by thick bush. So I swung the light one more time and made the wombat come towards me. I felt totally confident, totally in control. I planned to walk backwards slowly as the wombat came in my direction. The wombat hadn't read my script though. For no apparent reason he started charging, overrunning the spot of light on the ground. Maybe he saw me, but I really don't think so. Wombats give you the feeling they're just about blind. But they could be tricking of course.

At first I thought it was a joke, and I started going backwards a bit, getting faster as the wombat accelerated. Then suddenly I decided I was in trouble. It didn't seem to matter any more what I did with the torch. The wombat had torn up the rule-book. He'd stopped following the rules and he'd definitely stopped following the light. The whole situation was out of control. I forgot about my dignity and began to panic. A wombat at full gallop is surprisingly scary. Considering that they look like stuffed cushions on four little legs they actually get up to quite a speed. So I accelerated a bit myself. Ignoring the wild laughter of the other four, I swung around so I could make a high-speed getaway up the wall of Tailor's Stitch.

And I fell over my own pack.

I fell quite hard. The others were pissing themselves. I have to admit I was genuinely scared. I thought I was about to get torn apart by a wild wombat. The way he was grunting sounded seriously unfriendly. And I'd landed on my bad knee, which hurt. For a moment I expected the wombat to leap on top of me and tear my head off.

But he didn't. He swerved off his line and disappeared deep into the bush, having had enough of humans for one night. I struggled up again, with no help from anyone. They were still all falling around laughing. They can be pretty stupid and juvenile sometimes. I brushed myself down, put my pack back on, and started walking. I left it to them to decide whether to follow or not.

The weird thing was that Kevin seemed to feel better about me after that. He was laughing more and talking more and including me in his conversation. I don't know why he apparently decided I was an OK person again, but it seems like he did, and I thought that made the close encounter with the wombat almost worthwhile. Almost, but not quite.

IN THE MORNING KEVIN WAS IN A SULK AGAIN. WE STOPPED just before 5 a.m. and had a bit of a rest. We didn't put up tents or flies, but we spread out the bedrolls for a snooze. I think I slept for maybe an hour. I woke just in time to hear the first blowie of the day buzzing around. You know the night's over when you hear the first blowie. As you get into summer the earlier they come, and the more there are.

So I got up and pulled out a few things for breakfast. Nothing exciting, just dried apricots, fruit roll-ups and scroggin. We'd stopped about three hundred metres from a creek. It was something Ursula taught me: never camp right next to a creek, because the noise of the water will stop you hearing anyone sneaking up on you.

By the time I'd finished fiddling with the food and moving a few more things in my pack — I was always trying for a perfect arrangement of stuff in my pack; it had become a major hobby — the others were up too. None of us was much good in the morning, except Fi. She seemed to wake up and start functioning straightaway. Not like a diesel four-wheel drive. She'd get up and immediately be moving and thinking and talking at normal speed. Lee was the next best but he wasn't in Fi's class. Kevin and I were the worst.

So I grouched around, mumbling occasional comments to the others, as we each threw together our bizarre variations of breakfast.

We hadn't bothered with a sentry, because we were still in deep bush, though we were quite close to the Wirrawee-Holloway road. But while they were eating I went for a walk, to see what I could see. Despite the blowies it was a nice morning. It still had that fresh coolness you get early in the day, before the sun dries everything and bakes the air, and even the blowies have to give up and find shade for themselves. I had a good little stroll and managed to wake myself up at least, although the only interesting thing I saw was a trout breaking the world high jump record with a leap out of a pool to grab a passing insect. Talk about Cazaly. This fish was a metre out of the water. Well, almost a metre.

When I got back, a full-scale argument was raging. I could hear them from a hundred metres away, which worried me. We'd trained ourselves to speak pretty softly these days. In fact I didn't recognise their voices for a minute, they were so loud. I had a terrible spasm of fear that we'd been found. Once I realised it was only them I went on in to the campsite, but not very willingly. I'd just had my nice walk and I didn't want to get involved with something bad. I could hear Homer yelling at Kevin: "Christ you're pathetic Kevin. You never want to do anything."

"You'd better not make so much noise," I said as I arrived. "They'll hear you in Wirrawee."

Lee was standing against a tree. I've never seen him look so ugly. He had his arms folded and was staring with a terrible expression of contempt at Kevin. Fi was sitting at the creek, trailing her bowl in the water as though she were washing it, but not moving her hands at all. Homer and Kevin were standing facing each other like two bad-tempered dogs meeting for the first time. If they'd had hair down their backs it would have been bristling. Come to think of it, Homer does have quite a lot of hair down his back, but I couldn't see if it was bristling.

Anyway, I shouldn't make jokes about it. It was all too serious.

"What's the problem?" I asked, when no one answered my comment about the noise.

"Kevin's got cold feet," Lee said. "Again."

I was a bit startled. Seemed like it was OK for the boys to say that to Kevin, but it hadn't been OK for me.

"I haven't got bloody cold feet," Kevin shouted. "I've done everything you guys have done and more. I'm being realistic, that's all. Just because of what happened with Lee's parents he wants to rush off and kill anyone he can find. Well, that's fine for him, but I'm not in a hurry to commit suicide."

"We're not that stupid, Kev," Homer said angrily. "We've outsmarted them just about every time."

"Oh sure," Kevin said. "That last trip to Wirrawee was a huge success wasn't it? We did nothing, we achieved nothing, it's a bloody miracle we survived at all."

"You can go back to Hell if you want," Lee said, "but I'm not going back. Whatever we find out there, we'll deal with it. I hope we find Ellie's mother, of course, but I hope we find some targets we can attack too."

"Oh you're such a bloody hero," Kevin sneered. "Listen, Lee, things have changed. The invasion is successful. It's complete. They've won. It doesn't matter where we go, they're going to see us, chase us, catch us. And kill us. Don't you understand that? There's no point anymore. Hell is the only safe place left. Everywhere else we go they'll sniff us out. I tell you, in six months they'll have bushwalkers coming through these mountains the same as we used to do, and you'd better pray Colonel Finley has sent a chopper by then, because that's the only hope we've got."

Even Fi flared up at that speech. "It's not over yet," she said, without looking up. "I still think we can win. The New Zealanders think so too."

"I don't think we'll ever win it all back," Homer said. "Our best chance is that some day there'll be a ceasefire, and they'll split it up and we'll get some back. And the way Colonel Finley explained it to me, the more land we're holding when that happens, and the more we've got them on the backfoot, the more land we'll get in the big carve-up."

"Colonel Finley — fat lot he knows," Kevin said. "He just says what we want to hear. Whatever he thinks will get us to do what he wants. It's like your mother saying 'Eat your vegetables so you'll grow up big and strong.' Doesn't mean anything."

"It worked for you," I said, trying in my usual tactful way to lighten the atmosphere. I might as well not have spoken for all the notice anyone paid.

"Kevin, can't you get it into your thick head that we don't have a choice?" Lee said, speaking through gritted teeth. His mouth was pressed together so his lips were just one thin line. I'd never seen him so angry. "If we don't do anything, if we just wait to be taken back to New Zealand, we're pathetic. We're worse than pathetic. And if we never get taken back, then we're dead. Dead meat. Sometimes there aren't any questions anymore. Sometimes there's nothing to debate. If we have any choice at all, it might be as simple as this: to die fighting or to die as cowards. Not much of a choice, I agree, but if that's the way it is, I know which I prefer."

Lee's statement shocked us into silence. He put in words what I'd felt for some time, but I hadn't faced up to it quite so directly. We rolled up our mats and put the remnants of breakfast back in our packs. Then we walked on, still with no one saying anything. It had seemed a nice morning half an hour before, but now it didn't look quite as attractive.

Kevin still trailed along. If he had ideas of going back to Hell alone he didn't have the guts to put them into practice. I remembered something my hockey coach, Ms Sanderson, said, that it's the timid players who get injured. I wondered if that was a bad omen for Kevin. Mind you, I'm not sure Ms Sanderson was entirely right, because Robyn was the one who got the most injuries on our team, and she was definitely our most aggressive player.

We came out to the Wirrawee-Holloway road and turned right. This part of the road had thick bush on both sides, so we were in a good position to avoid vehicles, by diving behind trees as soon as we heard them. We trudged along silently, lost in our own thoughts. I'd started this trip with a sense of excitement, but I wasn't feeling too good now. I think I'd had a vague idea that we'd come out here and find my mother and everyone would be ecstatic and we'd all live happily ever after. I hadn't thought it through much.

I walked with head down, watching the dust slide over the toes of my boots with each step. Good faithful old boots. The guards took the laces out of them when I was in Stratton Prison, but when I got out I still had the boots. Now, months later, they didn't have a lot of life left, maybe just a few more miles. They looked unloved, which wasn't true, and uncared-for, which was. They had once been an olive-green, very dark. You felt you could almost see black in their depths, if you peered hard enough. Now they were a lighter drier green. The colour had been bleached out by the hard life they'd led. They were scuffed and worn and dull, especially round the toes. I could have used a whole tin of dubbin on the toes alone.

The boots were a bugger to get on in the mornings, like most boots, but once on they were the most comfortable pair I'd ever owned. Not glamorous, but strong and very supportive. I didn't want to ever give them up. They were one of the few links I still had with home.

Ahead of me, Homer, who was leading, came to a halt. I nearly cannoned into him, then realised why he'd stopped. We'd reached the edge of the bush and it was opening into farmland. I'd just walked four k's without noticing anything except my boots. Life's funny like that. Sometimes, before the war, we'd drive from Wirrawee to Stratton and I'd notice nothing on the whole trip. We'd arrive in Stratton and I'd have no idea how we got there, no memory of the road. Now I'd just done the same thing on foot.

I figured that we were about three k's from Holloway West, which was a dot on the map about five or six k's from Holloway itself. I searched my mind to think what was there. A service station and a general store, a school that had been closed by the Government just before the war, a couple of churches, and maybe forty houses. At least that was my memory of it, and when we slipped into the trees and took our packs off for a break, it seemed like no one else could remember much more.

There was a fairly easy route for us though. The old road, just a bush track now, was a few hundred metres back in the scrub, running parallel to the new road. I knew it went to the tip and after that I thought it kept going somewhere out Micklemore way, to the old Soldier Settlement blocks. There wasn't much to interest us in that country, except some good places to hide, and perhaps the chance of finding a few shacks unlooted. Some funny people had lived out there: old-timers, hippies, and people from the city who didn't want to mix with other humans.

So we cut across to the old track. It wound around trees and over a creek or two. It was a friendly road, corrugated and dusty, and it made me feel friendly towards the people who'd carved it from this dry scrub so many years ago. The bush is meant to be beautiful, and it often is of course, but this part wasn't. Just lots of small and medium gum trees, hardly any undergrowth, and shades of dull green and dull brown with no bright colours. I couldn't even see any birds.

Still, I felt at home in it, and it was safe. We walked along slowly, mainly because we were tired, but also I think because we didn't have any special goal. At night we planned to spy on the farms until we could find some prisoners to talk to. We hoped they could give us information about my parents, as well as anything else that would give us an idea of where to go and what to do. Until then we were stuck for suggestions.

We came to the intersection, where a dirt road from the main road met the track we were on. The dirt road led to the tip. It was quite a big tip this one — well, not big by city standards — but it served both Wirrawee and Holloway. Even before the council amalgamations the shires shared the tip.

We cockies didn't use it much because, like all farmers, we had our own tip on the property. There was a gully in Nellie's that we'd been dumping stuff into since my grandfather bought the place. You could stand on the edge of the gully and see the history of our whole farm in a big pile below your feet. Some day maybe an archaeologist would dig the lot up and write a book about our family. Mum and Dad's first car, a cream Valiant ute, was still rusting away, for example, along with a smashed Laminex kitchen table that a drunken shearer had fallen on in the shearing shed. There were sheets of roofing iron torn off by the willy-willy of 1994, tanks with holes in them, a few other cars and tractors, and bits of machinery. There were the remains of my disastrous attempts to make ginger beer — dozens of exploded bottles — and the pump that burnt out when the body of a drowned sheep got caught under the foot valve and lifted it from the water. The sheep went in the gully too, on top of the old computer that we'd tried for eighteen months to sell. Dad had finally lost his patience with it and hoicked it in there, in a fit of temper.

One Christmas holiday I tried to do a jigsaw of the ocean. After three weeks I'd had enough. I scooped up the thousand pieces, marched down to the gully and ceremoniously dumped the lot.

It was a kind of agricultural museum I suppose. Dad reckoned there was a story about every object we chucked in the gully.

The only time we came to the Wirrawee-Holloway tip was when we had toxic stuff to dump, like chemicals. They had a special container for that. And if Dad had to go to Holloway for something else he'd sometimes put a load for the tip on the back of the ute. "All the rates we pay, might as well get something for it," he'd say.

I'd been here with him just about every time and I quite enjoyed our trips. It was better in the old days though, before they cleaned it up. Back then, the tip was open twenty-four hours a day and there was stuff everywhere; you never knew what you'd find. Then there was trouble with the Environment Commission or someone, and the council had to hire a bloke to be there and keep it tidy. It got a bit boring after that. It was only open five days a fortnight, because we shared Darryl, the bloke who worked there, with Risdon. He did five days at their tip and five at ours. He did a good job too, there was no doubt about that. A month after he started he had the bottles in one area, the papers in another, and the cars all in a huge pile at the southern end. Inside the gate he built a galvanised-iron shed where he put anything that might have value, like old fridges and car seats and bits of timber. He was so organised.

One time Dad had to go to Holloway, so he thought he'd call in at the tip. He wanted to dump some sheep dip that was way past its use-by date. And seeing he was going anyway he decided to take the old Aga. It took an hour of struggling and sweating and swearing to load it onto the ute. He had to use the gantry in the end, and with its help and my help he got it on. Then he chucked in the drums of dip, and we drove out there. We dumped everything OK, and as we were leaving Dad asked Darryl it he had any old carpet. Mum wanted it to put on the garden to suffocate the weeds.

"Drop in on your way back from Holloway. I'll have some pulled out for you by then."

"OK," said Dad, "thanks a lot."

Two hours later we were back and we headed up to the northern end to collect the carpet. When we got to the bulldozer there was a bloke with a one-tonner. "Oh mate," he said to Dad, "you couldn't give us a hand for a minute could you?"

"Sure," said Dad, "what can I do for you?"

"Well, mate, have a look at what someone's chucked out over here. You wouldn't believe what people throw out. Some people sure are idiots, hey?" And of course he led Dad straight to the Aga.

Dad looked at me with eyes that burned, and there was no mistaking the message. It was like, "You say one word young lady and you'll be chipping burrs for the next three years."

So I stood there trying not to laugh as Dad and the man struggled and sweated and swore and finally loaded it onto the one-tonner. I must admit I even helped a bit. The bloke was so grateful to Dad. He kept talking about what a great score it was, and how the bloke who'd dumped it must be so stupid. When they'd tied it down and Dad closed his tailgate for him and the bloke drove away, Dad turned to me and said: "Don't you dare tell your mother about that, ever."

"OK, Dad," I said, "trust me."

"On this?" he said. "I don't think so."

He could never laugh about that one, and when I tried a few weeks later to make a joke about it, he cut me off before the first sentence was out of my mouth.

So here we were, back at the tip, twelve months on, and what I wouldn't give to see Darryl at the gate and the same bloke rabbiting on about his lucky find, and Dad sizzling as he loaded the Aga on the one-tonner.

It was nearly lunchtime. The thought of going into the tip made me a bit nauseous. I had an image in my head of the rotting piles of food that were always scattered around the place, and the clouds of flies. But I couldn't let my imagination take control of me: I had to be careful about that these days. Imagination and memory had become enemies. Before the war they had been my friends. Now, in all kinds of ways, I had to control them both. If I didn't I'd never have another peaceful night again, let alone a peaceful day.

The tip was the same as ever. Magpies and crows strutting around like they were in charge. Huge mounds of dirt heaped up by the bulldozer BTW — before the war. In among the papers and plastic and rotten food, those weird-looking piles that you could never identify. Grey and white and brown: piles of mouldy-looking stuff that was like nothing you'd ever seen before, and nothing you ever saw anywhere else.

So we just sort of wandered in, the way we'd been wandering all morning, not sure of what to do or whether we were looking for anything in particular. As we did I wondered why we were bothering. I mean, what was the point? We sort of drifted along aimlessly, I don't know, hoping to find something maybe. After all, scavenging was a way of life for us now. In times to come we might be grateful for the chance to sleep in a cardboard box at the tip. "You had a cardboard box? Luxury!"

Despite that we spent a fun hour in there. It wasn't exactly Disneyland but it had some good stuff. Even Kevin brightened up again, for a little while, although he didn't want to give us the satisfaction of seeing it. Fi found a cane basket full of wrecked soft toys — teddies and Humphreys and monkeys and tigers, all of them multiple amputees — and she and Homer started chucking them at each other. I had a good time reading some old newspapers. They were yellow and dirty on top but once you got down into the pile a few centimetres they improved. It was a bit depressing and it made me homesick again, but it was also weird. The things we got upset about back then! One of the sports articles started, "A tragic knee injury to Barry McManus has cost the North's fullback any chance of playing in this year's finals."

"Tragic!" I thought. "I'll show you tragic. Tragic is Lee losing his parents. Tragic is Robyn and Corrie and Chris being cheated out of fifty or sixty years of life. Tragic is one country invading and looting and overrunning another. That's tragic."

I gave up on the papers and wandered through the tip, kicking stuff aside with my feet, occasionally stopping to look at something more closely. Fi and Homer had gotten tired of their game and wanted to go. They were already at Darryl's hut at the entrance, calling to the rest of us. Kevin was nearly there and Lee was leaving whatever little playground he had found and heading in that direction too. With a sigh, I turned my back on a bunch of old photos scattered across the ground and went to join them.

I was the last to get to the hut, and I nearly didn't make it. The thick scrub surrounding the place was a good screen, muffling any noise from the road. I was walking towards the others with a big smile, wanting to tell them about a Far Side cartoon in one of the newspapers, when I saw Homer's face contort suddenly, as though he'd been stung by a wasp.

"Ellie! Look out," he yelled.

Almost at the same second I heard it. The roar of truck engines, in low gear. At first I thought it was just one truck, then I realised it was more than that. Homer and the others disappeared inside the hut. They seemed to fall backwards into it, in one move, like circus clowns. If there'd been time for jokes I could have turned that into one. But there was only time for fear. I leapt at the hut myself. It was stupid to put ourselves in such a deathtrap but we had no choice. Around the hut was clear ground. The nearest cover was scrub, sixty or eighty metres away. If we'd run for that we'd have been seen before we got halfway.

As it was I didn't know if they'd seen my back and heels when I dived into the little galvanised-iron shed. I would have been in their line of sight. And movement stands out so strongly. It always catches the eye. I'd got there as fast as I could; I just didn't know if it was fast enough. I fell on top of the others, knocking Homer and Fi half over. But no one wasted words discussing those little problems. As soon as we'd sorted ourselves out we got in positions where we could see what was happening. Already the trucks were going past the shed: that's how close it had been.

My position was down near the floor. I was looking out of the corner of the little shed, through a gap in the iron. It was enough of a view to get a fair idea of what was going on. I counted three big trucks but I thought another three had probably gone past before I found my peephole. I saw two big Dumpsters and a furniture van. These guys were making a serious visit. This was probably their major outing for the week. It might have been all the garbage from Wirrawee. It seemed too much for little Holloway.

The last truck stopped just past the hut, out of my line of sight. I tried to tell from the sounds what was happening. I think they were queuing to dump their loads. Homer was pressed up hard against me. I became aware of his elbow jammed in under my rib. I moved a little to get rid of the pressure.

"What are we going to do?" Fi whispered desperately.

No one answered. We were all in such total shock. One minute we'd been mucking around, no pressure on us, having a good old casual time at the tip, and the next minute we were looking down the throat of death. I could see its tonsils. We'd been close to death before. I realised though that this might really be it. I'd had this funny idea for some time that when we got caught (these days I thought in terms of when, not if) it would probably be in some stupid, casual way; not dramatically or spectacularly, not while blowing up a bridge or taking a hostage or attacking a convoy, but while we were asleep, or sitting on the dunny. Or we'd turn a corner on a path somewhere in the middle of the bush, the place where we felt so safe, and there'd be a thousand soldiers with guns pointed at us.

And here it was, happening. It had been such an innocent situation, but suddenly we were completely trapped. A drop of liquid fell on me: it was Homer's sweat. It felt hot. I couldn't do anything about it; it didn't matter anyway. At last though someone answered Fi's question. Surprisingly it was Kevin.

"Just stay here."

It wasn't much of an answer. If a soldier came into the hut we were gone, we'd had it.

None of us reacted to Kevin's comment. But it seemed we were going to get an answer from outside. A soldier came walking into my line of vision. He walked slowly, casually, like he was bored. A roll-your-own was sticking out the side of his mouth. He was coming straight towards us. It was so obvious what was happening. He had decided to check out the hut.

He was five metres from the door when I heard someone yell. The man stopped, looked towards the voice, then shrugged and turned around, and just as slowly went away again.

There was a rumble of a truck in low gear, and the sharp piercing beeps of it reversing. I could hear other engines revving too. I guessed they were moving up in the queue as each one finished. The soldier coming to check the hut had probably been ordered to shift his truck forward.

Suddenly one of the trucks appeared in my view. I figured it was the first empty one. It stopped right opposite my peephole, with a squeak of brakes and a grinding noise. It was another furniture van, but a very long one.

And again a driver came towards us. The man from the furniture van got out, stretched, and walked towards the hut, a little more purposefully than the other guy. I was rigid. What were we to do? We couldn't kill him. The others would be onto us straightaway and it would be all the worse for us if they found we'd killed one of their buddies. The best we could hope for was that they wouldn't kill us on the spot. If they took us into Wirrawee they'd work out fast enough that we were the ones who'd killed the officer there, even if it had been an accident, sort of.

They might pin a lot of other stuff on us too, if they did some investigating.

Yet the best we could hope for was to be taken to Wirrawee, because at least we might have a chance to escape on the way.

The driver kept walking straight towards the door. He wasn't a young man — about forty maybe — and he wasn't in uniform. I guessed he wasn't a soldier. No reason why they'd need soldiers to drive the garbage to the tip.

He passed from my view, because my peephole didn't give me much of an angle. I was so tense I couldn't breathe. There was a weird pain in my lungs. I was staring at the door, expecting it to open. But it didn't. A minute later the man walked back towards his truck. Now he was carrying a whole pile of hessian. I remembered seeing a heap of packing by the shed door, out of the weather.

The man climbed into the back of his truck. He was in there only a moment, then out he came, and walked towards us. Once again he got a big armload and took it to the van.

This time, while he was in there, Lee slipped over to the door, pressed himself against the wall, and took a tiny glance outside. Then he whispered: "They're all busy, unloading a truck by hand."

No one said anything. Lee seemed to be waiting for one of us to speak. When no one did he said: "I think we should try to get out of here, next time this guy's inside his van."

I felt Homer move, but he still didn't say anything. His sweat rained down on me.

"Where would we go?" Fi asked.

"Around the other side of the truck. Then try and get into that bit of scrub against the fence maybe. Or over to those wrecked cars."

"But . . . " Kevin said.

"Sshhh," Homer said.

The man was coming back. His third trip. As soon as he returned to his truck with another armload Homer joined Lee at the door. It seemed like the two of them had made the decision for us, something that always made me mad.

But this was no time for arguing. I followed them to the door, and I could feel Fi and Kevin pressing up close behind me. When the man climbed the step into the van, Lee opened the door. He took another quick glance to the left. Apparently the men at the other end of the tip were still busy, because he took off straightaway. Homer went after him, without even looking, which I thought was pretty amazing. I sure looked. Only for a moment, but I did look. There wasn't much to see. Just a truck with a long tray backed up to the dumping area, and a couple of blokes chucking stuff off it. From behind, someone — Fi or Kevin, but I'd bet on it being Kevin — gave me a shove. I felt a surge of anger, but again there was no time for emotions. I put my head down and ran.

Like the two boys I went around the front of the truck. I found them on the other side, leaning against the long body, trying not to pant. They both stared at me with huge eyes. They looked like chihuahua eyes, they were so big and out of proportion. My eyes probably looked the same.

Fi and Kevin suddenly arrived in a rush beside me. We all pressed ourselves into the metal side of the van, hoping no one had seen us, hoping the driver hadn't heard us. I got down on the ground and had a look underneath, trying to see what was happening. Sure enough, a second later I saw his feet. He was walking along the other side, then he veered away, towards the hut. We had a moment to plan our next move. I stood, and used sign language to show the others what was happening.

They just stared back, looking terrified, all with those huge wide eyes.

And I realised as I looked around what the others had already figured. We'd struck a big problem. The scrub against the fence was too far away. Like, fifty metres. We'd be in full view of the other drivers for forty-nine of the fifty. And the car bodies Lee mentioned were no better. They were as far as the fence but in an even more dangerous direction, back towards the truck being unloaded.

There was no other cover anywhere.

I could hear footsteps so I dived down and took another look under the van. The driver was returning. He took his load up the step again. I could hear him moving around inside. His boots echoed through the aluminium body. Then out he came, and back to the shed.

This time I stayed on the ground and kept watching. I saw his feet go straight to the door of the building and straight into it.

I knew what we had to do.

"Inside the truck," I hissed at the others.

They stared at me in horror.

"He's finished loading the felt," I said, although it was a huge gamble to say that. I didn't really know if he'd finished. I just assumed he had, now that he'd gone into the hut.

"Quick," I added.

Taking a leaf out of Homer's book I forced them to follow by going ahead on my own. I pushed past the two boys and sprinted around to the back of the vehicle. The door was still open, thank God. I went up the step and inside, knowing that someone, I didn't know who, was following.

Inside it was like a church, dark and silent. But the smell was musty and hot. It made my skin prickle. Or maybe it was the fear that did that. I don't know.

4

THE GUY HAD OBVIOUSLY BEEN THINKING LIKE A GOOD removalist, stacking up felt he could use to protect his loads. Tied in each of the front corners was a neat pile of blankets and hessian, and more felt. The stuff he'd collected today wasn't tied; just dumped in piles on the floor. Maybe he was taking it back to wash it. I hoped he was, for the sake of any future customers. Some of it was pretty grubby.

I burrowed in under a heap of felt. There was so much of it and it was so dark in the truck that if he glanced in he might miss us.

At least one thing was for sure: Lee had made the right move getting us out of the hut. The way the driver walked straight in: we'd have had to overpower him and run for it, or give up. And giving up was still unthinkable. Even though there were moments when I almost wished we'd be caught — just so the whole thing would be over and done with — when it came to the crunch, I'd do anything to avoid capture.

Someone burrowed in next to me. Someone light, probably Fi. I could feel her boots touching mine.

I was feeling hot and prickly and sweaty. The stuff was so dusty I was afraid I might sneeze, like I had in the fuel depot in Wirrawee, the night we'd tried to sabotage the jet fuel. This time I thought I could control it, but what if someone else sneezed? Was Fi allergic to dust? Her whole family was allergic. Her little sister got asthma pretty badly.

After a few minutes came the sound that would decide our fate. The sound of footsteps. There was a pause. I remembered a lady in New Zealand telling me about her little son, who had pins and needles in his legs. He complained: "Mum, I've got lemonade legs." Well, I had lemonade everything, right now. My skin fizzed. It felt like lice were crawling through my scalp, then I got the horrible idea that maybe the packing material was full of lice. It wasn't impossible.

There was a creaking noise, then a slam, and sudden darkness. He had shut the door.

I started breathing again. The itching in my hair stopped, so I assumed that maybe I didn't have lice.

I sat up, throwing off the covers. It was too dark to see what the others were doing, but gradually my eyes got more used to it. I realised Fi was next to me, like I'd thought, and she too was sitting up.

The truck shook as the driver got in and slammed the door, then it shuddered as he started the engine. We moved forward, but only about fifty metres, and sat there for another five minutes, with the engine running. I thought he was probably waiting for the other trucks. No one dared speak. We couldn't be sure how thin the wall was between us and the driver. Above the throbbing of the engine I heard the whoop of a truck horn. It seemed like this was the signal, because a moment later our truck lurched into gear — I don't think he had a lot of synchromesh in his gearbox — and away we went.

In peacetime, BTW, the airlines offered mystery flights, to fill their empty seats. You'd arrive at the airport and only then would they tell you where you were going. It was at the big city airports that they offered it of course, not at Stratton, and certainly not at Wirrawee, but Mr and Mrs Mathers had gone on a few of them.

And now we were on our own mystery flight.

My mind headed into full-on panic. I knew the first thing was to get control of my mind, control of myself. I breathed deeply and tried to concentrate. It took a while, but at last I felt calmer and able to think. I wriggled over to the middle of the van. By grabbing any limbs I could find I got the others to meet me there. And so we held our strangest ever meeting, whispering to each other as we lay in a star shape on the hot jolting floor of the truck.

"What are we going to do?" Fi asked.

It was one of Fi's standard questions. No one answered.

Finally, however, Homer said: "It's pretty easy to open the door from the inside."

"Can you do it quietly?" I asked.

"I think so. It didn't make much noise when he shut it."

"But we can't open it as we go along, because the trucks behind will see us," Lee said.

He'd obviously had the same idea as Homer, that we could jump from the moving truck, but he'd also realised that it was hopeless.

"All we can do is hide again under the felt when they stop," I whispered, "and hope the driver doesn't come in the back here."

"And then what?" Fi asked.

"Wait for a while and then try to get out. Maybe wait till dark."

"There's one thing I noticed when I got in," Lee said.

"What?"

"There's a little hatch between this part and the driver's

cab. So if we knew the driver had got out we could get through that and into the front while he was coming round to the back."

I was silent. It was a useful piece of information. It mightn't save us — nothing might — but it did give us an extra glimmer of hope. I was grateful for any glimmer at that stage, however slight.

The truck kept going. It was quite a straight road and it was bitumen. That could mean Wirrawee, but there was no certainty about it. It could equally mean Risdon, or West Stratton. The only thing I was sure of was that we weren't on the main road to Stratton itself.

Lee took a look through a crack in the door and came back to report that he could see at least one truck behind us. That finally closed the option of jumping out. Even if it hadn't, did we have the guts to do it? I doubted it. At best we'd break nine ankles between the five of us. The truck was doing a good speed.

"We'd better get any weapons we can find," said Homer. "Or anything we can use as a weapon."

"OK," I said. "But hide them in the felt. If we're caught, we want to look innocent. Don't have anything in your pockets that they could call a weapon."

I don't know what the others came up with but I didn't have much: a fruit knife, a box of matches, and a fairly heavy torch that maybe I could bounce off someone's skull. I moved the torch into the side pocket of my pack, the matches into my jeans pocket, and then, despite what I'd said to the others, I slid the knife down inside my sock. I figured if we were busted I'd try to dump it fast.

It was such an impossible situation. We could be on the road for ten minutes or ten hours. I was getting fairly desperate to go to the loo, but I had to tell myself firmly that there was no way. It was just nerves, I knew that.

My mind started to wander, like it always does. It's very annoying sometimes. And dangerous. I remember when I was leading the New Zealand soldiers up the track to Tailor's Stitch and on into Hell. I'd spent half that time daydreaming, and then realised I could have had them killed by being so casual.

Dad used to yell at me across the paddock all the time: "Ellie, are you still in the land of the living?"

Still, there wasn't much danger in daydreaming now. There was nothing we could do to help ourselves for the moment. No way out of this dark and musty cell. I tried to picture what the country outside would look like. End of November, moving fast into December, it'd be pretty busy out there. Irrigation'd be in full swing, milkers letting down milk by the tanker-full, and summer crops like soybean and sunflower going in. On our place we'd be dipping the sheep.

I wondered if they were still doing those things. I guess the trees would still produce their fruit and the sheep would definitely be mating and having babies, that wouldn't stop, war or no war. I never tired of the sight of new lambs. They were one of the best things about life on the land. They looked like they were made from pipe cleaners, tottering around, trying to pretend they could do gymnastics when all they could manage was to stand up straight.

One thing I wondered about was the irrigation. BTW — before the war — you were allowed to take a certain amount of water from the river, or from the irrigation channels. It was strictly limited, so people farther down the river didn't run out and the dams didn't go dry. Everyone had meters on their pipes, for the Commission to check that farmers only took what they were allowed. If no one was checking anymore it'd be a huge mess, with some people having great crops and others having droughts.

Our place was quite a way from the irrigation properties, but we had fairly good rainfall. Four years ago was the last bad dry spell. We usually averaged 500 millimetres a year.

This season looked good so far. There was a lot of good spring pasture around.

And now we were the spring lambs, maybe on a premature trip to the abattoir.

My daydreams suddenly got interrupted. The truck started to slow down. I felt the brakes come on, then I heard their squealing noise. They gripped hard and the truck stopped. The engine rumbled away but I couldn't hear anything else. By then I was buried under the felt anyway, hoping the others had the sense to do the same.

There was a pause. Above the rumbling bass of the engine I heard human voices, calling to each other. It was a conversation between three voices, one of them a woman. It lasted only about a minute, probably even less. Their voices were so light and cheerful they might have been talking about the weather.

Clunk, suddenly we were in gear again and moving. But we didn't gather speed like we had when we left the tip. We rolled along on a very smooth road, much smoother than the one before, but much slower too. I stayed under the felt. We went maybe a kilometre. Then we stopped again. The engine was switched off. There was a long terrible silence. There were no sounds from the other trucks. All I could hear was the clicking noises as the engine cooled. They seemed magnified, which made me think we were in a shed or garage. After a few minutes I heard the driver cough. He cleared his throat and spat. I felt a little sick. I've always hated it when people do that, always hated the noise, let alone the sight.

Then the man got out of the truck and slammed the door. I heard his footsteps. They echoed, again making me think we must be in some kind of garage, but a big one. He sounded like he was walking on concrete. Then I heard another door slam, and that was it. Silence, except for the engine ticking.

I thought it was time for quick decisions. I threw off the prickly hot coverings and whispered, just loud enough for the others to hear: "Let's check it out before they find us."

I knew it was a risk to do that but it seemed a hell of a bigger risk to stay where we were.

No one answered, though I could tell by the sudden stillness, the way they all stopped breathing at once, that they'd heard me. I realised that it might have to be me who did the checking out. Feeling with my hands in front of my face I made my way across to the rear door. Then Homer was suddenly beside me whispering: "It might be safer going through the driver's cab."

I thought, "Yes, maybe he's right."

We could be more secretive in the cab. If we opened the big rear door, there would be a moment when we'd be exposed to anybody out there. But by slipping into the driver's cab we might be able to look around before anyone saw us.

So I groped my way forward again, this time with

Homer close behind. There was a small sliding panel in the middle of the front wall. A crack of light showed down one side, so I had no trouble finding it. It slid to the left, and although it was stiff and hard to move I got it open. It was quite dark in the cab, which proved we were in a shed or garage. I wriggled through the hatch. I don't think it was made for people to go through, more for the driver to open and have a look at what was happening behind him. I grinned as I landed on my head in the front seat, thinking of the trouble Homer would have. I was rapidly losing my immediate fear because there was something about this place that said "EMPTY." Just the stillness of the air, the way the slightest sound echoed.

The cab stunk of humans: stale cigarettes and a bit of sweat, mixed in with last night's garlic, the vinyl smell of the seat and the musty hessian that followed us through the hatch. It wasn't an unpleasant smell, but it had its own identity, the way a wombat hole or a rabbit warren or a dog kennel does. I felt that this guy probably spent a lot of time in his truck.

Homer came through behind me, grunting and cursing. If anyone had been there with a rifle Homer would have been an easy target as he struggled through the hole. It seemed to take him about three minutes, but it probably wasn't that long.

OK, it was about fifteen seconds.

There we were: crouching in the cab. It was a bit late for caution, considering the noise we'd made. Or rather the noise Homer made. But we crouched there in silence, looking out over the shelf and the dashboard. There were three little soft toys hanging right in front of me. I couldn't see them very well in the dim light, but the one my nose was bumping against was a blue and green bird with horrible pointy eyes. I felt that at any moment he would start flapping his wings and squawking to warn the soldiers we were there. I had an urge to grab him and wring his scrawny neck. I think it really dawned on me at that moment how much this war was brutalising me.

I gave my head a tiny shake to clear away these stupid thoughts. "It seems OK," I said to Homer.

"Yeah."

He wriggled over and quietly opened the passenger door. I mean, I know he did it quietly, it was just my overheated nerves that had me thinking it sounded like a tractor reversing over a pile of galvanised iron. I had been about to open the driver's door but I hesitated when I heard the noise he made. "No point adding to it," I thought.

Instead I followed him. He was already outside the truck, so I quickly crawled along the seat and went through his door. As I did I caught a glimpse of Lee squeezing from the hatch into the cab.

Homer and I were standing on a vast concrete floor. This was the world's biggest garage. One of my questions had been answered already: there was nothing this big in Wirrawee. We were somewhere else. I was puzzled though. We hadn't been in the truck very long and I couldn't think of any place close to the tip that was this size. Still, that was something to worry about later. At the moment keeping ourselves alive was the big priority, the only priority. I followed Homer a few steps away from the truck and did like he did: stood and gazed around, trying to see in the dim light, trying to find a way out.

It sure was big. I don't think it was quite finished. Down one end I could see a pile of raw timber, for crossbeams maybe. There was a workbench against the wall to my left, but there seemed to be nothing else in the whole place. That's another reason I thought it was unfinished, the fact that this huge building was so empty. I still couldn't figure out what it was. The walls and roof were just galvanised iron. Opposite the wall with the workbench, was the other long wall that seemed to be the front of the building. I realised after looking at it for a moment that in fact it was a long door: the whole wall was a door. In the middle of that door was another little door, just the normal size for a person, but it looked pretty small in this place.

I guessed that the driver had left through the little door. I ran over there, as lightly as I could, and had a closer look. The big door was in segments on rails, so that you could slide open just one panel or every panel. If you opened up every panel you'd have opened more than half the building. Weird. I couldn't imagine why anyone would build a place like this. It was like a mega version of our machinery shed. Maybe it was some new way of storing grain. I looked back at the truck. It seemed tiny. Everyone was out of it now. Kevin and Lee were standing by the driver's door, arguing about something, Fi was standing halfway between me and the truck, and Homer was investigating the little door. He squeezed it open, took a tiny peep out, and quickly shut it again. Obviously that was where the action was. I ran over to him.

He looked shocked. He stared at me without saying anything. It was hard to tell in the dim light but I actually thought he looked pale, which is not easy for Homer, being Greek and all.

"What is it?" I asked him. "What's wrong?"

"You know where we are?" he said.

"No, of course not. That's why I'm asking."

"We're at the bloody airfield."

I stared back at him, equally horrified. Then I did what he had done, sneaked the door open a fraction and peeped out.

And I saw what he'd seen.

Hectares of grass and concrete runways. High-powered jets in a line on one of the runways. Buildings and building sites everywhere. And a big two-storey brick building in the distance, with a round section on top.

It hadn't been too long since I'd last seen Wirrawee Airfield. I'd been amazed then at how much it had changed in a short time. They'd expanded it from a little strip for private planes owned by cropdusters and rich graziers, into a huge military base. And from the quick look I got, it seemed they were still expanding it. This shed was evidence of that. And there was plenty of evidence outside the door. There were even more runways, even more buildings than last time. This place was bigger than Cape Canaveral. Not that I'd ever seen Cape Canaveral, but still.

I stared at Homer in horror and disbelief. This was the place we'd wanted to destroy. The place the Kiwis wanted to destroy. When they failed — at least we assumed they failed, because we'd never seen them again and there was no obvious damage to the place — when they failed, we'd had a go. And got absolutely nowhere. I wasn't surprised now, seeing it from the inside. It looked a hell of a lot bigger from the middle.

Well, we were in the middle of it, no doubt about that. Fair and square in the middle. And no way in the world did I want to be there.

5

I WENT A BIT CRAZY WITH FEAR WHEN I REALISED. WE were in an awful situation, I knew that straightaway. In a huge building with no cover at all, nowhere to hide, and no way to escape either. This would be the most heavily guarded area for a thousand k's. We were in a wasps' nest that covered one hundred and fifty hectares and we didn't have so much as a can of Mortein between us.

Back in New Zealand Colonel Finley had explained the significance of the airfield to me and me alone. I don't think he was exaggerating, but he said the enemy controlled half the state from this airfield. He said if it could be knocked out the skies would be opened up for the New Zealand Air Force. They would have virtually free access to half a dozen cities. Fifty or more factories could be bombed, as well as bridges, railway lines, Cobbler's Bay, and a missile launching pad being built near Stratton. Of course the enemy had other defences besides the airfield, but this was the key to it all. Through a cloud of pipe smoke Colonel Finley said to me, "Ellie, if I were to bomb those factories today, I'd have forty per cent casualties. But if the airfield was taken out I'd have five per cent."

I remember thinking how odd it was that he talked about "I" and "me" when he wasn't actually going out and bombing anyone. And it sounded so cold-blooded, talking about human lives in percentages.

I'd been willing for us to have a go at the airfield because I kept thinking about people like Sam and Xavier, the helicopter pilots. I could picture their faces. I saw them or their mates sitting in planes on the way to bomb targets and I saw enemy fighters screaming up behind them and the missiles, like little black darts, pouring towards the planes and I saw the planes lurch and stagger and fall sideways, and the faces of my friends as the jets spun out of control at ever increasing speeds, falling out of the sky to meet the rock-hard earth: the explosion as dirt and fuselage and trees and flames and human bodies detonated in a huge fatal horrible fireball . . .

Yes, I'd been willing for us to have a go at the airfield.

But it was different then. We'd been in control. We were free agents, moving around Wirrawee in the dark, going where we decided, doing what we wanted. Now we had no control. Sure we were in the place we'd been aiming for, but we were here with no weapons, no plans, no hiding place. This huge hangar wouldn't protect us for long.

Homer had done a quick tour of most of the building, jogging around its vast perimeter, and now he was back at the little door. Every couple of minutes he opened it a fraction and snuck another look. "This is the only entrance, I think," he said to me. "That's good. Means they've got less chance of surprising us. We can make our plans from here, while we watch them."

I was impressed by that. I thought, "You're not bad sometimes, Homer. Right now, when there's every reason to panic, you're thinking about tactics and survival. A lot of people would have given up."

And I was feeling like one of those people. But his strength gave me strength. I felt myself grow a little, get a little tougher and more determined. I said, "You keep a lookout. I'll get the others."

I ran to them and broke the news. "I hate to tell you guys, but we're slap bang in the middle of Wirrawee Airfield."

They took it in their different ways. Lee trembled slightly and didn't say a word, Fi put her hand to her mouth and sat on the step of the truck, and Kevin swore at me as if it were my fault. I realised a moment later that he thought it was, as he said: "If you hadn't told us to get in this bloody truck in the first place . . . " He stopped and stood glaring at me. But Fi turned on him angrily.

"How dare you? You know perfectly well there wasn't any choice. Just because you're scared. Well, there's plenty to be scared about, but don't take it out on Ellie."

There it was, the "scared" word again. It was getting quite popular.

Lee ignored all this. He was good at ignoring things he didn't want to know about. He was probably in the world's top ten for that. Already he was on his way to the door, to join Homer. I thought the smartest thing for me to do would be to go over there too.

We held a quick conference at the door. First the others had to open it and sneak a look through the crack, as if they didn't quite believe me, as if they thought I'd made the whole thing up. But their pale faces and trembling lips, after they'd had their peep, made it pretty obvious that they believed me now.

Even Lee looked as though this was too much to cope with.

"What are we going to do?" Fi asked, as usual. Was it my imagination or was her gaze fixed on me, in the dim shadowy light? No, it wasn't my imagination. And not only Fi. The three boys were gazing at me too, even Homer. I'm not sure when it first happened, this promotion of me to the position of the person with ideas, the person who'd get us out of tight spots, but at some stage it had happened, and now they seemed to take it for granted that I'd have inspirations on cue. It was like Homer had the positive energy and I was meant to have the positive ideas. But this time I gazed blankly back at them. Finally I said, pretty weakly, "Well, it should be easier to get out than in."

"The truck, it's our only hope," Kevin said. "We'll have to wait till it goes out again, and hide in it."

"I don't know about that," Lee said. "If he loads stuff in it here, where do we hide while he's doing it?"

"It might be weeks before it goes out again," Fi said. "We'd have starved to death by then." She looked around, wrinkling her nose. "There's not even a toilet."

"Well, we can't walk out," Kevin said. "And we can't dress up in stolen uniforms and bluff it, like they do in the movies. If we don't get out in the truck we're done for."

Our meeting was suddenly interrupted. A rumbling noise outside and a slight vibration of the building were our only warnings. We looked at each other fearfully then turned and sprinted for the truck.

We tumbled into the back of it just in time. A moment later I heard the rattle of a metal door sliding open, and the low rumbling became a loud throbbing. Homer was again watching, this time through a crack in the van door. "There're more trucks coming in," he reported, " . . . a whole bunch of them."

It got pretty loud there for a while. The shed — or hangar I suppose I should call it, because I was beginning to realise that's what it was — amplified the engines, causing their noise to echo around the walls. I could smell the fumes too: they seeped into our truck and made the air pretty foul for a while.

Gradually though, things started to quieten again. The engines were shut off. I could hear footsteps, and a few comments shouted as doors opened and shut. Someone walked past our truck actually drumming a tune on the side with his fingers. Fi, crouched beside me in the dark bowels of the van, half covered by felt, stiffened as though she'd had 240 volts put through her. I must admit I felt like I'd had an electric toaster dropped in my bath water.

Then there was nothing for a minute, until the sound of the sliding metal door again.

Then complete silence.

It seemed we were alone once more. Maybe. Homer gently opened the back door a centimetre and had a little peep. Then he opened it about ten centimetres. Then thirty. Finally he was satisfied, and opened it the whole way. We all got out.

There were now twenty trucks in the hangar. They still seemed small in the huge shed. They were a variety of shapes and sizes, from tray-tops to semis to vans. There were some genuine Army trucks in green and khaki camouflage paint, and some from businesses in Wirrawee and Stratton. Trucks that had become part of the war souvenirs these guys had scored for themselves. I saw an old prime mover with HHA Holdings written on the side. HHA Holdings was Mr and Mrs Arthur's company: they owned "Random Hills," a property about three kilometres away from the Quinns' place, next to the Ramsays'.

We had a quick look around the different vehicles. It didn't seem to help us much, having them there. So we had twenty to pick from now, instead of one. Did that make any real difference? None of them had any great hiding places.

In the middle of the hangar Lee said to me, quietly, where the others couldn't hear, "We have to approach this whole thing differently."

He'd obviously been doing some thinking. More than I'd been doing. My mind was chaos: it was a mess in there. Maybe Lee was going to take over as the ideas person. He was welcome to the job.

"How do you mean?" I asked cautiously.

"We have to see it as an opportunity."

"Oh no," I groaned to myself. I hate it when people talk like that. "Turn your negatives into positives." "Don't bring me problems, bring me solutions." "Become the person you dare to be." Iain, the leader of the Kiwi soldiers, talked like that a bit. "No, wait a minute," I thought. "You're overreacting. Lee hasn't started sounding like a preacher from a Sunday morning TV show . . . yet."

I still hadn't spoken and when he realised I wasn't going to say anything he went on.

"We're in an amazing situation here. By a complete accident we've got ourselves into the place that Colonel Finley most wants destroyed. We shouldn't be worrying so much about getting out. We should be thinking about how we can do something huge: something that might change this war in a big, big way. You can see that can't you, Ellie? You know that's the way to go?"

Funny, I'd never heard him talk like that before. It was like he was begging me for support. I wondered if he wasn't sure himself, if he didn't know whether he had the strength and courage for it. He was talking about suicide really, about our deaths, I knew that straightaway. There was no way anyone was going to attack this place from the inside and survive. You didn't have to be Einstein to figure that out.

When I still didn't say anything he kept going.

"I could never look anyone in the face again if we ran out of here like scared rabbits. I mean, we've achieved what the Kiwis couldn't, and all we can think about is saving our own skins. Imagine going back to New Zealand and saying to Colonel Finley 'Yeah, we got in there but then we chickened out.' I don't want to act like a frightened little mouse."

"Make up your mind," I said. "Are we chickens or rabbits or mice?"

I walked away from him then. I needed time to think. My skin was prickling again. It's not an easy thing to face your own death. Not when you're feeling young and alive and healthy. But I hardly had a moment to think before Fi came over to where I was standing. I don't know whether she noticed the way I was shaking, but she didn't comment on it. She just said, very quietly, so quietly that I could hardly hear, "Lee wants us to attack the airfield I suppose, does he?"

I nodded, hugging myself. Fi started trembling too. In the same soft voice she said, like she was whispering to herself, "I thought he would."

To my own surprise I said: "I think he's right."

"Now why did I say that?" I thought. I didn't know I'd already made up my own mind. Didn't think I'd even started to make up my mind. "Who's going to tell Kevin?" Fi asked.

We both glanced across at where Kevin was poking around at the end of the hangar. He'd opened a little door and as we watched he went through it. It was so inconspicuous that we hadn't noticed it. It looked like a storeroom or something.

Homer and Lee were talking urgently over by the main door. No prizes for guessing what they were talking about. Fi put her hand on my arm. She didn't say anything. She didn't need to.

Kevin didn't say anything either when we told him. And that was the first problem: we told him instead of asking him. In New Zealand, when Fi and I returned from our run and Homer told us we were coming back here with the Kiwi guerillas, I'd reacted the same way. I'd gone off like a willy-willy in a wheat field. Yet here I was, only weeks later, doing the same thing to Kevin.

Kevin took it a bit differently from the way I had back in Wellington though. It's hard to write this, to say what actually happened, but I've always tried to be honest when I write this stuff, and I guess I'd better not stop now. So what happened with Kevin was that he had some kind of breakdown. Andrea, my friendly counselor in New Zealand would have had a name for it. Nervous breakdown I guess, except I've never been too sure what that means.

The conversation started well, because Kevin came back quite proudly. He even cracked a little smile. All because of his great discovery. The little room he'd found contained a toilet and some cleaning stuff: a couple of big brooms, a few buckets, junk like that. Having a toilet was huge news. Funny how such a trivial thing could be so important. But the excitement didn't last. Kevin realised something was going on. We were giving him all these congratulations for finding the toilet but he knew it was fake because he suddenly cut across what we were saying.

He looked straight at me and said: "You guys are planning something."

I looked straight back and said: "We're going to attack the airfield."

I'd seen a few people go pale since this war started. Fi when the soldiers at Baloney Creek had them all bailed up, for instance. Lee when he was wounded, shot in the thigh. Corrie when she started to realise that the invasion had happened. And of course Homer when he looked through that little door. They were just some of the white faces that rolled through my mind when I thought about people going pale. But Kevin went through pale, into grey. He looked like an old man. His face almost collapsed. He used to be quite fat in the face until recently, when the war turned us all into compulsory weight watchers. But for a moment his head looked more like a skull. Then he put his face in his hands and stood there with his shoulders shaking. He didn't seem to be making any noise, just shook like he was standing on a fracture zone in an earthquake.

None of us knew quite what to do. In the end Fi took him by the arm and led him away to the truck we'd arrived in. He lay in there for the next twelve hours. I don't think he even used the toilet that he'd been so proud of discovering. For a long time I don't think he moved at all. Every half an hour or so someone — usually Fi or I — would go and check on him, but he seemed to be in a sort of coma. A vegetable. A Jerusalem artichoke. I mean, I shouldn't crack jokes about it, but what else can you do? Things were so frightening, and our future seemed so nonexistent, that sometimes jokes were all we had left.

When we weren't checking on Kevin or using our nice

porcelain toilet we spent our time in the most urgent, frantic conversations we'd ever had. We dreamed up a lot of different ways to attack the planes — even a couple of ways that might possibly almost work. But we also clung to the desperate hope that we could do it and get away with our lives. That was optimistic of us, greedy, but I think we felt that if we strained our brains hard enough we might come up with something. We were like people hanging over the edge of a cliff, knowing the only way we could save ourselves was to pull so hard we'd dislocate our shoulders.

We were willing to dislocate our brains if it gave us the slightest chance to survive.

While we talked we kept the closest possible watch on what was going on outside. We used a Phillips head screwdriver from the trucks to make tiny peepholes in each wall, and that gave us a 360 degree view. In twelve hours we were interrupted only three times: once when a woman came in to get something from a truck, another time when two mechanics came in and worked on an engine for half an hour. And the third time when a man came in to hide from something. I don't know what it was, nothing too sinister I wouldn't think, but you could tell he was hiding by the way he snuck in, looking back over his shoulder in a guilty way. Maybe he was trying to get out of some boring job. He looked pretty much the way I did when I was avoiding choir practice at school.

During each of these interruptions we hid in the same truck. I don't know if that was a good idea, but whatever we did was a lottery: a terrible game of Russian roulette.

When we had the luxury of being able to spy on the base we learnt a few things that might be useful. There seemed to be about sixty aircraft out in the open, two-thirds of them great huge things that were probably bombers or troop carriers. The rest were little fighters, like wasps. They were in three lines along a concrete apron that stretched for close on a kilometre. They were packed in pretty tightly, and I remembered Colonel Finley saying that as fast as these people kept expanding the airfield the more planes they crowded into it.

Behind the concrete apron were three giant hangars that could have contained anything from the officers' grog supply to another squadron of planes. It was a fair bet though that at least one hangar, probably more than one, was used for aircraft maintenance.

When a flight of bombers landed, a bunch of fuel trucks raced out to fill them up. The planes taxied to their parking spots. By the time they got there the fuel trucks were waiting. As the pilots and crew walked away the fuel was already pumping into the huge planes.

"There's a hundred million bucks' worth of aircraft sitting out there," Homer said.

He was probably underestimating. I guessed that planes like these would cost at least two or three million dollars a pop.

As it got darker we learnt the nighttime procedure. When a plane landed, runway lights were switched on, but they were very dim and were only on for a couple of minutes. The moment the plane touched down, out went the lights. Too bad if the pilot couldn't steer a straight line.

We gradually began to work out what the different buildings were, and Lee drew a rough map. I didn't like him doing that — I was paranoid about anything being on paper, because I'd read a story when I was little about a spy in World War One being executed when they found a map stitched into his clothing. But this one time I bit my tongue. Everything was so urgent, so excruciatingly desperate, that normal rules had to be suspended. I understood that.

So we figured out that to our left was the dining room or canteen. We guessed that because of the smells, which made our mouths water, and because when it got darker, around teatime, various soldiers wandered past our hangar, all heading in that direction. Half an hour later, back they came. They looked hungry when they went there and well-fed when they came back. You can tell, somehow. I don't know how, but you can. We snacked when we got desperate enough, with more of our New Zealand food, but we hadn't brought much with us, as we'd wanted to preserve our little stores in Hell. And scroggin wasn't quite as satisfying as the fried chicken I thought I could smell wafting down the road.

I found I was too nervous to eat much anyway. Only Homer seemed to have a real appetite. As I looked at the food disappearing down his throat I wondered what we'd do when the supply ran out.

To our right was a big fibro building with only a few lights. And they just seemed to be security lights, on all the time. We thought it might be a storage place. Farther off was the control tower — the building with the round top — which we could see clearly, higher than everything else.

Opposite us was a long low wooden building with small windows. We worked out fairly early that it had to be a barracks. There was music blaring, shirts hung out of windows to dry, and from time to time we had glimpses of half-dressed men coming from showers or getting changed.

Beyond that were the planes.

A plan was starting to form in my head and I started talking about it to the others. We were all trying to be brave I think, except for Kevin, who disappeared into the truck and seemed unable to move. Lee was really angry at him. At one stage he said: "Just leave him there. Let them have him." I was horrified. It wasn't the first time Lee had scared me. But this time at least I could understand his being so angry. I spent half the time feeling sorry for Kevin and half the time thinking he was gutless. I mean on one level I knew he had a big problem, like a medical or psychological problem, but at another level I was angry that he deserted us when we needed him most, leaving us to do all the work and take the risks. Of course when we were caught he would be too, but it was hard to see it that way.

We all had goes at talking to him, trying different tactics, like sympathy, abuse, common sense, encouragement. I suppose the strategies we used said a bit about us. Fi was sympathy, Lee was abuse, I was common sense and Homer, to my surprise, was encouragement. But none of them worked. The only "progress" was that instead of ignoring us when we went into the truck he curled into a ball and started crying. That didn't seem like much of a step forward.

So we just kept going with our plans, our vague half plans. My main idea rested on a bit of knowledge I'd picked up when I was little. Back when Homer was young and wild he'd sometimes have target practice with a rifle. But shooting at the usual targets, like tin cans or tree stumps, was too boring for Homer. To make it more interesting he filled the tin cans with petrol and sealed them again. I must admit I'd taken the odd shot myself, when Homer generously decided to share one of the cans. It was quite addictive. More fun than cleaning out sheep shit from under the shearing shed.

What we'd learnt back then was now the basis of our plans. But they were still only half-baked ideas when suddenly we were dragged into action.

At 6 a.m. Fi and I were both awake. Kevin may have been, I don't know, but he was curled up in his corner of the van. Lee and Homer were asleep, stretched out near him. It was the first rest we'd allowed ourselves since being dumped in the hangar. We wouldn't have taken that if we hadn't been desperate, suffering from sleep deprivation.

I took one more look at them, then closed the door of the van and went back to the lookout point. I was officially on sentry but Fi and I were sharing our turns, because neither of us could sleep. We were only doing an hour each anyway, as a four-hour break was all we could afford.

Fi and I getting insomnia when we had a chance for some rest was typical of the tricks the war kept playing on us.

The only interesting thing during our combined sentry duty was that a whole lot of aircraft took off at about 5.30. I'd say there were at least twenty. They took off in waves, three at a time as far as we could tell, roaring over our hangar. We felt the ground vibrate under our feet. I had to put my hands to my ears, the noise was so extreme.

If that wasn't enough to wake the boys, then they were certainly awake by 6.01. A PA system ran through all the buildings, and at 6.00 it played a major piece of music that was obviously meant to get everyone on their toes, ready for another good day of bombing the stuffing out of anyone they didn't like. The music sounded kind of weird to me, but it was loud and military, so when you heard it you knew you weren't at a Brownies' camp.

Next thing, we heard these trotting feet. It sounded like sheep on the wooden floor of the shearing shed. Fi was already looking through a spyhole; I leapt to mine. A whole lot of soldiers were hurrying past the hangar. They were all men and some of them looked very young. They carried rifles. Within a few seconds they were gone.

By then Homer and Lee had joined us at the door. We looked at each other anxiously, wondering what was happening, what we should do. I said to Lee: "We've got to use this time. Take the chance."

"I agree," he said. "I'm going to follow them, see what's going on."

"All right," I said. "I'll check out the barracks."

"I'll look in the store building," Homer said, catching the mood quickly, realising this was our first chance, maybe our last.

"What'll I do?" Fi asked.

"Stay here," I said quickly, in case the boys came up with some stupid suggestion. Sometimes I had this funny wish to protect Fi, to take care of her. She'd have killed me if she'd known that.

Homer opened the door a fraction more and the three of us started to slip out through the tiny gap.

I went second, behind Lee.

"Be careful," Fi said. I bit back a desire to laugh, and just nodded.

Outside, the wind felt sharp, quite cold for summer. It was only a short dash to the barracks building, but I knew I had to use the buildings and shadows for cover, as much as I could. I bent over and scurried across the roadway. It was weird because I felt I wasn't able to breathe, somehow. Yet here I was, running, so I must have been breathing. I felt really paranoid, too, certain someone somewhere must be seeing me. I didn't know if it would be the people in the control tower or a helicopter overhead or a soldier still left in the barracks, but I felt I couldn't get away with this: it was too outrageous, too much, thinking I could run around in this huge and vital enemy installation doing what I liked. So I waited for the shout, the cry of alarm, the rattle of a rifle being loaded and armed and swung into position.

Then I was in the shadow of the doorway, and definitely breathing. Now my trouble was the opposite — I was breathing too hard: so noisily that anyone in the building must rush out, to see what was going on. I sounded like a set of bagpipes warming up. I sounded like Fi's little sister when she was crashing into another asthma attack. I struggled to get control but I could only give myself a few seconds. After about ten of those seconds I stepped out of the doorway's shadow and into the barracks itself.

It was like a dormitory. And so clean and neat! Every bed beautifully made, every bedspread straight and symmetrical, every table and chair squared off. The place stank of disinfectant, so much that my eyes stung. The windows shone. I couldn't believe men were this neat. I wished Homer could come and see it. This is how his bedroom could have looked but never did.

I scanned the place quickly. The slightest movement and I was in big trouble, having to make a decision to run or attack. Either way, I was cactus. I had no weapon, except for the fruit knife in my sock. But the room was still. I hurried along the gap between the beds, looking for something, anything, to help us. There were no obvious treasures. At the end of the row I pulled open two locker doors at once, one with each hand. The insides of the lockers were as neat as the outsides. Uniforms and casual clothes, neatly wrapped in plastic bags, hung on coat-hangers. Each locker had a top shelf, and on it were the soldiers' personal possessions: photos and books and pens and cigarettes and sweets, again beautifully arranged. "Gosh, if Mum could see this . . . " I thought, but there was no time for that stuff. I was scared of staying too long but I didn't want to go back to the others empty-handed either.

In the corner an open door showed the way to a little kitchenette, so I ducked in there and opened the fridge. Even it was clean and neat, but crammed with goodies. Fresh food was one of our major dreams, a full-on fantasy for us all, so I loaded up with everything I could carry that wouldn't leave conspicuous gaps in the shelves. "They'll think they're knocking off each other's stuff," I figured. "It'll start a major fight and they'll kill each other and then we can take over the airfield."

I got an avocado, some cheese, a small rock-melon, a bag of rocket and other greens, and some stuff that looked like rissoles and smelt like fish. Then I moved my ass out of there. I was in a real hurry to be back in the hangar. I didn't know how long it would be before the Papa Bears marched home with their rifles, to find someone had helped herself to the porridge. I did know that if they caught me I'd get treated a lot worse than Goldilocks.

On the way out I noticed one interesting thing, although I didn't realise what it meant until a bit later. Above each bed there were two brackets, about a metre apart. Or less than that, probably eighty or ninety centimetres. They were made of brass, and were screwed to the wall. They looked like they could support some weight.

I got to the door of the building, the door I'd come in by, and took a quick peep out. It looked clear, so I slipped through the little gap. Now I was in the open, on the outside of the barracks, a frighteningly exposed position again. I was a great target for anyone wanting to earn a medal. I looked to the right, I looked to the left, I looked to the right again. Then I slipped off the kerb.

And nearly got run over.

All that road safety training in primary school could have cost me my life. I'd become so used to looking to the right, which normally would be fine, but in this case wasn't. The soldiers had hurried off to the left, and that's the way I should have looked.

Fifty metres to the left two officers had appeared. You could tell they were officers. The morning sun glinted off their gold braid, but even without that you could tell. It was the way they walked, like they owned the place. They were completely at home. You knew no one was going to yell at them for being late for sentry duty, or for having dirty boots.

They were strolling along the road having a good old chat. They didn't have rifles, but although it was hard to tell from that distance, I thought they might have handguns in holsters on their hips.

I stood there having a little tremble. They still hadn't seen me. But even as I trembled I knew I had to do something. A voice of logic in my head was saying: "You have to be calm, think coolly. It's your only hope." I knew from working with stock that the men hadn't seen me because I was standing still. You can get away with a lot by not moving. It's amazing what you can get away with. But although my stillness had saved me so far it wouldn't save me as they got closer. A teenager standing in the doorway with a pile of food plundered from their fridge? Yeah, sure, they were going to walk right past and ignore me.

I started to ease back into the building. I'd closed the door behind me but the tongue hadn't gone all the way into the catch, which was a bonus. So it opened quite smoothly and quietly. I was still in the shadows and now I slid a little farther into them. They were only thirty, maybe thirty-five, metres away. A jet screamed overhead and although they didn't look up I thought it might distract them slightly and give me the moment I needed. As the noise hit maximum decibels, and the jet crossed the roadway on its way to the landing strip, I did a quick fade into the dormitory, closing the door behind me.

There was no yell of alarm from outside. I ran to a window and peeped out. The two officers were still coming, totally absorbed in their conversation. That was fine, except that now I was in a building where I didn't want to be, couldn't afford to be. Not if I wanted to stay alive.

Which I did.

I ran to the back windows. There was nothing much there to look at: all open space, a huge expanse of airfield. The jet I'd just seen was now taxiing to a halt, smoke puffing from its wheels. Soon it would start swinging round to go meet the fuel truck.

I ran to the front again. I was feeling like a rat in a trap, and acting like one too. All this frantic running backwards and forwards, an animal in a cage, hoping against hope there'd be some little hole she hadn't noticed before.

This time from the front window I saw an even more

frightening sight. The officers were angling towards the barracks. They were on a course that would bring them through the door in seconds. I had another rush of panic: paralysing, frightening panic, and again I had to fight madly to keep it down, to suffocate it. They were only ten metres away.

I looked around wildly. The kitchenette was on my right but there wasn't much cover in there. At the other end, on the left, was what had to be a bathroom, but I hadn't bothered to check it out. I could fit into a locker, thanks to all the weight I'd lost in this war, but that was too much of a cage for my liking. Too claustrophobic. No hope if I was found in there. Looked like it had to be the bathroom. I ran towards it, on swift, silent feet, still clutching the food. I didn't dare drop it now.

The bathroom had a swinging door, like in restaurant kitchens, and as I swung it open I heard the men open the barracks door, behind me. It was as close as that. A photo finish. Had I been snapped by their eyes? I had to know. I turned and grabbed the door to stop it swinging and put my eye to the crack.

I couldn't see them, and for a moment my imagination went into a crazy and horrible fantasy where I pictured them creeping down the sides of the room until they were either side of me, ready to launch a big assault on the bathroom. Then one of them crossed my line of vision. He bent down and checked the corner of a bed, as if to see how neat it was. "Of course," I thought. "They're inspecting the place. That's why everything's so immaculate." I remembered Mike, the big black-haired Maori or Samoan soldier who Fi liked so much, and how he'd said the best thing about coming on the mission was that you didn't have to worry about inspections any more. Sounded like life at home with Mum sometimes.

I left the door and fled to the other end of the bathroom. There was another door here, another swinging door, and I pushed it open after only a quick peep. I had to hope no one was in there.

I was in a room that was like an annexe to the main dormitory. But it was completely different. It had a lived-in feeling — that's just a polite way of saying it was a mess. Beds unmade, clothes scattered everywhere, an open jar of peppermints on the floor, and at my feet three or four pages of a letter written on light blue aerogram paper.

None of that was important. Only one thing mattered. Above each bed, resting on the same kind of brackets I'd noticed in the other room, was a rifle. Dark, black, heavy things, so sinister. Magic wands of death. But they had magazines in them and I knew they could just be the only hope I had. I didn't hesitate. I jumped onto the nearest bed, grabbed the rifle and lifted it down.

First things first: I checked the magazine.

It was loaded to the brim. It looked like as many as twenty rounds in there. For the first time that morning I felt some sort of satisfaction. If this was the day I had to die, then at least it wouldn't be helplessly; I wouldn't be gunned down with only my bare hands outstretched to fend off the bullets.

I took a peep through the bathroom door. No movement yet. I didn't know which room I should hide in. Neither had an exit door, and the windows were too small and too high up. One thing or sure: there was nowhere to hide in here. Just four bare walls, eight beds and eight lockers. I couldn't get under the beds, because they went right to the floor they had drawers under them. And even if I changed my mind about hiding in a locker, I wouldn't be able to fit the rifle in as well. But I didn't want to change my mind about that.

What it came down to was a huge gamble. If the officers were doing an inspection they might not bother with this room. Obviously there was some reason it hadn't been cleaned up: maybe the guys who slept here were away on a mission or something. And the officers would know that, wouldn't they? So they could easily say to each other: "No point checking in there; they've gone to bomb New Zealand." If they did that and I stayed in this room then I was home free. On the other hand, if I stayed here and they came in, someone was going to die.

On the third hand, if I went in the bathroom and hid in a cubicle — the only place in the bathroom where I could hide — they might go right past and never know I was there. They might. All the cubicle doors were closed. I'd especially noticed that. I could get up on the dunny so my feet wouldn't be seen under the door.

They might also open the cubicle door and find me crouched on the dunny, wide-eyed, like a kangaroo caught in a spotlight.

I didn't have time to sit down on a bed with a piece of paper and make a list with two columns: "Points For" and "Points Against." I didn't have time to make a careful, calculated assessment of the situation. I'd already taken a couple of minutes to get the rifle and check the magazine. I had to make a decision.

"Ellie," I said to myself firmly, "whatever you decide, stick with it. No use worrying whether you've done the right thing."

In other words, I had to live or die on the decision I was about to make.

I went to the end bed and threw the food on the floor between it and the window. Then I lay on the floor, the rifle beside me. My right hand gripped it. I'd already flicked the safety forward and made sure there was a bullet in the breech. If they found me I'd have to shoot my way out. There were no other options. There seemed to be so few people around that I might just get away with it. But what then? My head started to hurt, thinking of the complications. I shut my eyes hard for a moment to block out those thoughts. I couldn't afford them. They were too distracting. I realised this was one of those times when I'd have to make things up as I went along; me, who always liked things to be organised, who wanted life to be planned, who'd been taught by my father that time spent in reconnaissance is seldom wasted.

Now there was no time for reconnaissance, no time to think of consequences, only a blind faith that if I got away with this action then maybe I could get away with the next, and the one after that, and the one after that, and so on. Of course something would go terribly wrong sooner or later. It would be like one of those cheap jumpers where you catch one thread on a nail and the whole sleeve suddenly unravels until you don't have a jumper anymore. I had to hope it would happen later rather than sooner, when maybe Homer or Lee would be around to help.

I suddenly held my breath, imagining I heard a voice. I realised, to my sick horror, that it wasn't imagination. It had to be the officers and they had to be very close. Were they in the room or not? I couldn't be quite sure. It was possible they had come in without my hearing the doors open. Just as I decided that no, they weren't in this dormitory, they must be in the bathroom, I heard a voice very close. They were here all right, they were about two beds from where I was lying. I nearly lifted off the floor in fright. I wouldn't have been surprised if I'd levitated way above the bed, where they could have a good view of me.

My grip tightened on the rifle. There had to be a shoot-out if they kept coming. I had the advantage of surprise. That would be worth a second. In that second I had to kill them both.

The same voice spoke again. He was still a couple of beds away. The other voice answered from way up the far end of the room. It wasn't a huge room, but it made my chances infinitely slimmer if I had to jump up and try to find him before I could shoot him. But, if that's what I had to do, then that's what I'd have to do. I was so hyped up now that I thought I really could levitate: I pictured myself springing up like I was on a trampoline and shooting both guys before they'd even moved.

My skin was prickling: lemonade legs again. Lice. I remembered my grandmother saying she suffered from something called prickly heat. I always thought it was a funny, interesting expression, so it stuck in my mind. Now I had prickly heat like my whole skin was burning, hot pinpricks all over me. I was keyed up to screaming point.

Then it happened. I went into automatic and lost myself completely for a couple of seconds. I was a robot, a terminator. I don't think I've ever experienced that before. There was a sudden shadow and all at once one of the officers was standing there. He was looking above my head at I don't know what, a mark on the wall maybe. He hadn't seen me. I swung the rifle up before he realised I was there. His mouth started to open with shock, but that was the only reaction he had time for. I couldn't miss at pointblank range. It was over in a split second. All I had time to notice was the way his hair flew up when the bullet hit him: his eyes closed and his hair went up like a sudden violent wind had gone through it. The force of the bullet sent him flying backwards over a chair. No human could have hit him as hard as that bullet did. But I didn't look any more. I didn't want to see the awfulness of it, and besides, I had another problem.

I swung round to the left, lifting the rifle a little higher as I did so. The other officer was in two minds, running to the door and at the same time reaching for his handgun. It seemed to be caught in the holster: he was wrestling it with one hand as he reached for the door with the other. He got the gun free as he pushed the door open. He swung towards me as he entered the doorway. I think he was hoping to get off a shot as he fled into the bathroom. But he had no chance. I was never going to miss. I squeezed the trigger. He went crashing through the door, leaving a smear of blood on it. I heard his body hit the hard bathroom floor with a terrible crash. I think he would have broken a bone or two as he landed, but he wasn't going to be worrying about that. It seems weird to think someone can break a bone after they're dead. I suppose it happens though, and it may have happened to him.

I knew now that there was no going back. I had knocked down the first two pins and the rest would have to be knocked down, no matter what it cost. I didn't know how I was going to break the news to the others that I'd signed their death warrants, but at least I'd do all I could to give us a fighting chance. The first thing I did was get four more rifles down from their racks.

I tried not to look at the bodies. I checked the one in

the bathroom, briefly, to make sure he was dead. The bullet had caught him in the neck, so he was dead all right. I won't describe what he looked like, but his body wasn't in one piece anymore. I'd shot the other one just below the chest, and he was dead too.

And just as I didn't spend any time looking at the bodies, I didn't spend any time thinking about what I'd done. I wasn't a robot or a terminator anymore, but I wasn't back to normal either. I still wasn't Ellie. I just got on with the job. I tried to be focused, to block out any ugly, frightening, nightmarish thoughts that would stop me doing my job effectively. I had to stay on automatic or I wouldn't be able to do it at all.

I grabbed the ankles of the man who was lying on the dormitory floor and dragged him in between two beds, where I chucked a blanket over him. I chucked some more blankets over the blood on the floor. It was all in the vague hope that people mightn't find the bodies for an extra half hour or so, because that could be absolutely critical for us. The dormitory was such a mess that maybe no one would notice the blankets scattered around.

Next stop was the bathroom. I ran towards the door. And it was at that moment, when I was just two metres away, that it flew back on its hinges. I hadn't expected that. I hadn't heard anyone coming. I didn't have any of the guns with me. There were all on the bed. I had two instant thoughts and I don't know which came first. Maybe neither of them did. Maybe they were simultaneous. One thought was that the enemy soldiers were back, returning to their barracks, and they were going to kill me. Tear me to pieces, at a guess. The other thought was that the soldier in the bathroom hadn't died after all: he had come back to life and was going to kill me.

What's that movie where you think the guy's dead and suddenly he rears back up at the goodie and everyone in the theatre screams? I can't remember. Maybe it was *The Terminator*.

My face went into a huge spasm and my left arm lifted up completely out of my control. It was weird. I could feel it happening but there was nothing I could do to stop it. I started to bend at the middle too, as if I expected a bullet to hit me there. That's how sure I was that my luck had finally run out for good.

7

IT WAS HOMER.

Oh Homer, there have been times in my life when I've been glad to see you and times when I haven't, but this time, yes, I was glad to see you.

Back in New Zealand there'd been a move to give us a medal or something. It seems like that kind of stuff takes about fifty years to organise though, and about sixteen committees have to consider it and you have to have heaps of independent witnesses. So we didn't think about it, although I'd like to have seen Robyn get one, a big one. But Homer that morning, he should have got one. He was truly brave.

Fi had seen the officers go into the barracks. Kevin and Homer were the only ones in the hangar. She ran and got Homer, who was on the toilet at the time. From inside the hangar, as he ran towards the little door, still pulling up his daks, Homer heard the shots. He knew they'd come from the barracks, and he knew they meant I was in desperate trouble. He didn't hesitate. With no weapons he crossed the road and stormed into the dormitory. When he found nothing there or in the kitchenette he went on through the bathroom, over the dead body, and into the annexe. That was a brave thing to do.

He didn't tell me that at the time of course. Every second was precious. We couldn't stand around having conversations. All he said was: "Are you OK?"

"Yes," I said, "but let's get the other one in here."

That was the first he knew that I'd killed two of them. But he didn't ask questions, just helped me wrap the two parts of the man in a bedspread and drag him out to where I'd put his mate. As we did I grunted: "They ambushed me." Homer just nodded. He was probably feeling like chucking up, which was the way I was feeling.

I used towels to wipe up the blood. It was a revolting job because he'd bled an awful lot, unlike the other man, who hadn't bled much at all. But I thought it was worth doing. It took five minutes, and if it bought us six minutes it was worthwhile.

"Do you think anyone else heard?" I asked Homer.

He shook his head.

"There was a jet went over just as you fired. Even Fi didn't hear."

That was good news, wonderful news, although I was amazed I hadn't heard the jet. Shows what concentration can do for you. Now that Homer mentioned it though, I realised that a number of jets were landing. There was one every thirty seconds. For all I knew it could have been going on for ages. I wouldn't have noticed.

When we'd finished our cleaning job we gathered the five rifles and the food. We didn't need to discuss the weapons. Homer knew what had to be done. We ran through the main dormitory again, carrying the guns, panting hard, knowing how deeply we were committed now, how those pins would keep falling. All we could do was try to push some of them in the directions we wanted. We wouldn't be able to push them all our way, that was for sure. At the end of the day the best outcome we could hope for was that we'd be alive.

From the door of the building we peered out. There was no movement along the road. We had to take our chances, keep going, so we put our heads down and sprinted for the hangar. As we belted in through the door another jet passed over our heads, so close I felt I could have touched it. The huge hangar acted like a sound barrier, so I didn't really hear the plane until it was right on top of us: I sure heard it then. I thought it was going to take my head off.

Lee and Fi were there. "Those planes are returning from a mission, I think," Lee said. They were his first words. Not "How are you?" or "Are you OK?" or even "Where have you been?" He was focused. It was left to Fi to ask those questions, and because there was such a sense of urgency she had to ask them with her eyes. There was no time for anything but the most urgent conversation. I gave her a quick squeeze then turned to Lee.

"We have to go for it now," I said. "Straightaway. I just shot two officers."

He calmly took a rifle and looked in the magazine. At least he seemed calm. I made Fi take one too, although she was definitely not calm. I could never quite get used to Fi holding a rifle. It was like Homer holding a Barbie doll.

Homer turned to Lee. "If they start refuelling the planes before they find the bodies, we've got a chance to do some damage . . ."

Lee cut in. "It'd have been better to wait till dark. But on the other hand, the planes are pouring in. There's a heap of them."

"By dark they might have found us anyway," said Homer. I think he mainly said it to make me feel better.

"Where are the other soldiers?" I asked. I knew Lee had gone to see what was happening. I wanted to know what he'd found.

"It's some kind of parade. Training for something.

They're still there, marching around in slow time, doing fancy stuff with their rifles."

"They're confident," Homer said. "They think they're safe in here."

"They're not," Lee said.

I was stunned. It was one of the strangest statements I've heard in my life.

This conversation was happening very quickly, in whispers. We were staring through our peepholes, trying to decide what was going on. There was certainly a heap of activity. A lot of planes were returning from somewhere. I could see three jets on the move: one just landing, one turning at the end of the runway to come back towards us, and one taxiing onto the apron where all the planes were parked. But it was crucial for us that refuelling started immediately. We only needed ten minutes to do what we had to do, but if the soldiers returned to their barracks after the parade and found the dead men, we wouldn't get our ten minutes.

"There's one," Lee said suddenly. I looked in the direction he was pointing but I couldn't get the right angle through my peephole. So I slipped across to his spot and he let me look. Sure enough, the first fuel tanker was already lumbering along the road towards the parked jets, like a big old dinosaur. Behind it I could see a second one nosing out of its depot. My stomach did a wild lurch, like my entire insides turned upside down. It felt like an earthquake had happened in there. These tankers were our death warrant. We wanted to see them, they represented our chance to destroy the place, but at the same time they were a death warrant. There was no getting away from that.

"Let's go," Homer said.

The four of us glanced at each other. What for? I don't

know. Just a check I guess, to make sure we were all up to it, all prepared. I have no idea what I looked like but I was a bit surprised to see that the other three had identical expressions: thin lips pressed together, pale complexions, sweaty foreheads, but steady eyes. I was encouraged by that.

We ran for the trucks. I'd completely forgotten about Kevin although we'd talked about him when we made our plans. He was coming with us, whether he liked it or not. That probably sounds brutal, but we had no choice. How could we leave him there?

It would have been ideal if he'd driven one of the trucks, because after me he was the best driver. But Homer was OK, and he'd have to do. Fi and Lee weren't too crash hot. Well, that was the trouble; they were very crash hot. They were dangerous. In fact they were so dangerous maybe we should have just let them loose on the enemy: they would have run over the lot of them.

There was no need for discussion. Fi and I ran to the furniture van, and Lee and Homer to the other truck we'd chosen, a high-sided Dumpster that weighed ten or twelve tonnes and looked solid. We started them up. That moment, turning the key: it was horrible, a terrible feeling. I gave a quick glance at Fi and looked away again, just as quickly. She looked ghastly. Like someone with a terminal illness.

Well, we were all suffering from that terminal illness.

As I started the engine there was a cry from the back. A wail of fear, like a baby who's burnt his hand. It had an hysterical edge to it. Like I said, I'd forgotten Kevin.

I glanced at Fi again. She looked grim now. "I'll go," she said, getting out of her seat. Before she could move, Kevin appeared at the little hatch between the cab and the main part of the van. He looked worse than Fi. Probably not worse than me, but I wasn't looking in the mirror. He had snot hanging out of his nose and he hadn't done his hair for about a week and a half, and during that week and a half I think he must have been running his hand constantly through it, messing it up as much as he could. His eyes were wild, staring at one of us then the other, as though he'd never seen us before.

"What's going on?" he squealed at me. "What are you doing?"

I didn't know if we should give him any sort of answer, because I dreaded his response. But Fi said: "This is it Kev, we're attacking the planes."

His whole face crumpled. In Science we'd done an experiment where you pump the air out of a tin can. The can crumples into a complete wreck. Well, that was Kevin. His spirit had been pumped out of him.

He ran his hand through his hair again and cried: "Ellie, this is crazy. Don't do it, please. This is suicide!"

But I put the truck in gear. Homer's Dumpster was already moving towards the big door. As it stopped by the door, with a piercing squeak of its brakes, Lee jumped out. He looked across at us, waiting till we got closer before he opened us up to the outside world. Once he did that, we were committed. And for the first minute or so we'd have nothing going for us but bluff. We had to hope that any soldiers who saw the trucks would assume we were on legitimate business. If they didn't, if they knew straightaway we were up to no good, we'd be wiped out before we got a hundred metres. We'd end up like feathers from a pillow when it bursts in a pillow fight. I knew that when the door opened we had only a few minutes to live. And a few minutes was our best-case scenario.

I didn't blame Kevin for going to pieces. I wasn't far off going there myself. Kevin had gone to pieces mentally and emotionally, but I figured we were all about to go to pieces physically. We'd end up looking like the dead officer in the bathroom of the barracks. I couldn't help thinking of Robyn, and the way she'd died. I knew it was the wrong time to think of her but I thought I'd be seeing her pretty soon.

We rolled forward. I glanced up at the rear-vision mirror to try to get a glimpse of Kevin; but then realised that of course there was no rear-vision mirror. There's not much use for them in furniture vans.

"Where's Kevin?" I asked Fi. She didn't answer for a minute: I think she was trying to peer into the back of the truck. Then she said: "It's hard to tell. It looks like he's under a pile of packing."

We were at the door. Lee gave us a nod and started to open it. "It's terrible," I said to Fi, meaning what we were doing to Kevin, the way we were taking him to almost certain death.

"Yes," she said, "it is."

I had to assume she knew what I meant, because there was no time to confirm it, no time for anything now except killing and dying.

The doors were sliding open. It was one of those arrangements where as you slid open one door, the next panel opened automatically. I took a quick look at Lee. He looked calm and beautiful.

I wondered if this was the last time I would see him. Or Homer.

The door was open enough for us to get through. I heard the loud revving of Homer's engine. He was giving it too much throttle, but it's hard getting used to a strange engine in a hurry, especially on a truck. The big dusty Dumpster started to roll. I noticed the dust and thought it was funny on a military base, where everything was so immaculate. I followed him out, then stopped and waited for Lee. He closed the door. There were a couple of soldiers down the other end of the road, but they had their backs turned. Lee jumped into the cab, with a last wave to us. I revved my engine and followed Homer.

Outside everything seemed bright and clear. It was like watching a very sharp movie on a very big screen. There was so much space. I swung the truck to the right, still following Homer, and peeped farther to my right, to where the soldiers were parading. For a moment I couldn't believe what I was seeing. But it had to be real. A crowd of men were at the end of the road, coming our way. I thought we'd been busted already, they were attacking us. Then I realised it couldn't be that. They must have finished their drill and were heading back to the barracks for a cup of tea and a good lie down. Bad timing. It meant the bodies of the officers would probably be found in three or four minutes. Not necessarily: they might not go into the messy dormitory, but I thought the odds were stacking even higher against us.

As if they weren't high enough already.

Homer swung off quickly to the left, down a side road. That was OK; it still took us in the direction of the parked jets. I followed him equally quickly, but at the same time worrying that we were driving too fast. We couldn't afford to draw attention to ourselves. We had to buy a minute and a half, at least, so we could get into position to cause the havoc that we wanted to cause.

And it was havoc we wanted. Havoc, chaos, destruction. If we succeeded, this airfield would be an inferno.

We had a chance to wipe out more aircraft in a couple of minutes than the New Zealand Air Force had wiped out in the last six months.

I could see them now. God, so many of them. That was good but frightening. I'd been feeling sick for so long it shouldn't have worried me anymore, but at this moment I felt I was going to lose everything in my stomach, and what's worse, lose it at both ends. The jets looked like hornets and I felt we were ants. Ants attacking hornets.

There were nine tankers fuelling planes, and another four planes in a line waiting to fill up. Thirteen altogether. Unlucky number for someone. There were about forty, maybe fifty, planes parked along the apron. This all fitted with what we'd seen before. We hadn't seen more than nine tankers out there and we suspected there weren't anymore. Their whole security depended on speed. They couldn't afford to have planes sitting on the ground for ages with no fuel in them, or with fuel lines running from trucks to planes. They were at their most vulnerable then. Colonel Finley and Iain had both made some comment like that to me, somewhere sometime.

We drove towards them. Homer's big truck lumbered on in front of us. Our speed was controlled by him. If he hadn't been there I don't know what speed I would have accelerated to. Probably about a hundred and forty. But the dump truck was a bit like the kind of person Homer had become. Solid and dependable and strong.

"I hope the bullets work," Fi said suddenly.

"How do you mean?"

"Well, just because it worked when Homer did it in a paddock with a tin can doesn't mean it'll work here."

I drove on, feeling I'd been hit over the head with a piece of four by two. Fi was right. This might be some special fuel, or they might have special shields on the tankers.

Homer veered to the left. This was as we'd agreed. We were now only four hundred metres from the nearest jet. Our plan was simple. Homer and Lee would take the farther group of planes; we'd take the closer ones. As the boys drove towards their target, we slowed down and moved out to the right, to get in the best possible position for firing.

Up until then we'd had an amazing run. No one had come near us or shown the slightest interest in us. But now things changed in a hurry. The next few minutes were madness: a wild sideshow ride where the winners got to live and the losers got to die.

8

THE FIRST SIGN OF TROUBLE WAS WHEN FI GRABBED MY arm. She whispered in my ear: "There's a car coming." I don't know why she whispered. It was hard enough to hear anyway, above the diesel rumbling of the truck. I glanced across to where she pointed and sure enough there it was: a green jeep with a canvas top, moving at high speed straight towards us. It was coming from the far side of the airfield and was still three or four hundred metres away. But there was no doubt it was after us. It was openly menacing, racing at us so directly.

I thought fast. I had to make my mind work as fast as that car was travelling, even faster. I don't know why your brain works sometimes and at other times it freezes up. It's not only danger and adrenalin; that time in Wirrawee when everything deserted me was a time of great danger and yet I fell apart. Here was another time of great danger and this time my brain functioned. But to be fair to myself, the time in Wirrawee wasn't long after Robyn died, and not long after I'd done something I really regretted with a boy in Wellington.

With the jeep, I didn't hesitate. I started making a big turn, quite gentle, so it wouldn't look suspicious, even slowing down a little, and at the same time said to Fi: "Get a good grip on something."

"What about Kevin?" she asked.

I hadn't even thought of Kevin. "Tell him too," I said.

There was no more time for conversation. Fi shouted into the back of the truck: "Kevin, grab a hold of something!"

At this stage we were facing northwest. The jeep was coming from the west. When we turned they slowed, then swung hard left to come around the front of us, maybe to get onto the driver's side of the truck, I don't know. I hadn't been expecting that, but it worked just as well for what I wanted. I think they still weren't sure about us, not knowing if we were a threat to their security or there for some legitimate reason. They probably couldn't believe anyone had got through their fantastic defences.

I started accelerating again, gently at first, then, when I judged them to be at the right point, I charged. Foot straight to the floor. The old truck did pretty well. Probably no one had ever asked her to do anything exciting or brave. Probably no one had asked her to go at full speed. Whatever, she surged forward with more power than I'd expected.

It happened so quickly that the soldiers in the jeep were caught unawares. I saw their startled faces. They were yelling at the driver and trying to get their rifles up. The driver thought he was going to get around the right-hand side of me, then did the worst thing possible: he changed his mind. He decided he wouldn't make it — he probably wouldn't have, it's hard to say — and he braked, slammed it into reverse and tried to back away at the same time as he spun the wheel hard to the right. It was a terrible, stupid decision. That's what I meant before, about how sometimes our minds work and sometimes they freeze. I don't know why he made such a bad move, such a bad call, at that moment of his life. And I'll never know now. Fi ducked to the floor, with her hands over her eyes, and

I shut my eyes for the last two or three metres. It was terrible. I was still accelerating when we hit them. Someone told me once that the police are trained to do that: accelerate when they know they're going to hit another car. That way they suffer less damage themselves. It's horrible, but I don't know where that leaves me, because I didn't take my foot off the accelerator until the very last second. I wouldn't have even then, but some reflex made me lift it off as we hit. It seemed too frightening to hit at full speed in that cold-blooded way.

Still, we would have been doing ninety when we rammed.

It was a massacre. The jeep fragmented; there were bits lying all over the tarmac. Some pieces were a hundred metres away. The biggest piece I saw was the door, and that wasn't very big, being from a jeep. And I saw the engine. It was sitting on the ground like a mechanic had lifted it out with a block and tackle.

There were bodies, too. I think there'd been four or five soldiers in the jeep, but I only saw two bodies, one lying completely still and the other sort of twisting from side to side, like a fish that's been out of water five minutes and hasn't got much left.

And I saw some bits of bodies.

Of course I didn't do a major examination of the crash site. My glimpses were just that, glimpses, and I got them at high speed as we turned a big circle. I had to swing the truck around fast, so we could line up the petrol tankers while they were attached to the jets. It didn't necessarily matter if they weren't attached, but it was better if they were. So I put the truck into a skidding turn, hanging onto the wheel like grim death even though I thought we had a good chance of tipping. I could feel the tyres lifting on the right-hand side and I thought, "Hello, this is it, we're over." But I didn't bring the steering wheel back even one degree, because I knew we had to go for it, all or nothing, no slowing down for any reason.

In a way it was like a roundabout. We got a view of everything as we spun, a full look at the entire scene. I saw the wreckage of the jeep, I saw the vast expanse of the runways and the security fence beyond them. I saw some soldiers piling out of the door of a big humpy-shaped shed near the control tower, I saw Homer and Lee's truck swinging wide to get a good position, and I saw the rows of planes and the fuel tankers.

That was where the action was. The rest of the airfield would get revved up sooner or later — the soldiers teeming out of the shed would be the first of many — but the guys on the tankers knew right away that this was life or death. Two or three just ran. Even though we hadn't done anything yet to threaten them personally, they weren't sticking around. The rest were going mental. They were jumping down off the wings of planes, they were unscrewing hoses off threads, they were running to the cabins of trucks. They knew that whatever we had in mind, they were the targets. They knew they had seconds to save their lives.

We had two problems. One was that as we skidded round we weren't in a good position to line up the rifles. Fi was trying to get off the floor and I was yelling at her: "Get up, get up," but with the centrifugal force of the turn she was very slow. The other problem was that we were now too close. Dangerously close. We could be incinerated.

As soon as we were far enough out of the turn I slammed on the brakes. Fi had just got up on the seat.

Now she lurched forward, hitting her head on the windscreen. We didn't need that windscreen anyway but this was not the way to get rid of it. I'd once seen a worker on our place punch his fist through a windscreen, when Dad sacked him. It was the windscreen on the old Datsun paddock basher. But Fi's head didn't even crack this one.

As I wrenched the gearstick into reverse I yelled at Fi again: "Come on." There was no time to sympathise about her head injury. With the truck stationary for a second, shuddering with the shock of what I'd done to it, Fi managed to twist back up onto her seat. There was blood running down her face and she looked as pale as a peeled banana.

"The guns, the guns," I shouted at her. I still hadn't found reverse. Bloody thing, where was it? It took me three goes. I thought our whole mad attempt might end there. Then with a crunch the gearstick went into its socket. "Thank God," I muttered. I hit the throttle again, foot flat to the floor. At least with hectares of airfield behind us there was nothing much we could hit. I didn't even look in the side mirrors. If there was another jeep behind us it'd have to take its chances.

We went backwards, wheels spinning, lurching violently, Fi bouncing like a cork in a spa. We did run over something, probably a bit of debris from the jeep. But I knew we had to stop about then anyway. We just couldn't take any more time. If we were too close and got barbecued, so be it. It was impossible to tell what was too close anyway. We didn't have a lot of experience with this stuff. But to keep reversing for another five minutes — well, it wasn't an option. If we were wiped out we had to do all the damage we could first.

So I hit the brakes again. This time I remembered to

warn Fi and she braced herself — just — by hanging onto the seat with one hand and the windscreen with the other. She held the rifles between her knees, pointing up at the roof but as we braked they both swung towards me. I hoped to God the safeties were still on.

So the moment had come. All those careful plans Colonel Finley and Iain and Ursula had made, so carefully, so long ago, so far away they came to nothing. Now it was up to us, using a plan we'd made up on the spur of the moment, using our own brains and initiative, and a lot of luck. Funny, the Kiwis had only wanted us to come on this trip as guides; they thought because we were young we wouldn't be much use. Even though we'd done so much already, they thought it was all a fluke. You could tell by the way they looked at us, and the way they talked. Like they knew so much more than us.

Well, here we were, inside the airfield, about to inflict major damage. I just hoped they'd build a big memorial to us after this was over.

I grabbed one rifle as Fi lifted the other. Fi was the worst shot in the Southern Hemisphere, but at least she was marginally better at handling a gun now, compared to when the war started. I checked that my safety was still on, then swung it round and used the butt to bash through the windscreen. It was wild. Glass flew. We got showered with it. But there was no time to check for scratches and cuts. Beside me Fi tried to bash out what was left of her part of the glass. But she wasn't aggressive enough. Or maybe she wasn't strong enough. Whatever, I swung my rifle again, nearly braining Fi, and smashed out all the glass I could.

And then we were ready. Ahead of us were five tankers. Coming from the right, around the corner of a hangar, were two more jeeps. I didn't dare look in the side mirrors. Anything could be happening behind us. I wished Kevin was functioning, so he could cover the rear. Or the right. Or the left. Anywhere. As it was, I had to make another quick decision, one of the most crucial I'd ever make. Fi was a lousy shot, sure. On the other hand, no one could miss these tankers. They sat there like big fat chooks in a nice line, like geese on their way to the dam. Although soldiers were rushing frantically to get the hoses out and move the trucks I estimated it'd be thirty seconds before they got rolling. These rifles could empty their magazines in a lot less than thirty seconds. But the two jeeps were coming fast. They were out of the cover of the buildings already, in the sunshine. I still wanted to stay alive. Stupid, sure, but it's the way I am. There was only one thing for it. I said to Fi: "You do the tankers."

She looked at me in horror. "Oh, but Ellie . . ."

"Just do it," I yelled at her.

Farther to my right, there was a massive blast. The ground rocked. A wave of hot air suddenly buffeted the truck, so that we rocked from side to side. From the left, I heard screams and shouts. Ahead of me, more soldiers started running away from the tankers. They knew what was coming now. Homer and Lee had struck, and they knew what we were going to do.

The force of the explosion made me realise we were probably still much too close, but it was too late to do anything about that. I didn't have time to look for Homer and Lee either; I hoped they were OK, but if they weren't there was nothing I could do. As Fi trembling and looking sick, raised her rifle, I wriggled around farther to my right and got into a comfortable position, head just above the bottom of the window and rifle resting on the sill. The jeeps were still coming and I didn't have much time.

No sooner was I in position than there was a second explosion from the direction of the boys. Then another one, almost immediately. Seemed like they were going to be finished before we'd even started. I took aim, but my mind was on Fi, begging her to get a move on.

I think we both fired at the same time. There was the familiar BOOM of the rifles: less smoke than with other weapons I'd used, but a big recoil. I braced myself, waiting for the huge explosion, thinking there was a fair chance the truck would be blown right over. There was nothing. The only interesting thing was that the leading jeep, a bit to the left of the other one suddenly lost its windscreen. It shattered and blew out. I guess I was pleased but I didn't have time to think about it. Instead I was looking around for Fi, to see what had happened.

She was distraught. "I missed," she sobbed. She was like a kid who's grazed her knee. I couldn't believe it. No one, no one, could miss at this range. They talk about people who can't hit the side of a barn. Fi couldn't hit the Empire State Building at twenty paces. From our right suddenly came a series of explosions that I thought would never stop. The sun seemed to disappear. Everything went dark. The truck was rocking and being pushed around like a bulldozer was attacking it. We were actually being turned around — a truck that weighed five tonnes, and we were being turned around. "Go again," I screamed at Fi. I looked out the front — that was how much we'd been pushed around — to see where the jeeps were. One had been blown right over, and there were soldiers clambering out of it. The other, to my horror, was only twenty-five metres away, stopped, and I could see rifles being levelled at us. You had to give those guys credit. I had about one second to get them. I'd have to waste some ammunition here. It'd be stupid to die with unused ammo in the magazine. I fired a few rounds but out of the corner of my eye I saw soldiers from the overturned jeep kneeling and preparing to shoot. I started taking aim at them and was about to fire when Fi finally had her second shot. It felt like she spent five minutes lining it up. It wouldn't surprise me, because she would have been so nervous about missing again.

But she didn't miss.

Our whole plan was based on the simple fact that when Homer and I, in our immature youth, fired at those tin cans filled with fuel they exploded instantly, into groovy little fireballs. I guess the spark as the bullet penetrated the metal was what did it. We figured that if it worked on a small scale with a tin can it ought to work on a big scale with a petrol tanker.

We were right.

And we got blown away. I was right about that too. We'd been much too close.

God, I'll never forget that feeling. Now I know what cyclone victims go through. The terrible noise, the complete loss of control, being shaken with bone-snapping violence, like a rabbit in the mouth of a terrier, like a sock in a tumble drier. Trying to keep my gun in the air so it wouldn't go off and kill Fi. You feel so helpless. You are helpless. It was like when the four-wheel drive crashed in Wirrawee, only a thousand times worse. I hung onto the steering wheel but soon lost that, and ended up on top of Fi. All I could think of was those guns. I was still holding mine, still pointing it away, but what about Fi?

Did she have a grip on hers? Once again, I'd forgotten poor Kevin in the back of the van.

I reckon we were blown more than fifty metres. Amazingly, the truck ended up the right way up again, sitting on its four wheels, if it still had four left. We were side on to the holocaust we'd created, but the other way around. I couldn't see anything of the tanker Fi hit — the flames were too intense to look at. I caught glimpses of dark skeletons of planes through the fire. All their fabric had been burnt away and you could only see black ribs, like a balsawood framework of a plane. Then there was another gust of wind and the planes disappeared again.

Almost simultaneously there were another two explosions, from inside the fire. I think it was probably the next two tankers. Or maybe they'd already gone up while we were being blown away. I wouldn't have noticed. Maybe it was some planes blowing up. They didn't seem quite as strong as the first explosion, but then we were farther away now. When they blew there was an amazing skyrocket effect, huge fiery orange comets burning into the sky, with this weird, whistling, sizzling noise. I guess that happened with the first explosion too, but I hadn't noticed among the spinning and rolling of the truck.

There were still two tankers the flames hadn't reached. One at each end of the inferno. With a feeling of fierce joy in my heart I put the rifle to my shoulder. I had been burning for revenge for a long time, and now I was going to do some real burning, to get them back for all they'd done to us. It was the most primitive feeling I've ever had. It went further back than primitive: it was primeval. I was cave-woman swinging the club around my head and charging at the jackals and hyenas.

It only took two shots. I figured I'd better do it fast,

because when the shock wave from the first blast hit us I wouldn't have a chance to fire the second.

It was unbelievable. When these things blew, they sure blew. With each shot came a huge flash of light, lasting a second or more, then a column of fire that went up a hundred metres, more blazing comets rocketing into the stratosphere, and a fireball that rolled across the ground like a giant blazing tumbleweed. There wasn't much smoke, but all of it was black. One part of the fireball met the rest of the fire and there was a sort of "wump" as they connected. It started burning even harder and hotter at that point, though a second earlier I would have said it was impossible for this fire to get stronger or hotter.

Then the shock waves hit us again and we rocked backwards and forwards. We were getting used to it, I suppose. I started wondering if I'd get seasick. But it wasn't too bad this time.

What was bad was the lack of air. It was like I couldn't get any oxygen into my lungs. The heat was so intense, even at this distance, that I felt I was getting burnt. I glanced at Fi and tried to say, "We've got to get out of here." I couldn't say the words but she seemed to understand, because she nodded.

Then she did something really heroic. First Homer, now Fi. I'm not kidding, we were in big trouble with air. I think the oxygen must have been sucked into the fire because I honestly felt I might suffocate. Fi looked very red in the face, but she suddenly started to climb through the hatch. I grabbed at her to ask her what she was doing, then I realised. Kevin! God, how could I have forgotten? As she disappeared into the darkness I forced myself up to peer after her. I couldn't see anything. I hesitated, then decided the smart thing was to leave Fi to fix up Kevin while I tried to get the truck moving. I didn't have much hope it would start, but I turned the key anyway. It actually whirred, which impressed me, but it didn't sound like it had a hope in hell of starting. Besides, even if it did, the tyres and suspension were probably wrecked.

I left it and stood back up, turning round to look through the hatch again. I still couldn't see anything. It was time to abandon ship. I went to open the driver's side door but the frame must have been buckled, because I couldn't shift it. So I struggled awkwardly through the window. My lungs felt like they were burning, like I was inhaling fire instead of air. They say smoking's bad for your health. I should have dropped dead on the spot from lung cancer.

It was such a relief when my feet touched ground. I ran around to the back door. I was sobbing for lack of air but at the same time trying not to sob, because I'd read somewhere that when you panic you use up more oxygen. There wasn't much of it left. I got to the back of the truck and wrenched at the doors. They wouldn't open: the truck was so badly buckled and crumpled across the top. I was really sobbing now, thinking I'd never get Fi and Kevin out.

OK, they could still get through the hatch into the cab, but it was dangerously short of oxygen, and dangerously hot up the front. Radiant heat, that's meant to be the big killer in bushfires. And I didn't know if Kevin would be that easy to move. If he was still in the middle of his breakdown he mightn't be too keen to do gymnastics through the little hole.

The roar of the fire sounded like it was right on top of us. Kevin and Fi must have felt they were in a microwave. I broke a few fingernails pulling at the door. The truck shook and shivered as another huge explosion, to my left, rocked the ground. The very air seemed to shiver and shake. There was a shimmer, like you get on a really hot day, when you feel there's a distorting piece of glass between you and what you're looking at. There were crashes and thumps all around me. I couldn't figure out what it was, then I realised: red-hot bits of jagged metal raining out of the sky from the last explosion.

I was trying to think, desperately. "What can I do to get this door open?" I needed a tool, but where could I get that? Then, suddenly, I heard a banging on the inside of the door. Fi or Kevin, or both of them, were hammering, trying to get out. But it sounded like all they had was their fists. It sure didn't sound like a sledgehammer, which is what they'd need. The sound made me even more desperate. They were going to die in there. They must have a lot less oxygen than me and I didn't have nearly enough. I flung myself against the door trying to push it back into shape. It didn't work.

Then I heard a voice. It came from above my head. Honestly, I thought it was the voice of God for a moment. It was actually the voice of Homer. Never do I want him to know I confused him with God. His ego's big enough already. His voice came from above my head because I was now crouched down, trying to rip the door open from the bottom.

"Stand back," he said. "Make way for a man."

Typical. I did make way though. Not because he's a man but because he had something I didn't. A crowbar. It was one of those jemmy-shaped ones, about a metre long, heavy and vicious. And very effective. It took him three quick moves, jamming it into the doorframe at three different points, and wrenching hard towards him with all his strength. With the third wrench the door flew open.

Fi and Kevin stood there. They looked pretty wild and pretty upset. Kevin shook like an old man trying to walk for the first time in six months. They stumbled out, down the little step, into our arms. But there was no time for charity. Once their feet were firmly on the ground they had to take care of themselves. I grabbed my pack — it was the only one I could see — and spun around. Behind us, its engine still rumbling away, was the boys' truck. Lee stood between us and the truck, his rifle cradled across his arms. He wasn't looking at us. He was looking in every direction, his head constantly darting backwards and forwards, waiting for the inevitable counterattack. One guy with one rifle ready for the swarms of soldiers who would soon be closing in. We ran towards the truck. I looked back once, and saw Kevin moving pretty well. He was actually a few metres ahead of Fi, so whatever nervous breakdown he was going through, it didn't affect his speed when he wanted to get out of danger.

I got to the cab of the truck. Normally, in situations like this I'd drive. But Homer would be used to this truck by now. Used to the clutch. If I got in and stalled it, we could all die, just because of one stupid mistake.

Behind me Homer called, "Have you got your rifle?"

"No, oh no. We left them in the van."

I glanced around to look at him. In a way I wished I hadn't. The view was horrifying. A wall of flame as high as the sky stretched to right and left, as far as I could see. It was all red, a vast flaring curtain. Somewhere there must be a top to it, but from what I could see it went up forever. Planes, tankers, hangars, sheds, barracks, everything must have been part of the blaze, everything in there would be incinerated. The heat was appalling. I felt as dried out as the beef jerky we'd brought from New Zealand for rations. Luckily I had a long-sleeved shirt on. I knew my face was burnt. My lungs felt burnt too, but that might have been the lack of oxygen.

We should have prepared for this like you would a bushfire, but we'd never dreamt it would be so huge.

I realised we must make great targets, silhouetted against the flames. All I could see beyond the truck was the grass expanse and bitumen runways of the airfield. To my left, where the administration buildings stood, I thought I got a glimpse of people running, but there was so much smoke and garbage floating around that I might have been wrong. I thought I could hear sirens wailing, but again, over the roar of flames, I couldn't be sure of anything. Our attack had happened so fast that they'd still be reacting. I guess the first thought of anyone remotely near the explosions would be to save themselves. Only then would they regroup, reorganise.

Homer swung himself into the cab of the truck. He grabbed his rifle and handed it to me. Then he jumped down again and helped Fi and Kevin up. As he was doing that I ran around to the other side. On the way I passed Lee. I'll never forget the way he looked. Unbelievable. Talk about Rambo. He stood there cradling that gun, legs apart, rock solid, his face expressionless, only his head moving as he scanned the airfield. I thought at that moment I could trust my life to Lee any time and he would never let me down. I continued on round to the passenger door and swung myself up into the cab. As I did, I noticed something funny. A row of holes suddenly appeared in the tray of the truck. A neat little row, like they'd been carefully lined up. Direct drilling. It took me a moment to realise what they were. Then I screamed at Homer, who'd just leapt into the other side again, "We're being fired at!"

"Took them long enough," he said calmly.

He shoved the truck into gear and the old thing leapt forward.

"What about Lee?" I gasped.

Homer shrugged.

"He can walk."

Only Homer could make a joke at a time like this. I glanced in the side mirror, and sure enough there was Lee, in the dump section, with the rifle at his shoulder now, in a firing position. I didn't wait to see if he fired. Instead I got busy doing the same thing: trying to save our skins. I brought Homer's rifle up to my shoulder too and searched the airfield, looking for the trouble I knew was out there.

Homer cut loose on the accelerator. It was insane. If I hadn't been shaken up already, I sure got shaken up now. One second I was thrown against Fi, the next against the window. He was doing the right thing though, zig-zagging wildly. The tyres on the truck were tested like never before. At any moment I was expecting at least one of them to blow. We lurched down hard on one side, then suddenly lurched down harder on the other.

Of course it was made a lot worse by the rough ground. We were racing at maximum speed across the grass of the airfield. Then there was another wild lurch, to the left this time, and to my astonishment we were suddenly on a smooth beautiful surface.

It took me a second to work it out. Then I realised. A runway. Unbelievable. I didn't know if this was a good idea. It meant we were getting away from the hottest part of the fires very quickly, and maybe getting out of range of some of their guns, but on the other hand we would be an easier target, going in a straight line.

Then Fi grabbed my shoulder, digging her fingers in like talons. She pointed, but she didn't need to, because I'd just seen it as well. I felt sick: my insides seemed to collapse.

It was a jet coming in to land.

I'd say it was about twenty metres above the end of the runway. Its wheels and flaps came down together, like a duck spreading its wings as it landed. It was a beautifully symmetrical thing, beautifully balanced, perfectly shaped. But there was still something vicious about it: it was more like a wasp than a bird. It seemed weird to me that it would come into an airport where almost every building was a raging inferno, but maybe it was out of fuel and had no choice. Anyway, it sure as hell was going to land.

And Homer kept right on driving.

At first I thought he hadn't seen it. But with us all screaming at him, that didn't seem likely. It only took one look at his face to realise he'd seen it. He was pale and sweaty and his eyes were fixed on the plane like he was hypnotised. "He's going to bluff it," I thought. This was like those awful games of chicken in American movies, where cars go straight towards each other at top speed. I can never bear to watch them in movies, but here, on the runway, in real life, it was infinitely worse.

With a little puff of white smoke from its wheels the jet touched down. It gave a slight skid, but that was its only hesitation. Suddenly it was screaming down the runway, right at us. It seemed to have a mind of its own. And I didn't know if that mind was going to change in time to stop us getting smashed to pieces. What speed would the plane be doing when it hit us? Two hundred k's? Three hundred?

We just kept coming. We would have been doing close on a hundred k's ourselves, every revolution that could be squeezed out of the old diesel. I put my hand on the door handle and glanced out the window. I didn't like the thought of throwing myself out of a truck going at a hundred k's, throwing myself onto bitumen. But I didn't like the thought of hitting this jet full on. If it came to the point would I be able to jump? I didn't know if I had that much courage.

Fi was screaming at Homer. She was actually screaming: "Stop! Stop!" which wasn't good advice, because if we stopped we still would have been wiped out. I think Kevin fainted. His eyes were shut and his face looked clammy, little drops of sweat all over him. He was leaning against Fi's shoulder like he had no control, like if she wasn't there he'd fall straight to the floor.

And Homer, good old Homer, he seemed set to kill us all. His eyes looked like someone on drugs. He gripped the steering wheel as if he wanted to squeeze juice out of it. He was backing himself to the maximum, using our lives as the stake. The truck didn't move one centimetre to the side, either way.

The plane came so fast. One minute it had been in the air above the airfield, the next it was racing straight at us. It got bigger and bigger. It stopped looking beautiful and symmetrical, and just looked plain frightening. Its windscreens were like bug eyes. They seemed to be staring at me personally. It was hard to imagine there were humans behind them. I know their brakes were on, because smoke was steaming from the tyres. I wondered if they noticed there was no smoke from our tyres. I grabbed the door handle again and actually began to open the door, to be ready. I was mentally begging Homer to spin the steering wheel, to swerve off the runway. Fi wasn't mentally begging him to; she was screaming at him. I had too much pride for that: even if it killed me I wasn't going to scream. I wondered if Lee in the back might already have jumped. I wouldn't blame him. The jet seemed so much bigger than us now. From a distance it had looked quite small. For the first time I realised Homer might deliberately smash into it. This might be a suicide mission. He might have figured we had no chance of surviving anyway, and our lives were a fair exchange for this valuable and deadly plane.

The gap seemed like nothing. There was no way we could miss it. The bluffs had been called. It was about to smash us apart.

And, at that moment, it lifted a little. Fi, who had been leaning across trying to snatch at the steering wheel, gave a loud cry. I started praying. I suppose a good soldier mightn't pray for an enemy jet to be saved, but that's what I prayed for. I just wanted that thing off the ground and in the air. But I didn't think it would get up. They'd left it too late.

I watched with all the intensity in me. I saw the nose quiver. It started to rise. I saw the tip go up a little and even saw daylight behind it.

But it was too late. I knew it was too late. I scrunched up my eyes, my face, my whole body, and waited for the impact.

It missed us by a centimetre, I'd say. They must have given it every last bit of throttle they could find. I don't know whether those things are turbo-charged or what, but this baby sure found something. The noise as it screamed over our heads was deafening — like a thousand dying pigs in perfect unison. It caused a terrible physical pain to my ears. And the slipstream! Unbelievable! The power of those planes was so great that I almost felt sorry we'd destroyed heaps of them. They were brilliantly made, perfectly put together. It seemed somehow wrong that a bunch of teenage hooligans could come along and destroy dozens of them as easily as you'd destroy a nest of European wasps.

The slipstream could have been fatal for us. We got blown along the runway with the engine racing, like a giant had exhaled behind us. In any lighter vehicle we would have been tipped head over heels, no risk. But the dump truck was so solid that it stayed on all four wheels. It even stayed on the runway.

And suddenly, there we were. Out on our own in the middle of the airfield, about a kilometre from the nearest fence, about a kilometre from the burning buildings and burning aircraft, about a kilometre and a half from the still-intact control tower. It felt very lonely. We were awfully conspicuous out there. And it didn't take a genius to know that our problems were just beginning.

9

WHEN WE STOPPED BEING BUFFETED BY THE SLIPSTREAM of the jet Homer swung the steering wheel. It seemed like we were going back into four-wheel-drive country. Sure enough, a moment later we were off the bitumen and bumping at maximum speed across the grass.

It was another teeth-snapping ride. The ground was very uneven, full of rabbit holes and ditches that we couldn't see in the long grass. There were no safety belts for anyone except Homer, and he wasn't wearing his. Maybe he wanted to show he was on our side, something I'd been seriously doubting the last few minutes. We grabbed onto anything we could, and I think both Fi and I were trying not to yell at Homer. We didn't want to put him off. We needed him to concentrate. It wasn't an easy piece of driving.

Kevin had slipped to the floor and was lying tangled around my feet. I don't know if he was conscious and I didn't care much, but he was probably having the best ride of anyone. He wasn't getting shaken around like me. But I pitied Lee, if he was still in the back. It wasn't the first time in this war that he'd had a painful and unusual ride. The time I'd scooped him up in the shovel of a truck, back in Wirrawee, when he was shot in the leg: that was rough.

At that moment Lee proved he was still with us. There was a sudden thump on the rear window, so loud and close to my ear that I thought the window was being smashed in. I spun around. Lee must have thrown something at the window, to get our attention. Now he was hanging over the edge of the Dumpster, gesturing madly in the direction of the runway. For a second I thought he was telling Homer to go on the bitumen again. But that didn't make sense. Lee knew Homer well enough, and trusted him to make his own decisions. There must be something else going on. Something we hadn't seen. So I looked to where he was pointing.

And I saw that the chase was on in earnest. Three jeeps were racing down the runway. At any moment they'd be level with us, and then they'd turn and come straight across the grass. They'd handle the four-wheel-drive stuff better than the dump truck. They'd catch up with us at a rate of knots.

I wanted to do something about them. I had to. The trouble was I could only see them by looking across through Homer's window. They were on the wrong side for me to get off a shot. The only reason I could see them at all was that we were going at a slight angle to the run way. Obviously Lee couldn't hold them off on his own, with just one rifle. But how could I do anything, from my side?

I heard a shot from the back. We couldn't afford to waste ammunition now, but Lee must have had a target for a moment. I couldn't see if he'd done any damage. The jeeps were starting to come off the runway and close in on us. They were like dogs rounding up a renegade steer.

Desperate times, desperate action. I still felt sure we were going to die so there was no point being a wimp. Might as well go out in style. And the window beside me was already open.

I became a stunt woman. It wasn't as spectacular as staggering along the roof of a fast-moving train, or getting out on the wing of a plane, but for me it wasn't bad. I said to Fi, "Give me the rifle when I'm out there," and I started squeezing through the window. That part wasn't too hard. The problems started when I got my centre of gravity — my bum — out. I suddenly felt very vulnerable, very unprotected — I was sitting on the window frame, facing back over the roof of the cab — so I reached across the gap between the cab and the truck. The gap was quite big and I realised I'd have to do a Tarzan and trust that I could grab the side of the Dumpster. Fi was watching anxiously through the window and I think she said something to Homer, because just as I held my breath and made the swing, the truck slowed down.

"I'll kill him," I thought. "If we ever survive this, I'll kill him." He'd thrown my rhythm completely out. Only the fingernails of my right hand caught the steel edge. My fingernails and the tips of my fingers. The ground was rushing past at frightening speed and if I fell I was dead. I'd be caught between the wheels of the truck, which wouldn't be pretty. It'd be quick, but not pretty. I dared not look down. I knew I'd only get one go at this. I tried to summon up all my courage, all my strength, all my energy. I've never done martial arts, but I know those guys break bricks by concentrating everything in their hand. I tried to concentrate everything into my swing. I knew if I waited too long the energy would drain away, so somehow, through all my terror, I had to make myself go for it.

One of the hardest things was keeping my eyes open. I was so terrified I wanted to close them. But that was a luxury I couldn't afford. With my eyes open, staring, I made the big leap.

I nearly got it OK. The height was less of a problem than I'd expected and I might even have relaxed a split second too soon, thinking I was going to make it comfortably. But I didn't quite get to the top. And the problem then was to get a grip. My fingers started slipping straightaway. I could feel the muscles on my right arm start to bulge and swell, with the strain of holding all that weight. I mean, sure, I didn't weigh much these days, but it was too much to hold by my fingertips for very long.

My hands were kind of operating separately, as though they were robotic. That *Terminator* feeling again. The right hand was told to grip, and it gripped, but it was also starting to slip, millimetre by millimetre. The other hand was scanning the surface of the truck as it slowly slid down, trying to feel by touch whether there was anything it could hold on to. It was weird. It seemed to me I was there for a long time, like I had all the time in the world to keep hanging and keep scanning. I felt quite cool, quite calm, quite detached — the only time during the whole morning that I'd felt that way.

It only lasted a few seconds. Suddenly I was back in the reality of it. The loud throbbing of the truck engine, so close to me; the thumping of the huge wheels over the grass; another massive explosion from the fires: my ears roared with these sounds again. I felt again the intense heat of the engine, which was working overtime. We hit a big bump and I nearly got thrown off right there: Homer wasn't slowing down now. We were shifting at a speed I wouldn't have believed possible. I think we were doing a big circle to get near the main gate. Homer probably figured he might have a chance to get through the gate somehow, with all the disruption the explosions had caused.

The tips of my fingers on my right hand had gone through pain and beyond, into some kind of extreme. I couldn't feel them properly anymore. I knew they were still digging in, but I knew they couldn't dig in any longer.

And my left hand kept scanning. And at last connected with something. Not much. By God it wasn't much. I think, some sort of metal pin. All I could tell for sure was that it was metal and it wasn't a regular shape. There was a hard solid bit and then a bit of wire or something.

It wasn't much to stake my life on. But there was nothing else. There wasn't enough to hold, or to get my hand around. All I could do was use it as a springboard. Something to push against, to give me the resistance for one last leap at the top, one last leap at life. It would have to be enough, because there wasn't going to be any other chance.

My left fingertips were pressing into the little pin. My fingertips were all I could get on it. As my right fingers finally gave way, suddenly with a horrifying irreversible quick slip, I pressed into the pin even harder and went for it. I was higher up than last time, but I was pushing against something so slight that I wasn't getting much lift.

With a feeling of wild and complete elation, I felt my hand get over the top. Funny how at times like that you concentrate on what's happening at the moment. Any second now we were going to get shot or blown up, but I was happy because I thought I'd saved my life. It figures: you have to be able to concentrate or you don't last long.

I sure as hell had concentrated this last minute or so, but my problems weren't exactly over.

With my left hand gripping strongly, and because I was a bit higher this time, I got my right hand up quite easily. Then I arched my back and planted my feet on the side of the Dumpster. I rested like that for a second, then dropped my feet, did another big leap, and got on top of the truck-side. With a wriggle I worked myself up until I was hanging over the top. The hard metal cut into my stomach. I panted and gasped, but got right over, doing a sort of slow forward roll till I landed on my feet.

There was one thing that was so urgent, I had to worry about it before anything else. I turned straightaway and leant back over the side, reaching out to the cab. Fi didn't fail me. I knew she wouldn't. She was already half out of the cab, holding the rifle towards me. She had the butt and I grabbed the tip of the barrel. Fi had worked out that I was stronger than her: if she tried to hold the rifle by the barrel I think the weight would have been too much and she'd have dropped it. That was a calamity we couldn't afford.

Even though I'm fairly strong, the weight was almost too much for me. I used every ounce of strength I had. I felt my muscles quivering with the strain. The rifle was going like a metronome as Fi let go and I tried to find the energy to bring it in. I imagine it was like landing a huge fish, except I've never landed a huge fish. But gradually, bit by bit, I hauled it up. I just hoped Fi remembered to have the safety catch on. With all this vibration it could easily go bang, and my guts would be splattered all over the airfield.

Only when I had it in my hands could I afford to look around.

It was a wild sight. Lee was there of course. I realised he hadn't even known about my struggle to get into the Dumpster. He had his back to me and was peering over the edge of the right-hand side. His rifle was resting on the steel rim. I don't know how many shots he'd fired; I'd only heard the one. I got my rifle round the right way then headed over to him. It wasn't easy, doing a run across the wildly bouncing surface of the truck, but easier than the little jump and climb I'd done to get there.

I touched Lee on the shoulder. He nearly fell off the truck. But he didn't say much, just: "Thought you'd never get here."

I don't know why boys love playing these tough-guy roles.

I peeped over the edge. The jeeps had fanned out and were chasing us across the airfield.

"The truck's bouncing too much," Lee shouted. It was hard to hear him now that we had our heads out in the open. "I can't get off a good shot."

That was true, but it also meant they couldn't get a good shot at us. I saw occasional flashes of fire, so they were definitely trying. I heard a couple of loud pinging noises, which were probably bullets hitting the truck, but they didn't seem to do any damage. We'd picked the right truck. If we'd been in the old furniture van we'd have had more holes than a colander.

I got my head down again. Even though they were missing us at the moment, someone could still get a lucky shot. They could miss a thousand times but one hit would be enough. I didn't want my last words to be: "There's no way they could get us from that far . . ."

I checked the breech of the rifle and flicked the safety forward. The ride was getting really wild now. Homer obviously figured that now I was in the Dumpster he could be creative. We were zig-zagging in crazy patterns. He was putting enormous pressure on the tyres. I hoped they could cope. But there were no more pings on the side of the truck. Then we suddenly straightened up.

Lee tapped me on the shoulder. "Don't look now," he shouted, "but he's going for broke."

I felt a shock of fear. Homer going for broke could mean anything. Nervously, I ignored Lee's advice and put my head up.

We were still a kilometre from the western fence, but it was obvious what Homer planned. The truck had a sense of purpose. We were going hell for leather at the fence. I couldn't believe it. The fence looked so strong, a high barrier with big steel poles and tightly strung wire. But I knew Homer was right; it was our only chance. And luckily this was a big truck. If anything had a chance of getting through, it was this baby.

Lee was looking grim as death. We'd had so many smashes already, so many near-misses, come close so many times. I didn't know how much more we could cope with, how much luck we had left. The pings started again, and what's worse, they were getting louder. Maybe they sounded louder because I was crouching down, but maybe it was because the range was shortening. Even though Homer had his foot to the floor I knew the jeeps must be gaining. I realised there were actually holes starting to appear in the back panel of steel. First there were dents, then some of them became holes. The metal was being forced open like flowers budding. One hole opened as I watched. Obviously it was time to stop watching. I gripped my rifle and stood, nervously, hunching up and peering over the tailgate of the truck.

The middle jeep was forty or fifty metres behind. The other two, to the right and left of it, were a bit farther back. They were starting to converge though. I tried to think of a way to do them some damage without wasting too much ammunition. The answer, I realised straightaway, was rolling at our feet. The fuel drums! We could miniaturise what we'd just done on such a big scale.

The nearest drum was a jerry can, flat on its side and, because of its shape, not rolling. I shoved my rifle at Lee, without even looking at him. Then I lifted the jerry can, which felt maybe half full, heaved it over the tailgate, and grabbed my rifle back.

Failure. The jerry can split the moment it hit the ground and its contents flew everywhere. Amazingly, it didn't ignite. Maybe it held water, not petrol. But I didn't stand there thinking about it. I gave Lee my rifle again and grabbed one of the round drums as it rolled towards me, hoicking it over in the same movement.

The jerry can had achieved one thing at least. The driver of the middle jeep must have got a shock when he saw it fly off the back of the truck. Maybe he guessed what I was trying to do. Wouldn't surprise me. So he slammed on the brakes for a second, which dropped him back quite a way and gave us a little more room.

The next can didn't burst. It bounced surprisingly high, then bounced a few more times. By then Lee had already fired twice at it, and missed. I fired once and hit it, when it was just ten metres from the jeep.

It gives me a lot of satisfaction to say that. I'm not the world's best markswoman, not by a long way. But this was a pretty fair shot. And the timing was perfect. The jeep driver must have gotten his confidence back, because he was coming on at full speed. The drum went up like a bomb: blazing fuel and bits of metal flew everywhere. There was no way he could miss it. He tried, of course. Who wouldn't? He swerved radically, spinning his steering wheel to the right, as hard as he could. Coward, I thought, conveniently forgetting the odd moment of cowardice of my own. Because this guy, by spinning the wheel to the right was getting himself as far away from the explosion as possible, but putting the man in the passenger seat in maximum danger. I'd put people in big danger once when I lost my nerve, but not deliberately like this.

Anyway, what he did was to roll the jeep. And it sure did roll. It went side over side — about three times, I think — and ended up on its roof, facing away from us, wheels spinning wildly.

There was no time to look any more. Lee suddenly yelled "Duck!" and I realised we were about to hit the fence.

He and I went down together. There was a thump, a cracking noise, and a series of wild twanging sounds, each one sounding like a gunshot, but actually high-pressure wires snapping. Horrible screeching metal noises. A wire whipped across our heads. If I'd been standing I would have been decapitated. I'm not kidding. But although I didn't dare stand up I knew that we had made it through the fence.

It was impossible, but we'd actually got out of the airfield. And as far as I could tell every one of us was alive. It didn't mean the terror of death had disappeared, because death was still very likely at any moment: much more likely than not. It was remarkable though that we had done such enormous damage, damage almost beyond my understanding, and despite it all we had actually managed to get out of the place.

I suppose the big difference now was that I let myself consider for a moment that we might survive. It seemed a dangerous thought, more likely to do harm than good, but it snuck into my head, and sat there like a little flower in a bitumen playground.

When the snapping, whining, singing sound of the broken wires was gone I slid down to the end of the truck and got up to have a look. It was difficult, because Homer still had us moving at full speed. Now things were different though, because we were racing along the road beside the airfield and already it was starting to climb and twist. Soon it would climb and twist more, as it ran up into the hills to the north of Wirrawee.

I was bruised and battered from being knocked around so much, but I had to ignore that and concentrate. It was desperately important to find out what was behind us.

The other two jeeps were right on our tail. I don't think they'd fired at us again since leaving the airfield, but they were right on our hammer. If the weren't angry before they would be now. Angry, and probably scared too. That didn't make them any less dangerous. Someone who's scared can be really savage.

I raised my rifle and started shuffling my feet, getting my legs wider apart so I'd be in a good stance to fire. As soon as I did, the soldiers in the back seat of the first jeep popped up and raised their rifles, aiming for me. I wondered why they hadn't been firing at us all the time. Maybe they were low on ammunition. They wouldn't have had much time to collect stuff. We hadn't given them much time to react. Maybe they were just trying to get their balance after the sharp turn onto the road. Or maybe they thought the bullets weren't penetrating the Dumpster.

Whatever, they were evidently going to make up for it

now. I ducked into cover as a volley of shots rained against the back of the truck. A dozen flowers blossomed in the steel tailgate. It was incredibly dangerous out there. Yet we had to do something.

I popped up, fired off two quick shots at their windscreen, and dived down, listening for the crash I hoped would follow.

Nothing. Just the roar of our engine, the thundering sound of every single part, from piston to fanbelt, working like never before. If I'd hit anything it hadn't made much difference.

Lee peeped over the top. We were into another series of curves, and the shooting seemed to have stopped again. One of the fuel drums rolled past me and I wondered if I should keep throwing them over. There wouldn't be time to take a shot at it but maybe it would burst and explode. Even though the other two hadn't.

Then Lee yelled something and beckoned me towards him. I scurried over. He pointed to the pin at the top of the back panel. Instantly I realised what he had in mind. "We won't have much cover," I yelled, but he shrugged, without saying anything. I think he was saying: "Worry about that when it happens."

I shrugged too and got myself to the other side. I began to work at the pin. If they saw my hand on the top of the panel they might guess what we were doing, but they'd have no hope of shooting my hand. They probably wouldn't see it anyway.

Lee already had his pin out. That increased the pressure on mine, and made it harder to work it up from the socket. The panel was in two halves, and we were working on the top half. There was nothing else holding it to the truck but my pin, and a bolt in the middle that secured it to the bottom half. My fingers shivered as I realised how close we were already to the moment when the heavy slab of steel would be free to fly wherever it wanted.

Well, that wasn't quite true. It would fly where the wind and the velocity of our truck took it. And that would be straight backwards.

Lee pulled the bolt free. But the pin was stiff and resistant. I tried to be patient. I wrestled and tugged at it. It didn't want to come at all. Maybe the panel knew what would happen to it. It seemed to have jammed completely. I fought desperately. I only needed it to come an extra three centimetres and I'd have it. But the bottom part of the pin felt swollen, like it was too big to squeeze out. My fingers were getting red and raw and sore.

Then, with a rush and a little grinding sensation, the pin came.

I stayed kneeling, feeling a bit silly, holding it in my hands. The panel hung as though suspended for a moment. Then suddenly it was gone. It blew out like a piece of paper. Lee and I were quite exposed now, watching with a kind of horrified fascination to see what would happen.

It was terrible to see what did happen. Obviously no one in the jeep had noticed our little fingers working at the top of the pins. Or they hadn't worried about it.

When they saw it coming at them they started to brake, but it didn't make much difference. The truck was going at over a hundred k's I'd say, and so were they. The steel panel flew into them at that speed. It was like the upper halves of the guys in the front seat just disintegrated. You'd have needed half a dozen plastic bags to pick up the bits. The guys in the back wouldn't have fared any better. I had a glimpse of the bottom halves of two bodies still sitting in the front seat as the jeep ran off the road straight into a tree and exploded.

You see some awful things in this war. Lee and I just looked at each other. If I was as pale and shocked as him I must have looked pretty pale. Probably even paler, given my Anglo skin. I think we were both stunned by how sudden and powerful and total the whole thing had been. It was one of the most dramatic and frightening things I'd seen. I don't know why it was so much more powerful than the fuel drum exploding in front of the first jeep, but it was. Maybe we'd seen so many explosions now and by comparison, this piece of steel flying into the car was such a cold and violent death. Death by explosion was hot and powerful.

The other jeep was still in sight. They began firing at us. Lee and I ducked behind the bottom panel and crouched there for a moment. Then I had another peep. Was it my imagination or were they hanging back a little? I wouldn't blame them.

When we went round a couple of tight corners we lost sight of them completely for a few seconds.

We were climbing steadily now and the truck was slowing. For these guys to keep back they'd have to use the brakes a bit, and I think that's exactly what they were doing.

I couldn't speak for Lee, but I knew I didn't have any cute tricks left. The road was still winding too much for us to use the fuel drums again. I got my rifle and lay down behind the remaining panel. After a moment Lee did the same. I figured we were in for a shoot-out, and we had to win. The sooner we got on with it the better.

When the jeep reappeared I fired off three shots. I heard

Lee's rifle too: twice I think. I aimed at the windscreen again — because that was the biggest and best target — and I saw it shatter, but I don't know if that was Lee's shooting or mine. Losing the windscreen didn't seem to make much difference — the driver was obviously alive and well and the jeep kept coming. But it did fall even farther behind. I began to worry about that. If it dropped right back and followed at a safe distance it would cause us enormous problems. Wherever we went, whatever we did, it would follow. When we did stop or try to hide, or even when we ran out of petrol, they'd be there. We simply had to shoot them out of the way.

I checked my magazine again. I had four bullets left. I raised my eyebrows at Lee, asking him how many he had. He held up one finger. I grimaced. This was desperate. I raised the rifle again, shuffled my body a bit to get the most comfortable position, and squinted through the sights.

This time I waited until we were on a straight stretch. When they came into view I had a good line on them even though they were quite a way back. Not till the blurred face of the driver was in my sights did I squeeze off a round. But as I did I heard Lee swear. Lowering the rifle I could see why. They'd started zig-zagging, just like Homer had at the airfield. My shot probably missed by metres.

In the next two minutes I tried twice more. I'm not sure what damage I did, but I saw something fly off the roof from one bullet and I thought I might have hit a guy in the back seat with the other. When we did finally stop them it was almost an anticlimax. Lee and I were both waiting, with our rifles to our cheeks, and when the jeep straightened up for a brief second we both fired, almost simultaneously. We'd agreed we'd aim for the engine, as that seemed our best chance now, at such a long range. The moment we fired, a cloud of white smoke, and then flame, erupted from it. The jeep stopped fast, like it had hit a wall, and I saw two soldiers jumping out. I didn't watch anymore.

I lowered my rifle and looked across at Lee. Still alive! It seemed impossible. Down to our last rounds, and still alive.

I wanted to relax. No, I wanted to let go completely and collapse in a corner and cry and talk and sleep and go hysterical — any or all of those. But I knew we were still in the most critically dangerous situation. Their radios and phones would be working flat out, going crazy, as they called up every man, woman and child they could find. All with one aim in mind. To kill us.

So there was no rest, no chance to draw breath. I went up the front to see how they were going in the cab. From the little I could see they looked OK. Then Fi turned, peering through the back window, and saw me. She put her hands together half-a-dozen times, clapping. I felt pleased about that, and I realised they knew we'd got rid of the hunters, for the time being anyway.

Homer drove on for another three minutes. It was pretty obvious what he was thinking: we had to get a safe distance away from the last jeep. But we couldn't go too far either, as enemy soldiers might be coming from the other direction. We'd be totally stuffed if they arrived. We'd been lucky so far. Maybe it wasn't entirely luck though. Desperation can take you a long way.

10

WE GATHERED ON THE THIN RAGGED GRASS LINE AT THE edge of the road. Even Kevin got out of the truck. Sure he was an emotional mess, but he was smart enough to realise there was no future for anyone in there. The truck had served us well, and maybe after the war I'd come back and find it and put it in a nice garage where it could live in comfort for the rest of its days. I'd feed it premium unleaded petrol, beautiful thick black oil, mineral water for the radiator, whatever it wanted. But for now we had to say goodbye. Homer had run it into some weedy-looking scrub, with trees about five metres high. It wasn't much, but it would have to do.

I grabbed my pack again and hoisted it on my back. Homer and Lee had their packs but Kevin and Fi's were somewhere at the airfield. That was bad news, not only for them, but for the rest of us too, because they'd had the last supplies of food.

Although we all had the shakes — we had such chattering teeth inside clenched mouths that hardly anyone could talk — we reached agreement quickly.

"We've got to leave the truck," was the first thing Homer said.

No one argued with that.

"Do we go bush?" Fi asked.

"I don't think that's enough," I said. "There'll be so many of them after us, and we're wrecked. We won't be able to go fast enough to get away."

"What, then?" Lee asked.

They were all looking at me again. I hated it when they did that. "We need a helicopter," I heard Fi say. That was no help. I racked my brains. I didn't just rack them: I spread them out on a woolclassing table, combed through them with my fingers, and checked every knot. And, to my amazement, I did suddenly get an idea. Nothing to do with helicopters. But in a distant corner of my brain, hidden under a whole lot of useless trivia, I came across one tiny, vital piece of information.

Like I said, desperation can do a lot.

"The river."

That was all I needed to say. They looked at each other for a moment — at least Fi and Lee and Homer did, Kevin was standing like a robot, gazing at the ground — and the next moment we were on our way.

Fi led. Being so light gave her an advantage. Lee was next, then Kevin, who we'd deliberately put in the middle, then me, and Homer lumbering along in the rear.

We were dog-tired. But we carried next to nothing. Our packs didn't have a lot left in them and the rifles were no good without ammunition. So at least we could move as freely as our exhausted bodies would let us.

The funny thing was — and I actually thought about this as I ran — we hadn't done anything to make us physically exhausted. We hadn't climbed mountains or swum oceans or played a grand final. We hadn't done any triathalons. Scrabbling from the cab of the truck to the Dumpster was the only physical exercise I'd had. But I was as wrecked as if I'd run a marathon. I guess the stresses we'd been through had taken everything: every gram of energy, every drop of strength, almost my life itself. That's what it felt like, as though I'd lost the lot.

Yet my tired legs kept moving. The bush we were in — only a couple of kilometres from the edge of Wirrawee — was light scrub and very dry. The gum trees were mostly medium-growth, with those silvery-olive leaves they get as summer goes on. A fire had been through a couple of years earlier, and lots of the trunks were still black. There wasn't much ground cover. It was poor soil, full of little stones, no rich dark chocolate earth. If you dug into it I knew what you'd find: the stones not much bigger than gravel and a reddish-coloured dirt that was gritty and dry. It made a hard surface, but quite a good one for us to run on.

Normally I would have expected helicopters to appear about now. They'd turned up so quickly when we were approaching Wirrawee to look for the Kiwis, not very long ago. But now, God knows what would happen. We couldn't tell how much damage we'd done, but it had been awesome. Not a single aircraft had managed to get into the air, I was sure of that, and I didn't know how many aircraft they'd have left. The only one that might still be up there was the jet we'd tried to head-on.

The last time we tackled the airfield there seemed to be some supersonic security system that let them detect people from an amazing distance. It must have convinced them the place was secure. In the sky, the RNZAF was getting beaten back across the Tasman. We didn't see them anymore. So the people at the airfield wouldn't have expected much bother from above. And their ground system seemed so effective. It was only by the greatest fluke that we'd beaten it. I could just imagine the conversation at the entrance gate between the guards and the truck drivers returning from the rubbish tip.

"Did you stop anywhere?" "No."

"Did you see anyone?" "No!"

"Just straight out there and back?" "Yeah."

"OK, in you go then."

And once we were in there, it was easy in a way. Maybe because they felt so secure they didn't bother taking many precautions inside the base. That was a lesson to me. Never think you've got it covered, no matter how much work you've done. I should have learnt that from working on a farm. Dad and I spent ages running hoses along the gutters around the house and sheds, installing them as permanent fixtures, then connecting them to a brand new pump. It was for protection against bushfires. You block the downpipes then fill the gutters with water. Every six months we tested the system. No problems. Then along came a fire, we switched on the pump, and there was nothing. We found out later some wasps had got inside the housing of the pump and made a nest. All the clay they used stopped the pump from working.

So I could understand how those guards at the airfield had stuffed up so badly. I just hoped they wouldn't get a note on their records about it. It'd be a shame for their careers to suffer.

Even as I thought about them I heard another explosion in the distance, from the direction of the airfield. I don't know what that was about. We came over a small rise, where some sheets of galvanised iron and the ruins of a fence were all that remained of a stockyard. Away to our left was a huge grey cloud of smoke. It was a funny shape, lying across Wirrawee like a thick table, a sort of slab of smoke. But it stretched for miles. We grinned at each other. Still there were no vengeful helicopters, no furious jets buzzing around, no movement in the sky at all. We must have done terrible damage to their fleet of aircraft, if they couldn't even get one off the ground to look for us.

Now our exhaustion started to get flooded by excitement. It seemed incredible what we had done. I found myself walking faster and faster, till I seemed to be going too fast. If I'd had an engine it would have been over-revving. Even Kevin picked up his pace. We could have been running on red cordial. Homer and I exchanged a few comments, only quietly, because we weren't too deep in bush, but we had to express how fantastic and enormous it seemed, how lucky we'd been.

I think that was the greatest source of emotion for me. We had survived! That was it. From being so sure for so long I would die, suddenly here I was still alive. Breathing! Smelling the dusty eucalyptus, feeling the hot burning of my own cheeks and the trickling sweat from my armpits, licking my cracked lips with my own dry swollen tongue. Life suddenly seemed wonderful. I wanted to keep experiencing these sensations for as long as I could. I really didn't want to die. The miracle of daily moments. Being able to look at the sky, or smile at Kevin's bum crack jogging along in front of me, or notice that the pimple on the soft part of my upper arm was getting better — these seemed such precious things. And even more special was the miracle of being able to make decisions, tackle problems, search for solutions. I had thought there was no hope. I had thought there was no solution. I thought death was the only option. Now I realised that by our own determination we'd made things happen. We'd found answers where there were none. I promised myself to remember this lesson forever.

And the time came soon enough when I had to remember it. We'd been running for maybe ten minutes when Homer suddenly clutched my arm from behind.

"There's someone coming," he whispered.

In a moment I heard it too. Not far back. They weren't making much effort to be quiet. I guess they'd decided that speed was more important than caution. I guess they knew we'd be in a hurry, so they'd lose us if they didn't get a move on. I cursed them though. In my heart and in my mind I cursed them. There was no point wasting breath doing it. But I had hoped we could get to the river without them knowing we'd taken that route. Somehow they'd worked it out. Maybe because it was just the more logical way for us to go — there hadn't been much bush on the other side of the road from where we left the truck — or maybe they were smart enough to pick up our trail. I thought that was unlikely though, on this hard ground. We shouldn't leave many footprints. Admittedly we might have helped them by following the natural lie of the land. We'd been too tired and anxious to do anything else.

I tried to think as I ran. It wasn't easy. I can walk and chew gum at the same time but I have trouble running while I think. I wasn't getting enough oxygen to do both. But at least I managed to figure out what we needed, and that was time. If we used the river we'd want a head start. Otherwise they'd be waiting for us a hundred metres downstream.

I sprinted a bit, passing the three in front and going to the lead. I figured we had to make a detour, taking the gamble that we could stay ahead of them for a few more minutes. And I quickened the pace. This was going to be a race for life, a sprint, and second place wasn't a good option.

Ahead of us, as we approached the river, the bush got thicker. There were more blackberries, and some dark patches of thick undergrowth. Beyond all that was a steep bank, almost a little cliff, and on the other side I thought we'd find the water.

If we kept going the way the land suggested, we'd turn left. That would point us back towards Wirrawee. There even seemed to be a faint track. Better still it seemed to lead away from the river again.

I didn't know if it would buy us much of an advantage, but anything was better than nothing. Without hesitating I went straight ahead, through the weeds and into the dark undergrowth. The others followed. They didn't have much choice. One for all and all for one, that was us again, as it always was really.

We had to tread lightly. If these people were tracking us they'd soon notice a whole lot of broken branches and torn plants. But we also had to be quick. In the end it was a compromise. We had about thirty seconds to make ourselves scarce. So into the dark hidy-holes we went.

I found myself crouched very low, in an awkward, uncomfortable position on a bit of rising ground. There was part of a broken tree stump hiding part of me, and some bracken covering the other part. I hoped I wouldn't be there for long.

I didn't dare look around. I had to trust that the others were settled OK, especially Kevin. God knows what he might be doing. Probably in a foetal position, like I was. I thought about him for a moment as I waited. The scary thing was that I didn't know what was happening with him anymore, and it was frightening to see someone I'd known so long crack up so completely. If that could happen to him, it could happen to any of us.

My thoughts were broken by the thudding of feet. I had some superstitious belief that if I looked at them they would be able to see me. But I couldn't resist. I made myself peep out.

There were six of them. With their heavy uniforms and heavy rifles, I think they were slowing down a bit. Certainly their faces shone with sweat, and there were big wet patches on their shirts: under their arms and across their backs. They didn't seem to be following our tracks though. Probably just following the lie of the land, like us. They got onto the path, sort of automatically, and ran along it.

As soon as the sound of their thumping boots faded, I was up again. I didn't signal to the others, just left it to them to see what I was doing and follow. So I charged through the weeds and started up the little cliff.

It was harder than I'd expected. The first bit was easy but after that it got steeper and more crumbly. Again I worried about leaving a conspicuous trail, and I hoped the others were taking as much care as I was. Kevin was still my biggest worry though. I kept glancing round at him but he seemed to be climbing stolidly, and after a couple of minutes, to my utter amazement, he passed me. He didn't even look at me, just kept going up like a big grizzly bear.

Despite that, the five of us reached the top more or less together. I was wildly relieved to scramble over the crest and hear, then see, what I hoped would be our lifeline: the big beautiful Heron River.

It was still early enough into summer for the river to be

quite fast and deep. By the middle of January its level would drop a lot, but the Heron was a reliable old river, and it took a long dry spell to really slow it.

We were standing above a straight stretch of water. It was about twenty metres wide. With no recent rain it was pretty clear. There were meant to be a few platypuses in the Heron, although I hadn't seen any since I was a kid, and I didn't see any now.

You would have expected a river that flowed through Wirrawee to end up in Cobbler's Bay, but through some freak of geography — the Blackman Hills, to be exact — it didn't. Instead it made its way across to Stratton, then kept going down to Lake Murchison. So it's quite an important river, because the water from Lake Murchison is used for the big power plants there.

But I didn't think about that. As long as it got us out of the Wirrawee district in a hurry, I'd be happy. Speed and action were our priorities. All I said to the others was: "Stick together. If anyone gets in trouble, give a yell. And everyone keep an eye on Kevin."

"I'm all right," he muttered.

I was encouraged that he'd said anything at all.

But I'd only just heard it, because I was already on my way. I didn't bother with a spectacular racing dive, mainly because I'm not very good at them. And besides, I wanted to stay close to the bank, for safety's sake. So I waded in quickly, till I was up to my knees, floated my pack out in front of me, flopped forward and swam a couple of metres. Then I swung right and headed downstream.

It's a weird feeling, swimming in clothes. I'd never done it before. In Cobbler's Bay, Homer and I wore light T-shirts and shorts. Now I was wearing the full outfit.

Water filled my boots, then my jeans. It came creeping up my legs. Everything got heavier and heavier. But at least it wasn't too cold. Because I'd run so far and been through such fear I was hot and stressed and sticky, and the river felt good. It wasn't only the coolness of the water, it was the way it washed the dirt and sweat off my body. It had been a long time since my last bath.

The Heron flowed strongly, without being too wild. There weren't any white-water rapids or waterfalls in the Heron. It wasn't that kind of river. Funny really, nothing about Wirrawee was wild or dramatic or spectacular, before the war I mean. We were such a quiet part of the world. Most people in our district didn't care what was going on anywhere else. They just wanted to be left alone, so they could live their lives. They wanted to be free to marry whoever they fell in love with, have their children, farm their land, be buried in the Wirrawee graveyard under the big dark pine trees, and have the possums run over their graves as the possums too searched for food, mated, and had babies.

That's the way the middle-aged and old people were. It's not the way I wanted to live. I wanted to travel to Asia and Africa and Europe, with Fi (it used to be Corrie), and come back and go to uni in the city, then get some interesting and glamorous job, and marry an interesting and glamorous guy — preferably rich. OK, maybe when I was forty or something I might return to Wirrawee and kick my parents off the farm and take that over. There was a lot to be said for living in Wirrawee. But I wasn't in a hurry to do it.

But the Heron River was typical Wirrawee. It just flowed along steadily, not doing anything exciting or unpredictable, no crocodiles or alligators or . . . Oh no! Snakes! Leeches! I put my head up and called softly to the others: "Watch out for snakes. And leeches."

"Thanks a lot, Ellie," Fi said.

It was the end of my feelings of peace and serenity. I started checking anxiously for leeches. I'd learnt my fear of leeches. When I was little they didn't bother me. If I got one I'd come out of the water and burn it off with a match. Being a nasty and sadistic brat I got some pleasure from watching them twist and writhe and shrivel and drop off. I wonder who first realised that burning was the best way to get rid of them? Must have been someone really charming.

One time I'd got out of the dam and walked to the house and gone to my bedroom to dump my things, and when I came back down the corridor I saw a trail of blood along the carpet. I thought it must have been from dog, maybe a bitch in season. "Mum," I yelled out, "has one of the dogs been down here?" She came to have a look. "Oh dear," she said. Then she had a closer look. "What's that on your leg?" Sure enough it was a leech, only half on me, hanging by a tooth or something, and letting all this blood flow away down my leg. I hadn't even noticed.

But Corrie taught me to be scared of them. Every time we got one she'd make such a fuss, screaming and running away, and after a while I started getting nervous of them myself, till I ended up worse than her. Crazy, but that's what happened.

Then Mr Kassar, our Drama teacher, told us this absolutely gross story about a friend of his in the Philippines. She had a little boy a year or two old, who always had trouble breathing and always had sinus trouble and colds.

They took him to a few local doctors who couldn't see anything wrong with him, so they finally took him to a specialist in the big city, who ordered an X-ray. They found that all that time a leech was living up his nose, like a permanent attachment, getting bigger and bigger as the months went on, with his own private drink machine. It was a disgusting story.

The funny thing was that on our Year 8 camp Mr Kassar got a leech. He'd been floating in a waterhole for a while, looking like a baby whale, and when he got out we saw this big dark red leech hanging off his back. We were dancing round yelling: "We'll burn it off! Get the petrol! Stay still Mr Kassar, you can trust us!"

He wimped out though, and made us use salt. Very boring.

So as we travelled on down the river I kept checking myself anxiously, looking at the bits I could see and using my hands to check the rest, running a hand over the exposed back of my neck and even reaching down to my ankles. I started imagining how they could get inside my clothing, which freaked me out, because after that I thought I could feel them sliming up my jeans legs, or down my top.

It could have been quite a relaxing journey but because of my stupid imagination it wasn't. I spoiled the trip for myself. The truth is, we were probably travelling too fast for leeches to catch us.

We did move at a good pace. We didn't have to swim much, only in the quiet patches, where the river took a long turn or widened out. Most of the time the water carried us at a steady speed. Sometimes we touched the bottom, other times it got narrower and deeper, but we had no real problems when it did. Homer and I were the only two who could swim well but the other three were OK.

We were going faster than walking but much slower than a car. Not that it mattered. By using the river I felt we were getting a big advantage. It was a secret road taking us a long way from the airfield. It was quick and silent and with a bit of luck it would be some time before they thought of it. Maybe they'd never think of it.

I underestimated them there.

After a while the nice warm soothing water wasn't so nice and soothing. My clothes got soggier and heavier and more uncomfortable, until they started rubbing and chafing. My pack got waterlogged, and although it still floated I had to keep one arm under it. The water stopped feeling so warm, and in some places — in the long dark stretches overhung by trees — it got extremely cold. I swam vigorously at times, but I hit a couple of underwater obstacles and banged my bad knee hard on a log or rock that I hadn't seen.

Nevertheless, we kept going. It was the best option. Face it, it was the only option. We had travelled probably fifteen kilometres in an hour, maybe more than that, before I swam a bit closer to Homer, to have a chat. Or rather a conference.

Until then no one had said anything, except for my comment about the snakes and leeches. Our silence was partly for security, but more I think because we were so shell-shocked after the airfield. We needed time to gather our thoughts, to get used to the idea of what we'd achieved. To come to terms with the fact that our lives would be different after this. The most obvious difference, in the immediate future anyway, was that we'd be the most hunted people in the country. Public enemies numbers one, two, three, four, five. A bit tough on Kevin, who hadn't wanted anything to do with it.

But I thought it was time we started talking again. We couldn't swim forever. We had to plan and think. We had to do that all the time, if we wanted to live till the next day, and maybe even the day after that. So I paddled across to Homer.

"What do you reckon?" I asked him.

He turned lazily onto his side so he could see me better. I think Homer's naturally lazy, so this style of transport suited him.

"Just float on down here forever," he said with a grin. "Where does it go anyway?"

"Didn't you ever listen to anything in school? It goes to Lake Murchison."

"Through Stratton?"

"Yes, exactly."

"Thought so. Thought I'd seen the name on the bridge at Stratton."

There was a pause, then he said: "How far from Stratton do you reckon we'd be?"

"I don't know. Probably forty k's."

"Yeah, you could be right. Although, I don't know, it depends on the river, doesn't it? If it takes a straighter line than the road it might only be thirty k's. If it winds around a bit it might be sixty."

"I think it's fairly straight," I said, trying to remember what it looked like on a map.

"You see," said Homer, "the trouble is, we have to go as far as we can. They'll have a net around this district that'll go for a bloody long way. And what I'm thinking is, if we go a long way, we'll be in Stratton. So do we get out of the water before Stratton or after it?"

"Or in it?" I added.

"Yeah, I hadn't thought of that. I suppose we could. Again, it's the last place they'd think of."

"We'd have to be ultra-careful," said Lee, who'd come over to join us. It was a funny way to have a war conference, floating down the river, but it took my mind off the cold and the aches and the chafing of my wet clothes.

"Yes," Homer said. "Stratton would be heavily guarded with all the factories and stuff."

"I don't know how many of those are still operating," I said. "The Kiwis bombed the crap out of it for a while."

"Saved our lives," Homer agreed.

"Cost Robyn her life," I said, which wasn't the normal kind of comment we made to each other, and it caused an awkward silence for a bit.

"I'm hungry," Lee complained suddenly breaking the silence.

"I know. I'm bloody starving," Homer said.

I realised I was the same, but there wasn't much anyone could do about it. But it helped explain why I felt cold and tired. I tried to remember when I'd last eaten, but couldn't.

"So what's the decision?" I asked. "How long do we keep going like this?"

"A long time," Homer said.

"Yes, I think we need to be another thirty or forty k's away," Lee said. "If it's possible. If we can stay in the water that long."

"That could take us to Stratton," I said.

"Oh don't let's go to Stratton," Fi said. She'd floated near us too. "I hate it there. It'd be too dangerous."

"My parents are meant to be somewhere near Stratton," Homer said.

"Oh," Fi said. "Yes. I'd forgotten that."

I didn't say anything because I didn't know what was best. But no one else seemed sure either, so we floated and swam in silence for a long time. In the end, like so many things in this war, the decision was made for us.

11

After another hour I was waterlogged. I thought I'd better get out, before I sank like a large rock. We'd had no more conversations, and it worried me that everyone was so quiet. We were getting too tired. I didn't think we should be screaming and laughing and partying exactly, but I thought there should be a bit more activity. I was really cold now. With no food in your belly, it's amazing, you lose so much energy, warmth, everything.

We passed a number of places that came right down to the river: holiday houses mainly. And I saw some walking tracks. But as we came around a long slow bend I realised that a ford was ahead. The river entered a wide shallow section. To prove it I found my knees scraping on gravel.

I stood and waded forward a little. I was incredibly soggy. Water poured from me. I'd thought before that this river had no waterfalls but it sure had one now. I was it. I must have weighed a hundred kilos. I couldn't wait any longer to get out of there, so I staggered up onto the bank. It was such a relief. I collapsed on the grass. Within a couple of minutes the others had joined me.

But no sooner had we sprawled along the bank, just next to the road, than we heard a vehicle noise, a light purring. It sounded horribly close. "Quick," Homer called, not that we needed to be told. We dived into whatever cover was available: mainly grass and sand along the bank. I found a fallen gum tree that stuck against another tree when it fell, so it wasn't quite lying on the ground. I got behind that, and thought I was fairly well hidden. Then I peered out, hoping to see nothing more ominous than a farm ute.

It was, unfortunately, a lot more ominous. It was another jeep, another of the big green insects that kept crawling into our lives. It held four soldiers, all men. And it stopped at the edge of the water.

I felt sick. I just couldn't take any more of this. I hoped against hope that they were stopping for a drink, but no. They made it obvious they were there for something special. Two took up positions on the other side of the river, the side they'd come from, and the other two drove the jeep slowly across the ford. Once they were over it they got out and found themselves good posies for watching the water.

From the way they peered so intently upstream it was obvious what they wanted. They had their rifles ready. Some genius had worked out our escape route. Right now they were probably rushing soldiers into strategic spots all the way down the river.

I gazed at them anxiously. I wanted so much to hate them. It's easy when you hate someone. You can persuade yourself that anything you do is OK then. Hassle them, pick at them, bully them: no problem, you hate them, it's fair enough, they deserve it. Sometimes at school Fi would say there was no one she hated. It always amazed me when she said that. Corrie and I, we could both hate, and Robyn too, even though she was so religious.

I wondered if Fi hated now, if she hated these soldiers. I looked at them again, trying to whip myself up into a frenzy of loathing. The two on my side had their backs to me but I could see the other two clearly enough. They could have been a father and son. One was about forty, a small man with a patient, calm face, who kept looking at the flowers as though he was more interested in them. The other was around fifteen. He seemed angry about something. He frowned a lot; well, glared really. I got the feeling he'd shoot a flower, given half a chance.

I couldn't even hate him though. He was in a bad mood, sure, but it was no worse than some of my moods. He looked like Steve, my ex-boyfriend, when he was fighting with his mum. Or Chris, when the bell went for afternoon school just as he got to the head of the line at the canteen. He even looked like me when Dad blamed me for a fox getting in the chookyard.

It wasn't often we got a chance to look at the enemy soldiers at close range, for a good period of time. Only when we'd been caught and chucked in Stratton Prison. And the more I looked at these two now, the more they reminded me of people I knew.

After all, how can you hate someone you've never met? That's probably the silliest thing there is.

It was already quite late in the afternoon: about three hours before dark, I guessed. Three hours doesn't sound like much, but I didn't know if we could stay in our uncomfortable little hiding holes for that long. We were all so wet and tired and cold. Sooner or later someone would sneeze or their leg would cramp up or they'd lose their nerve. It'd be utterly pathetic if we got caught by four ordinary little soldiers, after all we'd done, but it could easily happen.

I tried to put myself in their place. There didn't seem much point, but on the other hand, what else was there to do? It passed the time. If I was them, I'd be thinking, "Well, the chances of us finding them are about one in a hundred. They probably didn't go down the river at all or they probably didn't come this far or they're probably past this point by now or someone else has probably caught them already . . . But the boss said stand here and watch, and I'm going to do that, because they're very dangerous and besides, I'll get in huge trouble if they do go past and we miss them."

The jeep sat on the steep slope of the bank, quite a way from the soldiers, and I began wondering if I could get to it without them noticing, and whether it would do any good if I did. By the time I started the engine and put it in gear I'd be wearing bulletholes. So I continued to lie still, gazing at the jeep wondering what to do, getting colder and colder.

Then I thought I saw a movement. I stared even harder at the jeep. And after about twenty seconds I swore it did begin to move. I blinked several times, positive that I was seeing things. But no, it was definitely rolling. The handbrake must have failed! Amazing coincidence though. Maybe it wasn't the handbrake; maybe it was the power of my looking at it and thinking about it. Maybe I was a poltergeist.

The soldiers on the other side of the river saw it first, both at the same time. They yelled desperately, and waved, to get the attention of the other two. And those two, as soon as they realised, dropped their rifles and ran up the hill as hard as they could go.

The jeep accelerated quickly on the steep slope. It rolled steadily towards the river, but off the line of the road, heading straight for a pool that looked quite deep. So it wasn't surprising the soldiers were keen to stop it. They sprinted up on the track, yelling advice at each other, while the other two, on the opposite side, actually stepped into the water, watching anxiously and yelling more advice.

None of them saw what I saw. Lee's lean body, silent, stealthy, slipping out of the bushes and grabbing the rifles the two soldiers had dropped. Lee retreating quickly into the bushes and training one of the rifles on the two armed soldiers. Lee lying there, waiting, ready to shoot them when he felt like it. And after what had happened to Lee's parents, I felt he would be pulling the trigger sooner rather than later.

The jeep, travelling fast, careered past the two soldiers on our bank. Both of them made attempts to stop it. The older man ran alongside it for about ten metres. He had a hold of the doorframe on the driver's side and pulled back on it, trying to stop it with his own strength, but he had no hope. Jeeps are light, sure, but this one had built up too much speed. It dived into the water with a great splash and settled quickly, sinking straightaway with clouds of bubbles erupting around it, until only its windscreen and the top of the body were visible. It was well and truly sunk.

What happened then was fascinating. I'd realised by then that I wasn't really a poltergeist: Lee had worked his way around through the bushes, and caused the jeep's little accident. But from then on, I felt maybe I was psychic. Because the soldiers did exactly what I anticipated. At every step of the way, they were like characters in a play I'd written. It was as though they'd read the script. It would have been funny except that the whole situation was too serious.

First I thought: "Well, they won't want to admit to

their officers that they've been so stupid, so they'll try to get it out themselves."

And that's what happened. The two on the other side waded across the ford, with much shouting and arm-waving and arguing. They gathered at the jeep and stood staring down at it. "Look for a tree, guys," I thought. "That's your only hope." Sure enough, they started gesturing at the nearest big tree and it was so obvious what they were saying: "We could tie a rope or a chain to this trunk and haul the jeep out."

They still glanced up the river from time to time, so they hadn't completely forgotten what they were there for, but their main interest had changed a lot.

"They'll decide to get a winch," I thought, "and two of them'll go to get it while the other two stay here."

About a minute later, after more arguments, the two who'd been on my side of the river came down the bank to where they'd dropped their rifles. My heart suddenly felt pain. If they were going to look for a winch, why couldn't they have done it without their rifles? Now, because of their stupid attention to detail, because they were good soldiers instead of careless ones, we were back in the most awful situation. Lee would have to shoot all four of them before they could retaliate. The odds were on his side, with two of them unarmed, but it was still terribly dangerous. Even if he survived the gun battle, we didn't know how many more soldiers might be just over the hill. There could be an entire army. Besides, I was sickened by all this killing. My stomach rose, my gorge rose, at the thought of more blood. I couldn't take anymore, not today, please.

But I couldn't look away either. I stared at the soldiers.

When was Lee going to rise up from the bushes and start firing? Now Lee, better do it now, before they get any closer. Now Lee! Come on, hurry up, don't leave it too late, you need the advantage of surprise, don't throw that away. Lee, what are you doing?

The soldiers reached the spot where they'd left their rifles, bent over, picked them up, and walked back up the rise.

I was astounded. I was in shock. I lay there with my mouth open, gaping at them. Psychic powers, OK, but this was ridiculous. Was the rifle fairy operating around here? Was this cool shady clearing a magic place, an enchanted forest? I didn't know. I wasn't even sure whether the soldiers had rifles or not now. Maybe Lee hadn't picked them up in the first place. Maybe I was on another planet. Maybe I was hallucinating. I nearly pinched myself, but didn't bother. I knew I would feel a pinch, and I was already hurting enough from the bruises I'd collected at the airfield.

The two soldiers walked past their mates and on, up the hill and over, until they were out of sight. Seemed like they'd drawn the short straw.

The two who were left stood above the jeep, discussing its situation. They were very anxious. Their commanding officer must have been a real bastard. I think they were scared of going back to him without a jeep. Or they were just unhappy at the thought of a long walk back to base.

I had been so interested in what was happening that I'd stopped thinking about my cold and cramps and discomfort. I'd stopped thinking about the others too. So I was startled out of my brain when Homer and Lee suddenly leapt up and down out of the bushes, waving at me.

They were mad. Crazy mad, the worst kind. It was like those telecasts of football matches, where after the game the kids are behind the guy doing the interviews, and they act as if they're on pogo sticks, waving at their mums and screaming stupid comments.

Well, I'm glad to say Homer and Lee didn't scream. And they didn't hold up signs saying "Hi Mum" or "Molong Football Club." But they did everything else. They leapt around like they'd camped on an ants' nest and the ants had invaded their jocks. It was a dumb thing to do. But the soldiers were so engrossed in the jeep, and in looking up the river for us, that they didn't see anything behind them. Homer and Lee could have stripped and done *The Sound of Music* in the nude and the two soldiers wouldn't have noticed.

There was a point to it of course. Well, I don't know why I said "Of course," because those two idiots didn't need a reason for anything. But they were sending the rest of us a message. Then I realised they weren't sending the message to the rest of us. They were sending it to me. I saw that Kevin and Fi were behind the other two. They'd already gotten around the ford and were well past the danger. I was the only one left on this side.

The trouble was, that right from the start my position hadn't been as good as theirs. They'd all hidden higher up the bank. That meant they'd been able to get to the top, go over the crest, and work their way around. With me there was a big difference. I had so far to go up the bank that the risk was simply too great. I felt terrible being the only one there, being so alone, but I knew I'd have to wait for something to change for me to get away. It was good that the soldiers had been reduced to two, but they were still alert.

I stayed there for another half an hour. Homer and the others gave up trying to attract my attention. I was relieved about that. I didn't like people doing anything too crazy these days. It upset me. I wasn't even sure if they knew where I was hiding. It depended on whether anyone had seen me scuttling behind the fallen tree.

At last the two missing soldiers came back with a winch. I was impressed by that. I don't know how they found one in the middle of nowhere, but they had, old and battered though it was. And they knew how to use it. When they began to set it up, running the chain around a big old river red gum, I decided to make my move. If I didn't go now I mightn't get another chance. I started to slither and wriggle up the bank.

The blackberries were the worst. They always seem like they're out to get you. It's personal with blackberries. I hate them. They caught my clothes, my skin, my hair. And of course the more you get mad at them and try to rip away, the deeper they sink their claws in. I lost my temper with them half a dozen times but it didn't do any good. They love it when you lose your temper.

At least the soldiers were totally absorbed the whole time. They were doing quite a good job, I noticed, the few times I looked at them. Before I'd worked my way up to the top of the ridge they had the jeep half out of the water.

It was about then that I realised we had a big problem. I assumed Homer or Lee had let the handbrake off, to make the jeep run down the slope into the river. So far, so good. But what worried me was the reaction of the soldiers when they did the postmortem. I figured I'd better talk to Homer and Lee, and fast. As soon as I got across the ridge I started running. I'd only covered thirty or forty metres when Homer, then the others, popped up in front of me, looking very pleased with themselves.

"We're home free," Homer said. "Let's go."

"Uh uh," I said. "I don't think so."

"Why not?"

"In about one second they're going to check the jeep to see why it rolled down the slope."

They all stood there staring at me, looking puzzled.

"Oh yes," Lee said. Suddenly he'd realised.

There was no question in my mind that the soldiers were about to work out that their jeep had been sabotaged. And immediately my mind jumped to the next thought. They had to die, before they could tell the others we were in the district. More deaths. We had a problem, and these days I thought automatically of killing as the answer to every problem.

At least this time I wasn't going to be the one who killed them, I was sure of that.

"What's the problem?" Fi asked. "Why can't we go?"

"The soldiers are going to find the handbrake off," I explained. "And they'll know one of us must have done it."

"But it could have come off accidentally," Fi said.

"Don't think so."

"But why not?" Fi persisted.

I nearly didn't bother answering, but then said, "It just wouldn't. Not while there's still tension in the cable."

There was a pause, then Fi said: "What about if it came off again?"

There was another pause, a longer one, then suddenly her meaning hit me. I'd only been half-listening, while I tried to work out some way of stopping the soldiers. Tie them up, take them hostage, shoot them? We didn't even have a gun!

But then I realised what Fi was getting at. Without another word I belted back up the slope, dropping on all fours as I approached the crest. I knew I could get a nasty surprise if I came face-to-face with a soldier, but time was so short I had to take the risk. I slithered the last few metres, then peeped over the edge.

They'd got the jeep out of the water. It sat on the bank, looking wet and sloppy and sorry for itself. Two soldiers were inside, one was fiddling with the aerial on the back, and one was getting the hook from the winch off the towbar. "That's me," I thought approvingly and conceitedly, looking at him. "I'd be the one doing the boring job of getting the chain while the others have fun, inspecting the drowned jeep."

He was having trouble though. He was trying to free the chain with one hand while holding his rifle at the ready and looking around all the time. Next to him, the guy playing with the aerial slid it up and down as he called instructions to the man in the front seat. They seemed very excited, very anxious. Their attitude was certainly different from a few minutes back. It was like someone had dropped hot coals down their backs.

I put the clues together. They'd realised the handbrake had been released. They'd decided it was no accident. They knew we were around somewhere. They were trying to call for help.

One thing meant good news for us though. I think their only radio was the one inside the jeep. The soaking in the water had damaged it. That was a bonus.

Everything now depended on their next step. Would they get the radio working? Would they get the jeep started, and rush away for reinforcements? Or would they look for us first?

It might come down to a question of what would get them in the least trouble. Having to admit that we pushed their jeep in the water while they stood around doing nothing could be pretty embarrassing. However, if they came back with our bodies, dead or alive, no one would give a stuff about the jeep getting wet.

There was a lot of talk going on, even shouting at times. I guess they were debating the very issues that I was thinking about. All four of them kept looking around so anxiously all the time. They were very aware of us.

Their next step was to try to start the jeep. They didn't have much of an idea. For people who knew their way around a winch they seemed surprisingly helpless when it came to starting a wet engine. One of them sat in the driver's seat turning the key while the others stood by, alternately looking for us and shouting advice at the driver.

When it became obvious that the car wasn't about to start they went to Plan B. And that gave me my chance.

Plan B was a search of the area. I suppose they didn't like the thought of returning to base unless they'd done that much. And maybe they thought the car would dry out while they searched.

They started upstream. They did it methodically. They'd obviously been trained for this. Two stood at the back scanning the area, rifles held ready. The other two beat their way through the bushes using their rifles like sticks. Dad would have had a fit. He always kept our rifles in top condition. I'd dragged several thousand pull-throughs down their barrels over the years. One speck of dirt and I had to do it all over again.

But now was the time to make my move, while they were still a fair way away. I used the jeep as cover and went for a little darting run halfway down the bank to the first bit of shrubbery. I paused there, panting, and peered through the branches. So far so good. The soldiers were still on the job.

I put my head down again and waited a moment. I needed another charge of energy, another gulp of oxygen. But when I looked up again my stomach went into a spasm. The younger soldier, the fifteen year old, was walking straight towards me. I stared at him in horror. I flattened myself even farther, like an echidna, squirming against the ground, as though I thought I could press a hole into it. His gaze was wandering across a patch of blackberries, but it felt like a laser beam heading my way. In another second it would reach me. He would see me. His eyes would widen. His mouth would open. He would call out. I would be dead.

A plop saved me. A loud sharp plop from the water. In the middle of the biggest pool large, rough ripples were spreading. It was almost too big for a fish. I wondered if it might be a platypus. The boy frowned — something he seemed to do most of the time — and turned towards the river. He and his mates were so nervous that they would have jumped at a leaf falling from a tree. He took a step towards the bank, but then another soldier called out a few sharp and angry words. The boy screwed up his nose as though someone had farted. Mumbling to himself he walked back to the search party.

I thought I'd better make the most of my reprieve. I made my second dash, keeping so low to the ground I nearly got gravel rash on my tummy. I'd planned to stop again but once I started I just kept going. The last few metres were breathtakingly scary. But I made it to the jeep, crouching beside it, on the safe side. I peeped around the left-hand taillight to have a quick look at the soldiers. They were poking their rifles into some willow roots. It was a long way from where we'd been hiding, so I wasn't worried that we'd left any incriminating evidence. They were probably peering down a wombat hole. I reached into the jeep and released the handbrake. "You're a genius, Fi," I thought. I backed away slowly, but the soldiers were still interested in the willows. Before I knew it I was at the top of the hill. One last slither over the crest and I was with the others again.

I got a few pats on the back for that effort. But Lee was proud of himself too. "Did you like my shot with the rock?" he asked.

"Rock? What rock?"

Then I realised. "Oh. I thought it was a platypus. God, you took a hell of a risk."

We decided to stay and see what happened. It was too important to us. If these guys weren't fooled, if they were convinced we were in the area, it'd change our whole strategy. If we had successfully conned them, then we'd bought ourselves another chunk of time and space. We had to know.

It took half an hour to find out. In that time the soldiers, working carefully and methodically, covered the whole area up to the road. Then they at last decided to take a break. They came back down to the jeep.

It took another five minutes for anything to happen. For those five minutes we watched from our vantage points, sweating and wishing. If willpower could make those guys do what we wanted, they would have been moving at triple speed. But all our combined willpower didn't seem to make any difference. The soldiers lit cigarettes, and stood around talking, but still very watchfully, with rifles ready. I thought maybe they were losing enthusiasm. There wasn't much to encourage them.

It was only when one of them threw his cigarette away and went over to the jeep that things at last started to happen. He sat in the driver's seat and tried the key again. Again it didn't fire up. He continued to sit there. One of the others called something but the man in the driver's seat just shrugged. For another couple of minutes he sat gazing through the windscreen.

I didn't see him look down at the handbrake. But suddenly I heard his cry of surprise. Of delight even. He jumped out of the car, calling to the others. I felt Fi's hand grip mine nervously. This was so important to us. Especially to her, seeing it was her idea. It just had to work. We were too tired, too wrecked, to start another long bout of running and hiding. We had to buy that extra time.

Whatever the man said brought them all to have a look. There was a lot of excited discussion. But one thing was for sure: their attitude changed. They were relaxed, laughing, happier. I knew they didn't want to find us, any more than we wanted them to find us. To them we were vicious armed guerillas. Totally dangerous, totally deadly. Amazing. But I could see how they would think that way. They were just regular soldiers, used to cleaning their boots, marching round the parade ground, getting the barracks inspected, having rifle practice in the afternoons. Nothing would have prepared them for the kind of stuff we were doing. Nothing would have prepared them for the inferno we'd created at the airfield.

They were thinking now that they weren't going to find us. All they had now was a jeep with a faulty handbrake. That was cool by them. They were happy again.

There was more discussion. But at least two of them obviously wanted to go. With dark coming on, I assumed they were approaching the end of their shift. The first two were starting to wade across the ford, and urging the other two, the older man and the teenager, to come with them. They weren't as keen, but after a moment they started to follow. The five of us watched anxiously as they splashed across the river. Soon they were heading up the opposite bank. But only when they were over the top and out of sight did we relax. We lay back and laughed. The relief was huge, overwhelming. We had survived, without hurting or killing anyone. It was a big break.

12

No one was very keen to go back in the river. The darker it got, the safer the river would be — ambushes would hardly work when they couldn't see us — but we had become so uncomfortable and cold after the first trip that we weren't in a hurry to do it again. Instead we decided to follow the banks for as long as we could, then get some sleep. Funnily enough, no one even mentioned food. I guess there was no point. We knew we wouldn't be magically coming across any golden arches, so what was the good of whingeing? But I also knew our energy levels were a long way down, and we would need food soon.

We struggled along the sides of the river. It was difficult. There were big patches of blackberries in a few places, blackberries that stretched for a hundred metres or more. And in another place the banks were just too steep. Finally, while the rest of us struggled through another tricky part, where a clump of trees forced us into a big detour, Lee slipped into the water and swam around. It took him thirty seconds, but it took us ten minutes. When we got past the trees, Lee was waiting, comfortably stretched out on the grass. It was enough of a hint. At the next patch of blackberries we all took to the water.

We floated on for an hour and a half. By then the light was gone and we were terribly cold again. We needed to get out of the water. None of us had a clue where we were, but we hadn't seen any sign of habitation for twenty minutes, and the thick bush on either side of the river made us think we'd be safe.

We clambered out. We were so cold and miserable and hungry that when Homer said he was lighting a fire, no one objected. He looked straight at me, quite fiercely, as if he expected me to kick up a fuss, but I didn't have the spirit to say anything. And when I thought about it, as we straggled around the clearing looking for wood, it seemed like the right thing to do. It'd be dangerous to stand around in wet clothes. By the morning we'd have a few cases of pneumonia to worry about.

So Lee dived into his waterproof pack and got his matches. He'd said to me that I might be grateful one day for his waterproof pack, and he was right, as usual.

We lit a tiny fire and huddled around it to hide the flame, feeding it with dead twigs so there'd by no smoke. We talked quite a lot, in low voices, in case there were people closer than we realised. My first question was to Lee. "Was I dreaming or did you take the rifles from where those two soldiers dropped them?"

"Yeah, you must have been dreaming. I never touched them."

For a moment I actually believed him, which shows how tired I was.

"Yes, you did!" I said indignantly.

"OK, I did then. Whatever you reckon."

"Oh come on Lee, tell me, what happened? How did you do it?"

Homer finally took pity on me. "It was a snap decision. It looked like there was a good chance we could get out without any shooting, but only if we put the rifles back. So we took the risk."

I was relieved it was such a simple explanation.

We talked about the airfield, each telling our stories. What we'd done and where we'd made mistakes and how stunning and amazing it all was. We didn't rave or scream or have a celebration party. We just talked quietly. I knew we were probably hurting Kevin by having our postmortem right in front of him, but too bad. We needed to do this. We weren't trying to rub salt in his wounds, but the whole thing had been so overwhelming, so intense, so sudden and rushed, that we hadn't even begun to absorb it. That very morning we'd brought off what could be one of the most important hits of the war. We knew that from the Wirrawee airfield the enemy controlled thousands of square kilometres of land. We'd changed that. The explosions and the fires had been so vast and on such a scale that it was quite possible we'd destroyed every plane.

We were talking about the big hangar when Lee said: "We should try to contact Colonel Finley."

"Yes, good idea," Homer said, with sudden enthusiasm.

Lee went on: "They mightn't even know this has happened. And they'll need to know, because then they can take advantage of it. They can bomb the hell out of any targets they want."

"But they'll know about it," Fi said. "All that smoke! It'd just about have crossed the Tasman."

I think Fi's real worry was that if we used the radio we might give our position away. The New Zealanders had told us how easy it was to be traced, and how we should only use the radio in emergencies. To be honest, I did sort of want to call the Colonel, but for the wrong reasons. I wanted to hear a friendly familiar adult voice again, and even more than that, I wanted someone to say: "Fantastic! You guys did well. That was good!"

I hadn't heard any praise from an adult in quite a while.

"We'll be circumspect," I said to Fi. She just looked at me, like: "You're pathetic."

We decided we'd spend a maximum of four minutes trying to establish contact. That mightn't sound much, but the New Zealand Army maintained a twenty-four hour a day listening watch on the frequency we'd been given, so if we were in a good enough position and there wasn't much interference we might get through.

We were all still damp. Steam was rising from our clothes but the fire wasn't big enough to dry us out. We decided to go find a place for the broadcast, and hope that the walk warmed us a bit. Even Kevin seemed to brighten a little at the thought of talking to New Zealand, and he came along fairly happily. At the next bend of the river we trudged up a hill, occasionally whispering a comment, but mostly we were silent, thinking our own thoughts.

At the top, Lee took out the radio. He was so confident it hadn't been damaged during our assault on the airfield that he hadn't even checked it yet. But I was very nervous as he turned it on. If it was broken . . . well, I didn't want to think about that. The isolation, the fear, the loneliness of having no radio would be almost unbearable. Sometimes I thought the only thing that kept me going was the knowledge we weren't alone. There was an invisible link across the Tasman, a reminder that someone was on our side, fighting like we were, committed to the same cause.

The little red light came on OK. So far so good. Lee pulled up the aerial. He pressed the transmit switch and began calling. Our password was the password that Iain and Kiwi guerillas had used — Lomu. Lee would say it four or five times, then switch to receive.

He didn't have to say it for long. After the second group of "Lomus" his ear was nearly bitten off by the reply. It was a woman speaking, not a voice we recognised but she had the right response, which was "Zinzan." They were football names, I think.

Her first question was: "The Colonel wants to know if you've been active. Over."

Lee fired back: "Yes, very. Over."

"We thought so. We've had some interesting reports. Have you reunited with the Keas? Over."

I had to think for a moment. Then I remembered. Keas were the codename for Iain and Ursula and their group. But Lee was already answering. "No, we're still alone. We have no news of them, unfortunately. Over."

"But you've attacked their target? Over."

"Yes, correct. Over."

"Do you know how many units were destroyed? Over."

"Not exactly. We guess a minimum of thirty. Maximum could be anything, fifty or more. We might have got the whole lot. Over."

"That's what we're thinking. But some buildings are still standing, and we need to know what's in them. Can you help us there? Over."

"We only know about the ones in the northwest corner. Over."

"Yes, go ahead, that would be very helpful. Over."

"OK, the new galvanised iron hangar, about a hundred metres by fifty, next to a power line, is empty except for a few trucks. Across from that is an L-shaped wooden building, and that's the soldiers' barracks. To the south of the hangar is a store shed with aircraft parts, stuff like that. That's all we know about. Over."

There was a pause, then the voice came back. "Thank you. That's excellent. It was the first building we were worried about. What credibility rating would you put on your own assessment? Over."

"Huh?" Lee looked at me.

"I think she means, how sure are we that the hangar's empty," I said swiftly.

"Oh, OK," Lee said. Then into the radio, he said: "We're one hundred per cent sure. It was our home away from home. Over."

There was another pause, then the woman asked: "Did you sustain any casualties? Over."

"Now she asks," Homer said behind me.

"No, none. Over." Lee said.

"Do you have anything else? Over."

"No. Over."

I began to feel kind of empty. I wanted a whole lot of praise and gushing. All we ever seemed to get from them was this cool calm stuff, like a recorded voice on a phone.

"Cut it off," I said to Lee. We'd been on the air long enough.

But the woman was speaking again. "Can you call this time tomorrow night? The Colonel wants to talk to you himself. Over."

This was something, at least. Apparently we were still important enough for Colonel Finley to grant us a few moments of his precious time.

We trudged back to our little fire and got it going again. We were all dry enough now, so we didn't really need it. But it was comforting. I felt suddenly terribly weary. The radio call left me in the flattest of moods. Despite that, I heard myself volunteering to do the first sentry. It was incredibly generous of me. Everyone else seemed to be grateful, and so they should. They crawled off to their little hidy-holes, to try to sleep. I didn't know how successful they'd be. I certainly didn't know how successful I'd be in staying awake. I felt extremely aggrieved because we couldn't trust Kevin in his depressed state to do sentry, so even though we said we'd wake him, we had made a private agreement to leave him out of it.

Maybe a full night's sleep would help him get back to normal.

The night was a bit of a blank for me. Kevin didn't seem to care about being passed over for sentry duty — I don't know if he even noticed; he certainly didn't say anything — and I don't know if anyone got much sleep. I felt like I didn't get any. We were so hungry in the morning that the roar of rumbling stomachs was almost funny. I'm surprised it didn't attract hordes of enemy soldiers. But we had to get moving. The search for us wouldn't be scaled down for a long time yet. In fact they'd probably increase it. They simply had to find us, for their own sake. It was way, way too expensive to have us out in the bush getting ready for our next attack. If the last one cost fifty or a hundred million bucks, what would the next one cost? They'd be prepared to spend a few weeks on a search. That's how they'd think.

Before dawn we were stumbling through the bush, trying not to trip over, trying to be quiet, trying to stay awake and watchful.

We saw our first helicopter that morning, but it flew past to the west, very low, and going away from us, so I don't know if it was part of a search.

By then we were back in the river. It wasn't fun anymore but it was an effective way to travel: silent and quick and reasonably secretive. I fretted that all the time we were going farther from Hell, where the rest of our stuff was, and where I felt comparatively safe. But that was too bad. Like the song says: "If wishes were fishes, we'd all cast nets in the sea." Or, as my Stratton grandmother used to say: "If wishes were horses, beggars would ride."

I had the idea that drinking lots of water would fill my tummy and relieve the hunger, but it didn't work; just made me feel bloated inside as well as out. In a book I guess the hero would do something outdoorsy and boy-scouty, like make a snare for rabbits out of a young tree branch, or dig up roots using ancient Aboriginal knowledge, or tickle the tummies of a few trout. I wasn't that outdoorsy, although when I was younger I'd tried a few times to make snares for rabbits. They never worked. Anyway we didn't have time to sit around for a day or two waiting for an unusually stupid rabbit to blunder into a trap, after he'd had a few drinks with his mates. That was the only way we were ever going to catch one. A drunk rabbit would be quite handy, because it'd have marinated itself already. Save a lot of trouble.

An old bloke named Alf, who'd worked on our place, caught a dozen trout one afternoon by tickling their tummies. I had trouble believing it but he and Dad finally convinced me. The circumstances were a bit unusual though. It was a dry year and one of the tributary creeks on our property — a creek so insignificant it didn't even have a name — stopped flowing and was down to a series of little pools. Alf noticed that quite a few pools had trout in them, hiding under the bank as far as they could get, to be in the shade. So he stuck his hand in, gave them the old tickle, and flicked them out, one by one.

I'm not sure what the tickling did, hypnotised them I guess. At the Wirrawee Show there'd been a Tassie bloke giving a demonstration with snakes and lizards. He had one type of lizard where you just stroked its belly half a dozen times and it went into instant deep sleep. Totally relaxed. He put it on the ground and it lay there like an old drunk for nearly the whole demonstration. One time it woke up and started scuttling around so he picked it up, gave it another stroke, and exactly the same thing happened — instant coma.

I've hypnotised a few chooks over the years of course — I reckon every kid who's got chooks has a go at that. It is funny to watch. You put them on the ground, hold their heads down and draw a line out from their beaks, and straightaway they're gone. You can have them lined up across the chook yard doing Elvis impersonations, pretending their stripping their feathers off, or acting like they're madly in love with the rooster. No worries.

Years ago my Stratton grandmother had a dog you could hypnotise. You did it the same way as the chooks. He walked in circles, his head sticking out in front and his tail sticking out the back, completely straight. And all in slow motion. Funniest thing I've ever seen. We'd be on the ground in hysterics, but if you laughed out loud or made a noise it'd break the spell. The kitchen door slamming or a vehicle starting would be enough to wake him up. The dog — his name was Cob — would suddenly snap out of it. Life came back to his eyes, he'd shake himself vigorously, then sit down and have a good scratch, all the time looking a bit foolish, like he knew he had let down the doggy species by not acting with enough dignity.

In the end Dad stopped us doing it, because he said it wasn't good for the dog. He found Cob one day in a hypnotic trance of his own, just walking round the yard in a circle, in slow motion. So he said we'd better stop. Cob was becoming a junkie, couldn't do without his hypnosis fix.

Very strange.

These were the kind of dumb things I thought about as we cruised down the river. I passed a few hours like that, thinking and dreaming about the old times, BTW. It was a colder day and it felt warmer in the water this time. I found myself resenting the times I had to stand up and wade in the shallow stretches. The wind was so cold on my wet skin.

I was keeping half an eye out for soldiers, of course, but only half an eye. Around lunchtime — or what would have been lunchtime if we'd had any lunch — things changed.

But it wasn't soldiers exactly who changed them.

"THIS IS WORSE THAN THE FORTY-HOUR FAMINE," FI complained.

"Mmmm," I agreed. I couldn't be bothered talking. I'd been thinking about food a lot though, and in particular the smell of barbecues. I'd decided that right now I'd take that smell above any other in the world. I was dreaming of slightly charred sausages, fried onions and lots of potato salad.

The next moment though I was wide awake and talking, even if it was in a whisper.

"Go back," I hissed at her.

But it was too late. We were already too far around the bend and in a narrow deep part of the river where the water was moving quickly. Ahead of me I could see Lee surfacing by the right bank. He had seen the danger and swum to the bank underwater. He obviously planned to sneak out there, so I nudged Fi and we followed suit. I cursed myself for not paying better attention. We had nearly been caught. I should treat my life as worth more than that.

The problem was that we'd at last reached the outskirts of Stratton. It had been a long time coming, and although I hadn't wanted to get there it was a relief to break the monotony of the long swim. Ahead was a major bridge, built of concrete and steel, four lanes wide. I knew that bridge well, although I'd never seen it from this angle before. Beyond that was a series of rich houses all going down to the river. I figured the enemy officers had probably taken those over by now. In Wirrawee they'd helped themselves to the best houses.

On this side of the bridge was a factory that made ball bearings. Before the war anyway. I didn't know what it did now. It was the kind of target the Kiwis would love to bomb to bits, but nothing had touched it yet. Someone was using it, because I could see a couple of people standing talking on a brick wall out the front. And just before I dived I saw a truck backing down beside the building.

I got to the bank in one breath, which was pretty good, although I wouldn't like to do it too often. I came up just in front of Fi. I could see Homer and Kevin scrabbling up the bank already, so it seemed everyone was safe. I dragged myself out of the water and followed them, feeling as waterlogged as a walrus. Water poured off me. I think the river level dropped by half a metre when I got out.

We lay together in the bushes, gasping for breath. We were so tired and hungry that we didn't have the energy for these sudden shocks, these huge bursts of effort. It was cruel.

But it seemed our journey along the river had come to an end, for the time being anyway. We had no choice. We were in Stratton whether we liked it or not. Our second visit during the war, and I hoped it'd go a bit better than our first one, when I came so close to death, and Robyn crossed the line.

We had no idea what to do. We talked in low voices as we lay there shivering with cold. Trust our luck to draw the first cold day for ages. In the long run we all wanted to get back to Hell — the only safe place we knew — but it was obvious there was no chance of that at the moment.

I assumed we'd wait for night and keep going down the river, but the others, Lee and Fi especially, weren't very keen. Fi hadn't wanted us to go to Stratton in the first place but now she changed her mind completely. Maybe she felt safer in towns. It did seem a bit mindless to keep drifting down the river, with no goal or plan.

At one stage I mentioned my grandmother and Lee interrupted me. "Why don't we go there?"

"I guess we could. But I don't know that there's much point in that either."

"No, there probably isn't. But at least you know the area. All the shortcuts and hidy-holes. We could move around there with a bit more confidence. Your grandmother's sounds better than nothing."

"How far is it?" Fi asked.

"I guess maybe five kilometres. But it's a nice house, so it might have been taken over."

"It's out in the suburbs though, isn't it?" Fi said. "It's probably too far away for them."

No one else said anything and no one else seemed to have any ideas, until Homer clinched it. "I think we'd be safe in Stratton," he said. "They can hardly search the whole city for us, even if they think we're here."

It seemed like my grandmother was in for a visit from her granddaughter, and her granddaughter's rowdy teenage mates. Before the war Grandma, who was very formal, would have regarded that as a bit of a nightmare. Now, wherever she was, and if she was still alive, I don't think she'd have minded.

I doubted that she was still alive. She'd been about seventy-five when the war started, but she looked so frail. She was my bony grandmother. When you hugged her you felt the sharp bones. She was nice and kind of course — I think all grandmothers are, I think there's a law that says they have to be — but she hated any fuss, so if she slipped me fifty bucks for a new shirt I wasn't allowed to say anything except "Thank you, Grandma."

I was the one who did the hugging. She put up with it, but it wasn't her style.

No one told me exactly what happened to the Stratton people when the war began. In some cities people were gradually allowed to return to their homes, where they were strictly supervised, but because Stratton was such an important industrial area, all the civilians had been removed. I tried to imagine my grandmother in a prison camp, but I think she would have lain down and died in a place like that. Her pride would be hurt too deeply. Not just hurt: taken out, bashed, jumped on with hob-nailed boots, kicked to pieces.

They might have put her on one of the farms — like Homer's parents — but they would have thought she was too old for that. Maybe they were right. But with her spirit you'd never know.

We didn't start out right away. Instead we got onto the subject of food. How could we get some? It wasn't a long conversation, as no one had a clue. People sat around saying what they hoped, instead of practical ideas. "Maybe we'll find some shops we can break into." "Maybe there's a few houses that haven't been looted." "Maybe we can get in touch with a work group of prisoners."

I got sick of that pretty quickly.

"Oh, come on, this is a waste of time," I said, after the twentieth vague suggestion.

The journey to Grandma's place was dull for the first half. One of the many times during this war that had me grinding my teeth with boredom. Lee passed out some chewing gum from his waterproof pack, but that was all he had. I found myself cursing him because he hadn't carried more food, which was hardly fair, seeing I didn't have any.

The chewing gum only made me more hungry. Fi claimed that chewy always does that; she said it's because your stomach's getting messages from your mouth that food is on the way, but the food never arrives, so your tummy gets more and more frustrated. It's quite possible. Anyway it was a good theory.

Even though Grandma's was only five kilometres we took a route that would have been ten k's, easily. I didn't know the way too well, so I took decisions based on which was the quieter way to go. We ended up doing a tour of the outskirts of Stratton.

And that turned out to be pretty smart. We were about halfway there when we stopped for a rest in the corner of a large empty park. We were talking about the airfield raid again. Fi was wondering aloud whether our attack would make much difference. Then, as though Colonel Finley timed it just to impress us and to answer Fi, we got dramatic evidence that it had. There was a low rumbling away to the east. For a minute we couldn't work out what it was, then Lee said: "It's planes."

We jumped to our feet, poking our noses cautiously out of the shrubbery. We were in a good position, high above most of Stratton, with a view of the CBD. And before we'd even seen the first plane there was a series of explosions on the eastern edge of the suburbs. Flashes of red, like a giant camera going off, then the familiar mushroom clouds of dirty loam-coloured smoke. A moment later we heard "crump, crump, crump," and the droning of an aircraft as it gained height. Lee pointed up into the sun. "There they are," he said.

Some people said the Kiwis loved dropping bombs on us. They'd been wanting to do it for years, ever since we first won the Bledisloe Cup. Well, they sure went for it now. I don't know how many tonnes they dropped on Stratton but they let rip. It went for nearly ten minutes. They did it in waves: two planes at a time, beating across the sky like march flies, dropping their load, and droning away into the distance. We actually saw the bombs dropping; not great big round things with propellers on the ends, like in the cartoons, but more like black sticks, and lots of them. As each pair of planes disappeared, the bombs hit, there was another huge blast, the ground rocked and another red fireball erupted, followed by its shadow of smoke.

I actually saw one building fall in on itself. It was a big place that looked like a factory, and the walls suddenly folded in and slid down, collapsing like someone fainting. It was scary and exciting at the same time.

Considering the New Zealanders had just about given up aerial bombing, this raid was proof that we'd opened up the skies for them again. We grinned at each other in amazement. Homer's eyes were alight with pride. To think we had contributed to this! Our radio call had made it happen. Dial-a-bomb. Dial-a-plane. Dial-an-air raid. It was a bit too big to take in. I found myself almost hoping for the planes to go, so I wouldn't have to think about it anymore.

When it did finish we wasted no time getting on our way again. It seemed like a good time to be moving. A lot of people wouldn't be rushing outside yet. We made good progress for a while.

But for all that, our arrival in Doncaster Crescent came well after sunset. We'd had to slow right down again. It was frustrating, teeth-grinding stuff. As soon as we got into the settled areas the streets were busy. It was nothing like before the war, but it was hectic enough. This could have been New York, compared to what we were used to. People were hurrying along the streets, stepping around the piles of bomb rubble and litter. No one looked happy. They seemed keen to get somewhere else. I saw no smiles. There was something almost furtive about the way they scurried past. We didn't go in any areas where there'd been heavy bombing or recent bombing, but every street seemed to have suffered damage at some time.

The vehicles were all driven by soldiers, like they were on official business. Most of them were trucks, and most were in convoys of six or eight. There mightn't have been much petrol available for social trips.

So the trip to West Stratton took forever, and every metre was riddled with anxiety. We had to wait for ages for clear breaks, when we could make a quick thirty or forty metres to the next bit of cover. I felt like my head was a garden sprinkler, turning round and round all the time, to the left, to the right, ahead, behind. It was physically tiring but worse than that, it was emotionally draining. None of us even spoke to each other after the air raid. We were concentrating so hard, nerves at hair-trigger tension.

As I'd hoped, and half expected though, West Stratton itself was different. It was too far from the CBD for enemy soldiers. It seemed deserted, and the power was off.

Only when we were approaching the house did I at last allow myself the luxury of thinking about my grand-mother. I had a strong sense by then that she was no longer alive. I just felt that her spirit, which had filled the house for so many years, was gone.

In fact one of the impressive things about my Grandma was that her frail body had a spirit strong enough to fill this big old house. I swear, you could go to the farthest corner of the top storey and you'd feel her presence. It was like she was in every room, walking every corridor, popping up at every corner. I think Mum was quite relieved when Grandma moved off the farm and into Stratton. I don't know if the farm was big enough for both of them.

We got into the garden and I tiptoed up the steps to the front door. The flower garden was so overgrown that I found myself feeling glad Grandma wasn't there to see it. Then I told myself off for feeling glad that she wasn't there. Then I explained to myself that I was just trying to make myself feel better because she wasn't there, so that made it OK.

I exhaust myself sometimes, thinking like this. It makes life so complicated.

It was hard to walk along the verandah without every board creaking. The timber in the house was getting old. I took one step every ten seconds, praying I wouldn't wake a sleeping soldier, imagining him leaping out at me with his gun drawn. I peeped through window after window, but it was impossible to see anything. The darkness was so complete, the stillness so total.

I had to assume the place was empty. All I could hope was that somewhere deep in the pantry would be a can of baked beans or a jar of marmalade. Grandma was a good cook, but the one thing she could never manage was jam. Her jams were famous in our family for being too hard: we called them concrete and made lots of jokes about breaking our teeth when we ate them. But now, yes, a jar of Grandma's concrete would be very welcome.

I went back to the others, who were waiting in the farthest corner of the garden. In the dim light they looked thin and pale and unhappy. I knew a lot of that was lack of energy from lack of food, and I promised myself that as soon as we were settled in the house I'd get food. I didn't know how, but I knew I had to do something.

"It looks OK," I whispered. "There's no one there. Let's go round the back. It'll be easier to get in."

With the power off I wasn't worried about the security system. The backup battery would have died months ago. But I thought the kitchen door would be weaker than the sturdy dark oak door at the front. I led them to it. Kevin kept walking on my heels, and I had to bite my lip to stop myself turning on him and yelling, "For Gods sakes, Kevin, can't you look where you're going?" I guess I was as tired as the others.

The back garden was the vegetable section. For the first time I realised it might have vegetables self-seeded from last year. Well, I could cope with a vegetarian diet for a while. The way I felt right now I'd eat stewed gum leaves. I'd eat tree bark or crickets or compost. I'd eat the pickles from a Big Mac, that's how serious things were.

From my glimpse of the vegie garden as I led the others past it, I thought it still looked quite neat. Better than the front anyway.

The back door used to have a panel of glass in it. Not anymore. I took a quick look through the square where the glass used to be, but again it was too dark to see. I wasn't too worried by now. The place was obviously deserted. I jiggled the door handle up and down. It felt like the tongue was only just in the socket, as though one good shove would open it. I put my shoulder to it and gave a good shove, but it didn't move. "Come on," said an impatient voice behind me. But I didn't like to be too brutal: it seemed impolite in my grandmother's house. Then something hard was pressed into my hand. Looking down I saw a trowel. I'd used that trowel before, to help Dad put in the concrete path through the vegetable garden. But I took it now and shoved it into the door, using it as a lever. The damage we'd done at the school, as part of our practice for breaking into Tozers', stood me in good stead. I heard the splintering crunch of the door giving way.

I pushed it right open and took a nervous step inside. At that exact moment I heard a whooshing noise. Something flashed past my hand so fast and so close that it pinched my skin in passing, and crashed against the wall next to me. Fi, who was right behind, screamed and backed away. I think she knocked down Kevin, who was behind her. It sounded like dominoes. But most of my attention was on the kitchen. I still hadn't moved, except to jerk my hand away from the wall, and even that was pure reflex. Then, getting my senses back, I did move, crouching fast.

From the next room, the breakfast room, I heard rushing feet, like hail on a galvanised-iron roof. A moment later the shatter of breaking glass echoed from the other side of the house.

I crouched there in shock. For an instant I'd thought Grandma was still in the house. But I was so sure she must have died. I'd been mentally saying goodbye to her for the last half an hour, trying to get used to a new world where she wasn't around. Then I thought it might have been a ghost. But not many ghosts would be this active.

I felt around on the ground. I soon touched the thing that had so nearly hit my hand. It was a poker, long and heavy. I picked it up, grimacing as I did so. I was lucky it hadn't smashed every bone in my hand. I was lucky it hadn't hit me in the face.

I tiptoed forward. My feet scrunched on something broken. Behind me I heard the others following, equally cautious. It was reassuring to know they were there. But I wished we could have had some light.

The house was empty. It took us twenty minutes to prove it, but at last we were convinced we had it to ourselves. There'd been a lot of damage though. It looked intact from the outside, but the inside was a mess: broken plates, smashed furniture, Grandma's clothes scattered around. The toilet full of the stuff toilets are usually filled with. It was the kind of mess kids would leave. Someone had been using my grandmother's house for a camping ground.

Getting through the house in the dark was an obstacle course. I hit my shins about ten times.

Back in the kitchen we worked out a plan of action. We made the big decision, to stay in the house. I wanted to, so I could clean it up, and protect it. The others agreed because they were too wrecked to go looking for another place. Whoever was camping there was more scared of us than we were of them, that was one consolation. We got an arsenal of weapons together, anything we could find, pokers, walking sticks, knives. And we worked out how to barricade the doors. If these people came back they'd have a fight on their hands.

We didn't muck around with theories about what was going on in Stratton. That could come later. We elected Fi and Kevin to check out the vegetable garden. Lee and

Homer and I volunteered ourselves to go out into the mean dark streets and see what we could find. The three of us would start together, but if necessary we'd split up and meet back at the house in an hour.

So off we went. I still felt hungry but the need for action helped me overcome my hunger pangs. The night was even colder than the day, and the street really did feel mean and dark. We walked along silently, keeping to the shadows of the fencelines. We didn't know where to start looking for food. Lee suggested breaking into another house. That seemed dangerous, and unlikely to produce much, but no one had a better idea. We decided to check out a few streets first and if nothing looked promising we'd pick a house and bust in.

"I hope there's no one else lying in wait with pokers," I whispered.

I had a strong feeling a couple of times that there were people around. I don't trust my instincts too much but several times I stopped and signalled the others, convinced someone was following us. The neighbourhood that previously seemed so lifeless now had a different atmosphere. Maybe the later it got, the more things started to happen. It felt spooky, like some weird and unhealthy presence.

As for food, well, we didn't have any brilliant ideas. "Food doesn't grow on trees you know," Homer whispered at one point, which I later realised was his attempt at a joke. I was too tired to get it, let alone laugh.

We passed a big park, but it looked too sinister to go in.

After nearly an hour that was totally fruitless — oh, I just made a joke myself, not much better than Homer's — we chose a house to raid. It was no different from any others in West Stratton, which was probably a good reason for picking it. It was a brick veneer with a little verandah, a brick wall at the front, garage at one side, circular garden at the other. Boring but nicely solid. We tiptoed around the back. Even after being attacked with a poker we didn't take a lot of precautions. There was something about all these places that screamed "unoccupied," although of course that hadn't proved true at Grandma's place.

It did in this one though. The back door was completely smashed in, or to be accurate, smashed down. It lay on the kitchen floor. I felt strange when I saw it there. I knew why. It was because the house looked so solid from the front. So reliable, safe, secure. Just from looking at it, you felt you knew its life history, and the story of its owners. They'd be steady, responsible people. He'd work in an office and collect wine and drive a Magna and be into gardening in a big way; she'd be a doctor's receptionist and make nice salads and listen to Paul Simon and attend all the school council meetings.

Then you go round the back and you find the kitchen door on the floor and it makes you wonder about everything.

We went in, but again too many people had been here before us. Cupboards and drawers were opened and a few things tossed around, but it wasn't as bad as Grandma's. Only in the main bedroom had there been a thorough search. I guess it's where most people hide their valuables.

There was no food, just a few disgusting piles of mould in the kitchen.

We gave it up and retraced our steps to Grandma's. Fi

and Kevin were sitting at the kitchen table chopping up potatoes in the dark. Better still was some broccoli which we promptly crunched into, while Fi gave a quick summary of the state of the vegie garden.

"The potatoes were Kevin's idea," she said, beaming at him like a mother with a kid who's just learnt to count to ten. "There's only new little potato plants growing, but Kevin said if we dug we might find some from last season, and they should be OK to eat. And look, we got quite a lot."

We all beamed at Kevin then, like he'd learnt to count to a hundred. He didn't beam back, but his mouth twisted into an expression you could pretend was a smile.

I munched on some more broccoli as Fi continued.

"The trouble is, everything's so young. It's too early in the season. But there's quite a lot of stuff growing. Pumpkins and lettuce and zucchini. We'll get a better idea in the morning, when we can see properly."

"Are you planning to cook the spuds?" Homer asked. I could imagine what he thought of raw vegetables for a diet.

"Well, what does everyone think? We could light a fire in the dining room fireplace and turn it into a barbecue. We had a quick look and it seems OK."

"It should be safe enough," Homer said. "We just have to be careful not to make smoke."

"What about the smell?" I asked. "I don't know about you guys but I can smell a wood fire a kilometre from a house. We don't want our visitors to come back."

"Well, the dining room's in the middle of this house," Fi said. "So that might cut the smell down."

I wasn't convinced.

"Those people won't come back," Homer said. "Why should they? There's hundreds of places they can pick from. They don't want any grief."

I thought, "There are hundreds of places we could pick from too," but I didn't say it, because I felt quite emotional being in Grandma's house again.

Lee asked: "Is there any food in the pantry?"

"Oh, do you know, we completely forgot to look."

That gave us a moment or two of excitement, as we rushed in, thinking maybe we'd find a treasure trove of goodies. It wasn't quite that. There was half a bottle of vinegar, an unopened jar of chutney, half a jar of stale coffee and a packet of gelatine. And the spice rack, with most of its little bottles still nearly full, and Grandma's so-familiar row of blue-and-white kitchen canisters. I opened each one: flour, no sugar, half a cup of rice, a few grains of castor sugar, quite a lot of salt, that was all. It was a depressing collection.

In the end we did cook the spuds. We were so low on energy and spirits that we thought we should take the risk. Fi and Lee went out in the street as sentries while Homer and I did the cooking. I'm not sure what we'd have done if Fi and Lee came sprinting in to say there was a patrol of enemy soldiers, or a gang of squatters, advancing on the house. I don't think I could have left the spuds there for someone else. Maybe I'd have chased intruders away with the poker.

But we finally had a meal, and a hot one at that. Spuds and broccoli with salt and chutney, followed by coffee. Afterwards we trooped out to the back garden and tried to call New Zealand. I'd been excited every time I'd had a chance to think about this. It was our lifeline to the normal world, to sanity, to calm pipe-smoking Colonel

Finley in his book-lined study in Wellington. And somehow every time we called, I expected magic and miracles. I'm not sure what kind exactly, or why I expected them. Maybe because it seemed so miraculous that we could call them on the radio in the first place.

Well, this time I sure got disappointed. We'd allowed ourselves six minutes to make the call, and as usual we didn't stick to our own time limit. We tried for nearly twelve before Homer switched it off. All we got was different varieties of static again: loud, soft, whistling, crackly, humming, stormy. Maybe there was some problem with the weather. Maybe it was atmospheric disturbance. Worse still, maybe someone was on our wavelength. I was disappointed and relieved when silence again took over the chill night air.

Homer took first sentry and after we'd cleaned up a couple of bedrooms we found enough clean blankets and sheets in the linen press to make proper beds. It was a night of sheer luxury.

14

I GAVE FI BREAKFAST IN BED: COLD POTATOES WITH chutney.

She took one look at the chutney and said: "Oh, you put chutney on it."

"But you like chutney."

"No I don't. I didn't have any last night."

Downstairs, Homer and Lee had done a bit more exploring. We already knew the toilet didn't work, but surprisingly the water was still on, so we flushed the toilet with a few buckets of water from the sink, and put the bucket in there for the next person who used the dunny.

Kevin had at last found something he seemed to enjoy. Perhaps our encouragement the night before helped, but for whatever reason he was out in the garden digging for vegetables. He had quite a good little pile of spuds. Some were half ruined by a mouldy wetness and a lot were sprouting new growth, but some were fine and we could cut the bad bits off the others. Up the back of the garden were heaps of dead white canes with a bit of new growth at the base. I thought they might be Jerusalem artichokes, which are pretty boring, but they seemed like chocolate now. I gave Kevin the hint to check them out, and left him to it. I've never been keen on gardening, so with Kevin looking relatively happy I didn't push my luck by hanging around.

Fi and Homer and I talked Lee into doing guard duty

and we went up the hill at the back of West Stratton to see what was going on. It was dangerous moving through the suburbs in daylight again but we couldn't afford to stay in one spot, slowly dying. We had to make things happen.

Stratton didn't have a nice lookout like Wirrawee. It was about the only thing Wirrawee had that Stratton didn't. But from the hill we thought we'd get a good enough view. It was a kilometre and a bit from Grandma's, but it was in a different suburb. They called it Winchester Heights, and if that sounds pretentious, well, that's the kind of area it was. Huge new houses each bigger and grander than the next. No interesting wild gardens or strange secret places or funny little outbuildings. A billion bricks and a million roof tiles had gone into building those houses, and I reckon they wasted the lot of them.

The conditions there were very different to West Stratton. It was back to the tension of the previous day. That was good news and bad news. The good news was that I didn't feel the constant tingling in my back that I got around Grandma's: the feeling of being watched or followed. Here the dangers were obvious, out in the open. The bad news was that this area was definitely occupied. Seems like these spectacular new homes proved irresistible to the invaders. It all reminded me of the new-look Wirrawee, with families living in the houses again. Not "our" families, but if you didn't know that you wouldn't have guessed it. The same washing hung from the lines, the same cars were parked in the streets, the same flowers grew in the same carefully manicured gardens. I felt like we'd stepped out of the lightless world of West Stratton and into an American TV show.

Homer and I looked at each other from our hiding place in a creek bed. We were in a small park at the bottom of the hill.

"No point going up into that," Homer said flatly.

"I agree."

"Oh thank goodness," Fi said. "The way you two carry on I thought you'd want us to charge in and take them all hostage."

"Hmm, now that's not a bad idea," Homer said.

We withdrew as delicately as we could into West Stratton. It had once been an unfashionable nice old suburb. But it didn't feel all that nice anymore. Again I found myself looking around all the time. My neck could have twisted like a coil spring on a car.

"Do you get the feeling something's wrong around here?" I muttered to Fi, as we crouched behind a garden shed in someone's backyard.

It seemed, even to me, like a stupid question to ask in a war zone when your country's been invaded. Fi looked at me so strangely that I thought that's what she was about to say. But to my relief she said: "Yes, it's creepy. I feel like I've been drinking tonic water."

I've never drunk tonic water, but it seemed like at least we agreed there was a problem.

"I don't know what you're talking about," Homer grumbled. "I don't feel anything. Except hungry."

Fi and I grinned at each other.

From the backyard with the shed we took a shortcut to a lane that would get us within a block of Grandma's. We reached the entrance of the lane. Going into it I felt the strongest sense of danger I'd had since the war started. I don't know why I didn't stop right there. Well, I do know; it's because Homer and Fi were already twenty metres in and it was too late. I could have called out but it would have been noisy. I could have stopped where I was but I didn't want to be separated from them. I could have . . . oh I don't know. The point is I didn't do anything except follow along tamely. And I suspect the real reason is I didn't trust my instincts enough and I didn't want to make a fool of myself in front of Homer.

It did look safe. It was one of those narrow lanes that in the old days was used by the night cart for its pickups. A modern car would have trouble getting down there. The lane was only short but was lined all the way by high fences. The fences made us feel secure from a side attack but at the same time caused all my tension to be concentrated in a small area.

Whatever, halfway down, I'd had enough. I called softly to the other two: "Hurry up," and started running. Fi started too, before the first word was out of my mouth, so I knew she felt the danger. But as soon as we started, the lane erupted. It was the most frightening thing. Like lifting the dags on a sheep and finding it swarming with maggots. Like being bombed by a magpie you didn't even know was there. Like picking up a log and finding, not one snake underneath but a whole nest, mother and babies, writhing and rearing.

They came over the fences. I suppose we knew, subconsciously at least, that fully armed enemy soldiers in their combat uniforms couldn't come swarming over high fences like gymnasts springing off trampolines. That's the only excuse I can give for going down the stupid lane in the first place. But we didn't know how much things had changed in Stratton, in our own country. Because these weren't fully armed enemy soldiers in uniforms. These were kids.

They were a mixture of ages. The youngest might have been six or seven, but they were so skinny and undernourished that I couldn't tell. The oldest were probably twelve or thirteen. There were six that came over the fences and another two at the end of the alley, in front of us. When I looked around I wasn't surprised to find another one blocking the light behind us.

They were all armed. One even had a bow and arrow. Two had rifles, which they cocked as soon as they landed and aimed straight at us. The rest had knives. I thought they were going to shoot us on the spot, that's how frightening they were. They looked half mad.

I couldn't believe it was happening. These weren't the enemy. These were our people, the kind of kids you'd share the school bus with, the kids you'd muck round with at the Wirrawee pool. And they were attacking us. It was all wrong, horribly disgustingly wrong. I looked at them frantically. Stared at them. I was trying to find something I could recognise. I wanted to find one friendly pair of eyes, and then I would have said to them: "Hi! It's us! Let's talk. We've all been through the same stuff. We can help each other."

I found no face like that. Just glaring, wild, scary eyes. In some of them, yes, I thought I saw expressions more scared than scary, but that was probably me being overimaginative. There wasn't time to think about it anyway.

They were shouting and screaming at us to get down on the cobblestones. Homer and Fi were already down. A boy was pointing a rifle at me so aggressively, so viciously, thrusting it forwards with such violently shaking arms that I thought he was about to pull the trigger. His finger was already squeezing the trigger far too hard, and I dropped fast. "Oh God," I thought dumbly, "is this how it's going to end? Shot dead in a lane with no name, by the very people we thought we were helping?"

I lay on the cobblestones. I've never felt anything more uncomfortable. A rifle got pushed into the back of my head so hard that I thought it had broken the skin. Hands started wriggling into my pockets. They felt like little claws. I simmered, furious at my helplessness. "Turn over," a girl's voice said, and I did. She went through my shirt pockets.

I was trying to think, to come up with some way to calm the situation. It wasn't easy. I heard Fi say: "Stop it, you little moron." and Homer say: "Give up." It was weird. These were the words we'd have used to kids on the school bus if they started chucking their lunches at each other, or mooned someone through the back window. They weren't the words to use to violent thugs.

I focused on one of the older girls. She could have been any age between ten and twelve. I chose her not because she looked kinder but because she was a girl, so I assumed she might be more reasonable. "What are you doing this for?" I asked. "We're on your side, you know."

"Fuck off," she said, looking away.

"Haven't you got any food?" a boy asked me. It was the first time any of them had spoken in a voice halfway normal. He looked very young, and his voice was so helpless and unhappy that I did feel a bit sorry for him.

Still lying on the cobblestones, I shook my head.

"We just got here," I said. "We've been living out in the bush. We don't know where anything is."

I thought that if we could get them talking there might be some hope; we might get a calmer atmosphere.

"You must have food somewhere," a girl said. I couldn't see what she looked like. She was standing behind my head, quite a way back.

"Nothing, I swear," I said.

"We haven't eaten for three days," Homer lied.

"You're breaking my heart," the same girl sneered.

"Want a tissue, cry-baby?" another voice asked.

I was sure this was how they talked to each other. It'd stop the little kids from crying or showing weakness. After all, they'd survived, how long? I was losing track of time, but it was probably about ten months, probably without adults. Weakness wouldn't have got them far.

I asked: "Have you been on your own the whole time? Have you ever had adults with you?"

A boy started to answer, saying: "We had a couple of . . ." but a girl interrupted him. She barked a word that sounded like "Exit," but could have been anything, and suddenly they were gone. They might have been undernourished but they were as quick as rats. One moment there, the next a patter of feet, the next an empty alley and silence.

We picked ourselves up. Fi wiped a tear out of her eye and sniffed. Homer looked furious. "Those little mongrels," he said. "They've taken everything."

We did a stocktake, continuing it as we left the lane and found a hiding place in the backyard of a looted milk bar. They'd taken Homer's precious Swiss Army knife, as well as good knives from Fi and me. But the way Homer carried on you'd think he was the only one who lost anything.

They got everything I'd had in my pockets: a biro, a couple of Panadol in foil, my last tampon, a New Zealand compass, a photo of my parents, the ring Robyn gave me for my twelfth birthday and which I kept in my pocket, because I thought it was safer. Even my hankie. Worst of all, my watch, that had been a Christmas present from Grandma.

We'd been well and truly mugged, by a bunch of ten year olds.

To be on the safe side we took a really roundabout route back to Grandma's. We didn't know if the kids were still watching. We didn't want them to know where we were hiding, although I wouldn't have been surprised if they'd known our names, dates of birth, blood types and school grades. They'd been frighteningly efficient. I wondered if they'd been the ones squatting at Grandma's, but I thought there were too many of them for that.

When we got there and told Lee what had happened he was at first incredulous and then depressed. "Unbelievable," he kept saying. "After what we've been through. Unbelievable. God, what's going to happen to us? Even if we end up winning this war, the whole country's going to be a psychiatric hospital."

We sat glumly around the dining room table, where we had a view into the street. No one had the heart to disagree with Lee.

"Well, what's next?" Fi asked eventually. "We have to make plans. We can't just sit here for the next six months. We've got a lot of stuff to work out."

She looked straight at me as she said it. All I could think was how much we'd changed, and in such subtle ways. BTW, before the war, Fi would never have taken the lead like this. Especially not in front of Homer and Lee. She would have waited until we two were alone and then we would have talked it through between us. It was only a little thing and there was a time when I mightn't even have noticed it, but I noticed it then, and I felt a bit sad. So many things had changed that I clung even harder to the few things that hadn't.

"Well, we should try to stay here for a few days," I said. "Obviously we all want to get back to Hell but until the search dies down we daren't go back into that area."

"Food'll be a big problem here," Lee said.

"Yes, and security."

"Yeah, not just from the enemy, and the squatters, but from those bloody little sewer rats too."

"On the other hand. . ." said Homer.

He didn't finish the sentence and we were all puzzled for a moment until I suddenly realised and said: "Oh, your parents."

"Yep. I know it's a one in a million chance. . ."

He was right about that.

"We don't have to make a decision now," I said. "We should try to call Colonel Finley again tonight. He might have some suggestions."

"Yeah, so might Santa Claus," Lee said.

"Well he might."

I meant Colonel Finley, but it came out wrongly.

"It'd be a long hike to Hell from here," Fi said.

"At least we've still got food there."

"We hope."

"How can we get food in Stratton?" Homer asked.

"There's enough in the vegetable garden to last a week maybe. It's not exactly a gourmet diet, but at least we won't starve. And the longer the summer goes, the more new growth'll come up."

"Great," said Homer.

Homer wasn't designed to be a vegetarian.

"Those kids probably don't have a clue that vegetables

grow in gardens," Fi said. "They probably think they're manufactured out the back of the supermarket. There's probably lots of gardens around here where we'd find stuff."

That was a good idea, although there was something in Fi's voice that made me suspect she wanted to sit the kids down at a long table and feed them greens. It was a frightening thought.

"It's not like we're trapped in the middle of New York," I said. "If we follow that creek I reckon we'd be in the bush in an hour."

"Yeah," Homer said. "That's true. If we did use this as a base for a while we could butcher some meat and bring it in. I don't mind vegetarian for a few days if I know there's half a dozen lamb chops waiting at the end of it."

"Half a dozen!" Fi said, looking faint.

"We need a safer way to cook though," I said. "I think it's really dangerous having the smell of a fire wafting through the neighbourhood."

"Especially with those kids around," Fi said.

"Yeah, they're scary. We're going to have to do something about them."

"I've got an idea," Kevin said.

I nearly swallowed my tongue.

"Yeah?" we all said eagerly. Too eagerly. For a moment I thought he was going to back off again. But finally he forced a few more words out.

"Boucher's. The trout farm."

"Yeah, what is that place?" I asked. I'd been past the turnoff often enough but had never been down there. It was about eight kilometres from Stratton.

"I've been there," Fi said. I wish she hadn't said anything, because for Kevin to start talking again was such a big deal that I wanted to encourage him to keep going. But she took over.

"It's great. They have this big dam filled with trout and they give you fishing rods and everything, and you catch as many as you want, then you clean them in a little shed and take them home and cook them. The cleaning's yucky, but I just smiled nicely at Mr. Boucher and he did it for me."

"You're a disgrace, Fi," I said.

"Typical woman," Lee said. "You all pretend to be feminists until you want a guy to do something for you, then you go all gooey and girly and wear a short skirt."

This was such a boringly predictable comment from Lee that neither of us bothered to answer.

"Anyway it was a good idea, Kevin," I said. "If we could score a few trout it'd make all the difference."

"Ellie, do you do that deliberately?" Lee asked. "Cos it sounds so sterile."

"What?" I said.

"Oh you know, that primary-school-teacher voice. 'That was a lovely idea, Kevin. You are a clever boy.'"

Kevin got such a smug smile on his face that I could have hit him.

We hadn't had a good argument for a long time — we'd been too busy — but we sure made up for it then. Sometimes it seemed like Lee was just spoiling for a fight.

I went upstairs. I wasn't planning on having a sleep, but I lay down on a bed and went out like I'd had a general anaesthetic.

15

It took me a few days to get over the argument. Normally I don't think I hold grudges for long. But I felt especially betrayed by Lee. I felt he owed me a favour or two. To be totally honest, I sort of thought that the fact we'd slept together might have made a difference. OK, I know it means less to boys than it does to girls — well, that's what my friends all say — but I still thought it would have made a difference.

And Fi hadn't stuck up for me, either. That hurt. With only two of us against three guys I thought we needed to take care of each other. I'd have taken her side if Lee or Homer or Kevin had a go at her.

So I sulked for a while. I spent most of the time doing something that was very important to me. I hadn't said much to the others about my reasons for wanting to stay at Grandma's. Of course it made sense to hide there and not try to reach Hell just yet. But my main reason was a great desire to take care of Grandma's things, to tidy up her house, to restore it to a decent state. That meant collecting all her letters and papers, which were scattered around the house, and burying them in a small Esky in the garden. It meant wrapping her best clothes in any plastic I could find — the shower curtains were a big help — and hiding them in a dark corner under the house. It meant picking up the remnants of her jewellery and ornaments, and storing them in among the pink batts in the ceiling.

I couldn't help feeling bitter as I looked at the pathetic little pile of jewellery. I could hold it all in one hand. Grandma had owned many valuable and beautiful things, which would have come to me one day. Many times when I was little she had got them out, put them on me, told me their stories. There was a silver and emerald necklace, a pearl necklace, a white jade brooch, a heavy gold bracelet, at least a dozen rings. One of the rings had a ruby the size of a peach stone.

Now those treasures were reduced to a few broken earrings, four bangles, a Wedgewood brooch and an empty locket.

The dusting and sweeping and tidying took a lot of time and energy. There was so much to do that it wasn't hard to keep myself busy, and in fact I hardly saw the others. When I did they seemed much the same as me anyway: kind of switched off. Kevin really did do some good stuff in the garden, clearing and watering and fertilising. Fi became the main cooking person and Homer was surprisingly good at helping her. But all of us seemed to spend time sitting staring at nothing, in different parts of the house. Quite unexpectedly I'd come across Homer or Fi, for example, slumped in an armchair looking like they'd been hit over the head with a pile driver. They'd stay like that for hours. I was the same. I'd curl up in the big old brown leather armchair at the rolltop desk and suck my thumb, while I gazed at the wallpaper. After some time I'd find that three hours had passed, but I don't know where they went. Maybe into the limbo where lost hours are stored, where thoughts and feelings that can't be put in categories are sent for safekeeping.

It took me a few days more to realise something else: that Lee was hardly to be seen. I went missing mentally but he went missing physically. At first I thought he was going off into the garden, in the shed or up a tree. Then Fi told me he was going a bit farther than that. We were snuggled up in a double bed in a spare bedroom. It was very early, probably only 8.30 p.m., but that's the way we lived. The long hours on sentry and the lack of electricity and the lost sleep of the last few weeks: all those things had turned us into good little boys and girls who went to bed early.

Fi said: "Do you know what Lee's getting up to?"

"No. How do you mean?"

"Well, he's gone a bit feral. I think he goes into town on his own."

"Does he? What for?" I felt a little stirring of fear as I asked. Knowing Lee, if he was going into town it wouldn't be to visit the library.

Without waiting for Fi to answer my question I added: "What's wrong with him? Haven't we done enough for a while? When will he be satisfied? When he's dead I suppose."

I felt so angry and bitter suddenly, like I'd retched up something bad and swallowed it again. That's the taste of war.

"You can't blame him," Fi said. "Imagine if you found out the way he did. About his parents, I mean. It's amazing he's not totally crazy."

"Do you think he is a bit crazy then?"

"Oh no. Just . . . he's always been different. All that stuff you told me that his parents went through to get here, of course it'd make you different. It'd be strange if it didn't."

"He always seems so focused," I said. "I used to watch him playing his violin, in the school orchestra. It was like nothing else existed."

"Oh yes. You can tell so much about people by the instruments they play, don't you think?"

I'd never thought about that before.

"Guitar players are really loose," Fi said. "Like hippies or something. So alternative. And piano players are always perfectionists."

"Drummers are always idiots. Like Matt Cohen. He just got off on making a loud noise. Plus going to drum lessons got him out of class a couple of times a week."

"So what are violinists?"

I had to think about it. "Well," I said at last, "I think they're really sensitive, and kind of deep. The way Lee looked when he played. His eyes were just so focused and at the same time, a million miles away."

"You're still in love with him," Fi said suddenly. I knew what she was doing; testing for a response, teasing, curious to see what I'd say. I was going to give some stupid funny answer, but I didn't. Instead I thought about it seriously. I hadn't thought about it for ages, hadn't wanted to, but now I tried to decide: did I or didn't I? I love him, I love him not. Where were the daisies when I needed them?

On the one hand there were Lee's beautiful eyes and his slow smile, his long lean brown body, his intelligence and honesty, his strength. Strength inside as well as outside. On the other hand there was the fact that he could be so cold and violent sometimes. Even more than me, and I was bad enough these days.

Also on the other hand was the terrible thing I'd done with Adam in New Zealand, that I felt so ashamed of, and that had put me off boys in a pretty major way.

Anyway, Lee and I were too young to have a relationship that went for years. That might have been OK in the old days, in my parents' generation. My mother was eighteen when she got married and my father was twenty-three. But that's not what I wanted.

The biggest thing was always the war. Sometimes it seemed like everything came down to that. I couldn't concentrate on a relationship while all around us were flames and death and hatred. Sometimes days went past without me thinking about Lee or anyone else, days when I didn't dream of some boy or imagine myself in someone's arms or feel the slightest bit interested in kissing and being kissed. Thanks to this invasion I was going to end up a sterile cold lonely old woman.

Now I turned to Fi, shifting my whole body around and finding a more comfortable position for my head on the pillows.

"Maybe I still do. I don't know. I mean, sure that's the easy answer to give, the automatic answer, but I seriously don't know."

"Well, you're in a good position in one way. You've got no opposition. If Lee wants a relationship it's either you or no one. And I think he still likes you."

I ignored the last part of what she'd said and concentrated on the other bit.

"There's you."

"No thank you. I like Lee a lot, and I think he's one of the most amazing people I've ever met, but I've never been interested in him that way."

"Well, maybe he and Homer'll decide they're gay and start going out with each other."

"Maybe they will. And it'll be your responsibility."

"Oh, thanks. So his whole fate depends on me? Not to mention his sex life."

"Do you think they masturbate?" Fi giggled.

"Of course they would. I'm sure I've nearly caught Homer a couple of times. And I heard some interesting noises from Kevin's tent one day, back in Hell, when he thought we were down at the creek."

"It seems so funny. It's disgusting really. I can't imagine them doing it."

I went a bit red and turned my face into the pillow. Sometimes Fi seemed like she'd been born a hundred years too late. She belonged in the nineteenth century. Talk about innocent. She'd been in a war and killed people, yet a garden gnome would know more about life.

"So how about you?" I asked, to change the subject. But Fi misunderstood me. Her head came up from her pillow and she asked: "Do you mean . . . do I do that?"

"No! I don't want to know if you do or not. I mean, do you have any secret loves? Is it still Mike?"

Mike was a Maori soldier, or maybe a Samoan, I wasn't sure, but he'd come with us when we returned to Hell with the Kiwi guerillas.

Fi's head went back into the pillow and her voice changed, became sadder. "No. I don't think we're ever going to see them again."

This bloody war. There was no getting away from it. I tried to think of something to say, to change the subject a second time, but couldn't come up with anything.

To my surprise, Fi did it for me.

"I do have a secret love, though," she said.

"You do? Who?"

"You know. The same one: it's always been him."

"Homer? You mean Homer?"

She didn't answer, which of course was all the answer I needed. I lay back, mentally shaking my head. One thing about Fi, she was unpredictable.

"You seriously still like Homer?"

"'We have only one rabbi and he has only one son.'"

Fi was quoting from *Fiddler on the Roof,* a musical we'd both had a craze on for a very short time, in Year 8.

"You're mad," I said. "I think you're one of those people with a genius for picking the worst possible boy-friends. Like Sally. I bet you get married and divorced about six times."

"So you don't think it'd work? You don't think he likes me?"

I should have picked up on the tone of Fi's voice, but like an idiot I rushed on with what I was saying.

"Well, what I think is that Homer doesn't notice any-one in that way . . . he's just not into it at all. I think one day he'll turn around and marry someone but it won't be anyone he's known for a long time, it'll be someone totally new."

Fi didn't answer. There was silence for about two min-utes. I still didn't realise I'd said anything wrong until I heard a half-cough, half-sob from her side of the bed. Finally, I figured what anyone with half a brain would have known right away — that she was crying.

I was horrified.

"Fi! Ohmigod, I'm sorry, I didn't realise . . . Oh no, I can't believe how stupid I am sometimes. Oh Fi, do you really like him that much?"

She didn't answer.

"Oh Fi, don't take any notice of what I said. I don't know why you guys haven't thrown me off the back of a truck with a note around my neck for the Lost Dogs' Home. Honestly Fi, remember when I say anything you have to think: 'Oh that's only Ellie, good, I can ignore it.'

You just have to train yourself. It's not that hard. I've learnt to do it. Anyone can. Honestly."

"But you're right, I know you're right. That's why I'm crying."

"No, I'm not. It's jealousy, that's what it is. I've been mates with Homer for so long, I don't like to think of him going off with anyone. Not with another girl. I mean I don't want him for myself, not in that way, but I don't want another girl to have him either."

"You're just saying that to make me feel better."

"Well, of course I want you to feel better but it's still true, what I said, I don't like seeing other girls crack onto Homer. It's like: 'He's mine, rack off.' Even with you I feel a bit that way."

"You are lucky, the way you two get on together. You're so . . . comfortable with each other. It makes me wish I had a brother."

"But you know, if you want proof that what I said was totally untrue" — I was starting to get my arguments together now — "you only have to remember the way he got so rapt in you in the early days, when we were first camping down in Hell. God he just melted like . . . well, you remember when we microwaved that Easter egg?"

At last I got a little hiccuppy half-giggle out of her. One year we'd had too many Easter eggs, so we started mucking around and getting stupid with them. The one in the microwave melted into the most disgusting black toxic-looking liquid. It filled the kitchen with smoke, and a smell that didn't go away for hours.

I told Fi again all the things Homer said about her when he worshipped the ground she floated across. How perfect she was, how he wasn't good enough for her, how he went red every time she came near. What I couldn't remember, I made up. I felt like a mother telling a kid a bedtime story.

"I wish he was like that now," Fi sighed when I finished.

"Fi, those feelings are still inside him, believe me. They haven't gone away. It wouldn't take much to reactivate them."

"Do you think so?"

"Of course. You're just what he needs. It'd be the best thing, for both of you."

Sometimes I think I'm wasted. I should have been a saleswoman. I'd make a fortune. To be honest, I wasn't all that sure Homer with Fi was a good idea — even leaving my jealousy out of it — but by the time Fi drifted off to sleep I think I'd got her believing they might have a future.

When I went out to do sentry, four hours later, I took over from Lee. After the conversation with Fi I was curious to see him, to find out what he was up to. But I got nowhere. All he wanted was to get to bed, and it didn't matter how many hints I dropped, he still kept yawning and edging away through the trees. Eventually I had to let him go. But I was more conscious of him again now, and over the next couple of days I watched him keenly. Fi was right. He did go missing for long periods of time, and when he came back he looked exhausted. Exhausted, yes, but there was something else. It took me ages to think what it was, but I began to realise, gradually. He was excited. He really was up to something. He was alert, almost quivering with life, like a collie that's been working sheep all day but thinks there's a big mob just around the corner.

I asked Homer: "Where do you think Lee goes when he slips away for hours at a time?"

Homer looked surprised but not very interested. "Is he going off on his own a lot? Yes, now that you mention it, I suppose he is. But you know what Lee's like. Once a loner, always a loner."

This was another of those un-Homer-like comments, the kind of thing he never would have said before the war.

"Well, I'm worried, that's all. If he's doing anything that might affect the rest of us . . . I think he should let us know where he is."

I was horrified to hear myself say this: it sounded so like my mother. War sure changes your perspective.

"Why, what do you think he's doing?"

"I've got no idea. But he's obsessed with getting revenge for his parents. He could be sneaking off and blowing up factories for all I know."

"Doubt it. Why don't you ask him?"

That was easy for Homer to say but Lee was so difficult when you approached him directly. Maybe Homer talked to Lee that way, although I hadn't noticed it myself. Anyway, Homer didn't have the background I had with Lee. He certainly didn't. The conversation hadn't really helped at all.

But a day and a half later Lee seemed in a surprisingly relaxed mood and I thought I might as well try Homer's direct tactics. We were sitting on a garden seat watching Kevin dig over an old garden bed, spreading compost, and I said to Lee: "So where have you been flitting off to in your spare time?"

He didn't seem to mind my asking; he shrugged and shook the hair out of his eyes. "Just around."

"Around here? Or into the city? Or out of town?"

"Just around," he repeated.

"Any particular reason?"

"Yes and no."

I waited for him to say more. I was wondering if I'd been wrong: maybe he did mind my asking. I was tempted to start nagging, to say: "Don't you think we've done enough for a while? How do you know you're not putting us all at risk?" But I didn't think he'd take that too well. Instead I said: "So you're still going for it huh?"

"Why don't you say what you really think?" he said.

"Well, why don't you tell me, if you're such an expert on my brain?"

He looked at me levelly. I was simmering already; he was as cool as a mouthful of Minties.

"I think you're burning up because you want to know exactly what I'm doing and I'm not going to tell you."

"I don't give a stuff what you do," I said. "You can swim to New Zealand for all I care. But you shouldn't do things independently. It's not fair. It could affect us in all kinds of ways. What if you don't come back one day for instance, and we have to go looking for you? We wouldn't know where to start. What if you launch some action against the enemy and they come after you and suddenly we're on the run again, without having any say in it? What if . . ."

"Oh, what if this, what if that," he broke in impatiently. "You can go on all day with that stuff. What if the sun explodes? We're all dead then. I know what I'm doing. You ought to try minding your own business for once."

He jumped up, marched over to where Kevin was working, grabbed a mattock and started furiously attacking the hard dry clay at the end of the garden.

16

We were going along a quiet back street lined with old brick houses. They'd probably been neat and tidy a year ago but they were looking pretty sloppy now. One thing was interesting though, as I crouched in the shade of a rose bush with lots of little yellow roses: I could see so many insects! Bees and little native bees and dragonflies and a couple of butterflies. European wasps and a hornet and a few other things that I couldn't identify. A daddy longlegs danced along a branch of the rose bush. I was fairly sure that a year ago there wouldn't have been all these insects. I thought it was quite good really. I don't mind the odd insect once in a while; it makes me feel that the world isn't in such bad shape when there's insects around. It's only when they get in plague proportions, like the locusts in our paddocks two years back, that I don't like them so much.

Lee waved me on, and on the other side of the street Homer moved forwards too. Fi was checking the rear. We'd left Kevin at Grandma's. He seemed happy enough doing his gardening, and we had to hope he'd be safe. We were going out to the countryside to get a lamb, to satisfy Homer's cravings for meat.

It was still quite early, so we moved with maximum care.

We planned to try to call Colonel Finley again when we got back. We'd discussed bringing the radio with us but the trouble was those kids. We didn't have any rifles, and if they mugged us again and took our stuff — well, we couldn't afford to lose the radio.

It was infuriating and even embarrassing to be scared of little brats. But we had to take them seriously. God, did we ever have to take them seriously. The memory of those trembling fingers on the triggers of rifles, rifles with the safety catches off, the memory of those wild panicky eyes: there was plenty to be scared of in that.

They reminded me of some horror movie, where people were taken over by creatures from outer space. Or one of those stories about drug-crazed teenagers jumping off balconies because they thought purple monkeys were crawling up their legs. I wondered if these kids were on drugs, but I didn't think so. Not that I'd know. I've never seen anything heavier than dope.

I got to the next corner. There was another of these little lanes, like the one where they'd mugged us. I let my eyes travel along it carefully. I didn't know who I was more nervous of: the enemy soldiers or the kids.

My eyes turned back to the main street, but something on the ground caught my attention. I glanced down. Then stopped and stared. Then looked a little farther and saw something else. I called Homer, with a low whistle.

Homer moved quickly and lightly when he wanted. He was surprising for such a big guy. He could have made a ballet dancer in another life.

On second thoughts, maybe not.

When he saw what I'd seen he reacted the same way. He raised his eyebrows and looked at me, then suddenly glanced across the street.

"Let's move on," he said. "One of them's watching."

"All right," I said. "But I'm coming back for my things."

"Yeah of course. So am I."

We left the stuff there and hurried after the others. We met in a carport in a house at the end of the street. "What were you looking at?" Lee asked.

"My photo of Mum and Dad," I said.

"My lucky rabbit's foot," Homer said.

"My hanky."

"You mean, the stuff those kids knocked off?"

"Yeah, exactly."

"So what happened, they dumped it there?"

Homer tried to reason it out. "They've either met in the laneway to divide up the goodies and dump the rubbish. Or they're trying to ambush us."

"Doubt it," I said. "It's not a very good place for an ambush."

"Why didn't you pick it up?" Fi asked.

"I saw one of them watching," Homer said to Lee and Fi. "I reckon their hiding place could be somewhere around here. I want to track them down."

"Why?" Fi asked.

I thought he'd say: "Because I want to beat the crap out of them and get my other stuff back," but Homer all my life has been surprising me and I guess he'll keep surprising me till the day I die.

He said: "I feel sorry for the poor little buggers."

Fi leaned against the wall of the carport and fanned herself.

"Homer," she said, "I swear I'll never understand you."

I was relieved it wasn't just me.

"So what are you suggesting?" Lee asked. "That we go in and convert them? Save their souls? Open an orphanage and look after them?"

Lee had been in a very aggressive mood lately.

"Nothing like that," Homer said. He didn't seem too fazed. "But I thought we could try and give them a hand."

"It sounds," Fi said, "like jumping into a lions' cage and offering the lions our livers for afternoon tea."

"Look," said Homer, "how about this. We leave the stuff there while we go and get a lamb. By then it'll be dark. We come back and have a sniff around. If they're trying to ambush us, they'll have given up by then. I reckon they probably hide out not far from here. All I want is a bit of a look-see. If we can work out where they're living then we can keep an eye on them, and at the same time have a think about how to calm them down. I know they're dangerous, but it's only because they're a bit mad. We've got to be careful, but we shouldn't give it away as a bad job, not that easily."

That was the longest speech I'd heard Homer make for ages. There was a time when you couldn't shut him up, but that was a long time ago.

"I don't like the idea of leaving my only photo of Mum and Dad on the ground," I objected. "At first I thought I'd never see it again. I don't want to risk losing it a second time."

"But they won't bother picking it up," Homer said. "And it won't rain. It'll be safe for today at least."

"How about we ambush them," Lee said. "Drive them out of this district once and for all."

"Yeah," Homer said. "But there's something in me, I don't know what, that makes me want to give them another chance. If your little brothers or sisters were in that gang, you'd want to help them."

It reminded me of something I didn't think about very

often — that when Homer was eight his mum had a third little boy, but he only lived a couple of days.

So I backed him up and we went on out into the countryside, found a paddock full of sheep, and culled a nice fresh spring lamb.

Once upon a time Grandma could be relied on to have good knives. Must have been a hangover from her farm days — all farmers are fussy about their knives. But the only knives left in her house now were fruit knives and dinner knives.

So we did a rough job of butchering. We chucked away so much good stuff. We were too tired, and Homer and I kept arguing about the best way to do it. I wanted to bury the rubbish, to stop foxes and wild dogs getting it, but Fi said: "What does it matter if they do?" I thought, "Yeah, I suppose that's true." Just another change from the old days, from the way we used to do things. Dad would have killed me.

By the time we got back to Stratton it was really late. I didn't expect the gang would still be out and about. I suppose I was thinking of a world where kids go to bed at 8.30. But as we came down the wide avenue near the lane where we'd seen our things I again had the feeling of being watched, followed, haunted by little dark shadows. I was last in our group and I kept taking quick glances behind. Three times I saw a flicker of movement, like a wild cat darting away from the lights of a car. I knew there was a chance they would attempt to mug us again, especially as they could no doubt see Homer carrying the sack that held the lamb. Maybe they saw the little drops of blood that dripped along the footpath. Maybe they could smell the fresh raw meat. It wouldn't surprise me.

Such little savages probably could smell like feral cats or dogs.

We had our plans ready though. For one thing we were spread out very widely, about seventy-five metres between each of us. That made it difficult for them to attack. For another we moved irregularly, sometimes running half a block, sometimes crossing to the other side of the road with no warning, sometimes taking shortcuts through front yards. Even though they'd seemed organised when they attacked us, we assumed they'd fall apart in a situation where nothing was predictable. We'd made it easy for them the first time by going into the alley. We wouldn't do that again.

We had a quick conference, in the middle of a footy oval. I told them I thought we were being followed. We agreed there was nothing we could do. With all our precautions we'd hoped to be the watchers, instead of the watched; the hunters instead of the hunted. But I wasn't prepared to leave my photo on the ground any longer. It was time to forget whatever grand plan Homer was dreaming up. We did a quick check of the nearby yard, then Homer and Lee and Fi formed a protective cordon, while I picked up our bits and pieces. A pathetic little pile they were too.

Then we went back to Grandma's. It was nearly midnight. Homer and I spent ten minutes trying to call New Zealand while Lee got the dining room fire going again. Another risk, but the temptation of grilled spring lamb was hard to resist.

New Zealand was a washout. It seemed most likely that the airwaves were being jammed, but we couldn't be sure.

We had a good pigout on loin chops and half-cooked spuds. I'm exaggerating really: when you've been hungry for a while your stomach must shrink or something, because you can't eat much, you don't even want much. So I ate what I could, then went out to take over sentry from Fi, so she could have a feed.

When I relieved her, the first thing she said was: "They're out there."

"The kids?"

"Yes."

"Are you sure?"

"Yes. And I think they know I'm here. I think the smell of cooking might be attracting them."

"Like flies," I thought.

After Fi went into the house I sat quietly on the lowest branch of a peppercorn tree, watching and listening. It wasn't long before I knew Fi was right. Either there were some very big cats or some small to medium size humans around. It was quite weird. It made me uncomfortable. I wondered if maybe we could use cooking smells to attract them. If Fi was right about their ignorance of food, the attraction of a lamb chop might be hard to resist. We could put on a barbecue for them. I smiled grimly to myself as I pictured it. It'd be a weird barbecue. A bit different from the ones we'd had down by the river in the days of peace.

Part of our sentry technique in this kind of situation was to keep moving, so after a while I got off the branch and started patrolling, creeping around the garden. But the night passed slowly. I didn't have my watch anymore, thanks to these little mongrels, and it seemed like no one came to relieve me for many hours. Eventually Lee appeared, rubbing his eyes. "Sorry," he said. "My fault. I flaked out."

By then I was wide awake and wanting to talk but he didn't seem in the mood, so I gave up and went upstairs to bed. Then, of course I found I couldn't sleep. It was like that most nights. I started wondering about those kids again, and after a while, without planning it, without even thinking about it really, I got up and went downstairs again.

I slipped over the side fence, hoping Lee wouldn't see me, and went for a stroll up the street, keeping to the shadows. It was refreshingly cool after the warm day. Now at last the suburb felt free of its vicious wild-life. Perhaps even the street kids of Stratton were in bed.

I walked almost directly to the lane where we'd found our stuff. It still felt quiet. I went up the lane, very carefully. Halfway along it took a dogleg to the left. I inched my way around that. I certainly wasn't sleepy now. Every sense was on alert, every part of me wide awake.

And almost immediately I heard a sound. For a moment I thought it was a cat wailing, in that terrible way they do sometimes. But then I realised it was a child crying.

It went on for a while. It sounded like a young child, but it wasn't the crying of someone hurt or in a panic. It was a sort of tired noise. You had the feeling this kid might have been crying for a long time, all night maybe. All war maybe.

I tried to work out where it came from. That's the trouble at night — it's much harder to locate sounds. At home sometimes I had to follow the barking of a wild dog or the bleating of a distressed lamb or the bellowing of a calving heifer. And it is tricky at night. Here, in such a built-up area, it was harder again.

I decided after a while that the most likely place was a long dark building, which might have been an old stable.

It was about fifty metres ahead on the left. I started tiptoeing cautiously towards it.

When I was only twenty metres away I felt something grab at my leg. That's what it felt like anyway. I froze for just a moment. A second later a whole wall of stuff moved, right in front of me. It seemed to fall away, like an earthslip.

I jumped back. There was a hell of a crash. A sort of clattering smashing noise that echoed around the alley for the next half-hour. And kept echoing through the whole damn suburb. I heard it all right. I heard it as I ran for my sweet life. I thought it was following me, but I didn't need that to make me run. I kept thinking of the guns these kids had, the guns these kids held with shaking hands and crazy eyes. I didn't want those guns pointed at me again.

I was five blocks away before I ducked into the front verandah of a little semidetached cottage, and crouched behind its brick wall. I'd heard no sounds of a chase, and although I stayed there for nearly forty minutes, I saw no sign of one. But as I crouched there I figured out what had happened. Those cunning little brats had rigged up a booby trap. They had a trip-wire and a whole heap of stuff connected to it, so when I hit the wire a wall of pots and pans or whatever they were came crashing down. It was smart. Not only did it give them warning that someone was sneaking up on them, it also gave them time to get away. The soldiers would be so shocked by the noise that they wouldn't go rushing in. In fact they were more likely to rush away, like I'd done.

It was a high-risk system but it wasn't a stupid one.

I had a long walk back to Grandma's, because I'd run in the wrong direction when the noise went off. And I had to be incredibly careful. We hadn't seen many soldiers in West Stratton but if there were some who'd heard the booby trap, they'd be on the alert.

We whistled to tell each other we were on the same side. Like birds. It was the five note whistle from *Close Encounters of the Third Kind*, and I used it as I approached the house. Fi had taken over sentry, and she was startled to see me come slipping in from the darkness.

I was tired now but we talked for a while and I told her where I'd been. To tell the truth I was hanging out for another good goss, a good conversation. I still felt guilty about how I'd upset Fi when she talked about Homer. There hadn't been a chance to make up for that. We were always racing to keep one step ahead of death. And even though I knew I'd regret it in the morning, I nestled in next to her and we talked about Kevin, and the old days, and the airfield and the kids who'd taken our stuff. I felt a lot better these days than I had after our first, failed, attempt on the airfield. Not for the obvious reason that this time we'd succeeded, but because I felt a bit older, a bit more confident, a bit more in control. The issues had been clearer. There hadn't been time for agonising arguments about what to do, whether we were doing the right or wrong thing. We just had to do it and worry later.

Fi didn't feel the same though. As we talked I realised to my surprise that she was doing it hard; harder than ever. She started crying when we talked about the airfield. "It was horrible," she said. "All that blood. One man, I saw his legs blown off, right under him, his whole body just shook up and down like some sort of horrible dance, his face went all blurry, and he went down on the ground and I couldn't see what happened after that. And another man, I saw the flames whoosh across the ground like they were chasing him and they caught him before he'd moved even three steps . . ."

"Stop it, stop it," I said. She was bringing up all the things I didn't want to think about. "Stop it." Suddenly I didn't feel so good. But I had to shake her to shut her up. She wanted to talk about the jeeps crashing, about being trapped in the back of the truck with Kevin, about the officer she'd seen pull out a revolver and shoot himself as the flames closed in. I didn't want to talk about any of it. I'd more or less convinced myself it was all OK, that we were soldiers doing it for our parents and Colonel Finley and Iain and Ursula, and here was Fi dragging me back into the world of reality.

"Talk about something else," I begged. "We can't talk about this. Not here. Not now. Wait till we get back to New Zealand, or till the war's ended. Remember ages ago, back in Hell, Homer said we had to think brave? Well, we still do. If we let our minds go crazy, we're finished. We have to keep our heads together."

I was talking as much to convince myself as to convince her. I just wished Andrea, the counsellor I'd had in New Zealand, would materialise suddenly, so I could pour it all out to someone who understood.

Fi calmed down but she didn't say anything then; just sat there looking miserable. "I didn't mean to shut you up completely," I said. "I want to talk. But not about all the terrible things. I don't care what we talk about as long as it's not that."

"Oh," she said, "I know this stuff was happening in other countries when we were growing up: East Timor, Irian Jaya, Tibet. And I cared about it, I really did. But it's so different when it's right in front of you; when you see it. Or when it's your family and friends who get hurt and killed. Those kids, Homer's right, we should do something about them. Like he said, they could be our brothers and sisters."

I was glad she'd given me a chance to change the subject.

"They're pretty wild," I said. "Do you think we can do anything for them?"

"Well, why did you go there tonight if you thought it was hopeless?"

"I'm not sure. I just couldn't sleep for thinking about them. I suppose if we know more about them we can decide if we want to have a go."

"When that little kid said, 'Have you got any food?'," Fi said, "that was awful. I wanted to pick him up and hug him."

"Fi, they were mugging us at the time!"

"I know. But they looked so desperate. Do you think they really are starving?"

"They did look hungry. When we were eating the lamb I was trying to work out how we could leave some out for them, as a present, and then they'd trust us and know we could help them. At home I only fed the possums once in a blue moon, but that was all it took. They knew I'd never hurt them."

"Isn't it amazing the way the New Zealanders hate possums?" Fi said. She'd calmed down a bit, at last.

"Yeah, that surprised me, until I found out that they weren't native to New Zealand. They're imports. Like foxes and rabbits here."

"So why didn't you take some lamb to those kids?" Fi asked. "I would have if I'd thought of it."

"Because they're so off their heads that if we approached their hideout during normal times they'd shoot first and ask questions afterwards. And after the fright I gave them tonight I'm not sure how we can ever approach them."

"They mightn't have known it was you."

"True."

Although I was really sleepy I sent Fi off to bed and I did the last watch. Now that we were well into summer the dawns were longer and slower. It was nice seeing the grey light gradually turn orange, then pink, and red. Being dawn, the temperature dropped a lot, until I was shivery cold, but I didn't mind. I knew later in the day, when it got really hot, I'd remember this sharp coolness and use it to refresh me. As soon as the sun appeared the air started to dry out and I felt the first little tingles of warmth.

It occurred to me that maybe we had to try to help these kids for the sake of our own sanity. If we could do something good, something positive, we might be able to dilute the memories of the other stuff, the horrible stuff Fi had talked about.

17

We continued in a time warp. We couldn't get through to Colonel Finley and we assumed the airwaves were being blocked. And with no urgent priorities, no urgent purpose, we went into a bit of a coma. I'm sure Andrea, the psychologist, would have an explanation for why that happened. I guess it wasn't too hard to work out.

I figured in another week we could think about heading back for Hell. Until then we just had to stay put.

There were some good things and some bad things. Kevin certainly started getting better. He spoke more often, smiled a bit, made a few bad jokes that we laughed at as though they were from some brilliant American sitcom. Seemed like I was the only one who got into trouble for patronising Kevin. He still liked working in the vegetable garden and he explored a number of neighbouring gardens and found odd collections of vegies that had survived.

We did what Kevin suggested about the trout farm. It turned out brilliantly. The place, Boucher's, was a hell of a hike away but we went on a nice warm night, and once we'd done all the sneaking around to get clear of Stratton we relaxed and enjoyed the clean air of the paddocks.

The Stratton area didn't seem to be colonised like the land around Wirrawee. That was a big disappointment to Homer, who still dreamt he would walk down a road and run slap bang into his parents. But we saw no evidence of work parties. The trouble was that the Stratton district covers hundreds of square k's, so really, Homer wasn't much closer to his mum and dad than he had been in Hell. A fluke meeting was his best hope, probably his only hope.

I'm sure the reason there wasn't much colonisation was that Stratton had suffered so many air raids. Apart from the last few months, when the New Zealand Air Force had been driven out of the skies, Stratton had copped a beating. We passed many bombed blocks in the suburbs, and even out in the country there were huge craters from bombs that had missed their targets.

At one point we saw the dark outline of a crashed plane, in a corner of the next paddock. Without much of a moon we couldn't tell if it was ours or theirs, but we gave it a wide berth. There was no point going over there. It probably wasn't dangerous, but we didn't want to see any more death or horror.

The buildings around Boucher's were dark too, and we approached mega-cautiously, at about a centimetre a minute. It was the kind of place that settlers might have occupied. And in fact we didn't ever check out whether they had, because we didn't need to go to the main buildings. Fi and Kevin led us to the shed where the gear was kept, and we helped ourselves. Most of the good stuff was gone, but there were some old rods and lines. Kevin had a nice assortment of worms and witchetty grubs and crickets from Grandma's garden. My father would have turned his nose up — he was a fly fisherman who thought that any other fishing was cheating — but we weren't in the mood to be fussy.

I didn't know if there'd be any trout left in the dam, or if they'd bite in the middle of the night, but I guess they were hungry, because the first one hit my line so hard I dropped the rod. We reeled in ten in twenty-five minutes, and we were laughing so much that if there were colonists up in the house I think they'd have heard us.

"This is madness," Homer said, when Kevin pulled in the tenth. "We'll never eat all these. We've got no coolroom either. We should quit and come back another time, now that we know they're here."

We agreed with that, but the night was spoilt when we had a fight about where and how to cook them. I thought it was safer to make a fire in the middle of a paddock, and Lee backed me up, but the others wanted to do it at Grandma's. Lee and I won, but it did sour the whole thing a bit.

Still, the trout were beautiful. I'd brought lots of foil — one thing Grandma had plenty of — and salt and spice, so we reduced the fire to coals as fast as we could and cooked the fish in the foil. The flesh fell off the bones, and the flavour was strong and tangy. After we'd pigged out there was even enough left for us to carry a decent supply back to town.

So despite the argument it was one of the better nights. In this war the bad kept outweighing the good, but a night like that kept us going for a while. In the air there was plenty of action, jets streaking backwards and forwards. Some were ours, some were theirs. It seemed like things were definitely more equal than they had been. But one night a whole armada of aircraft passed overhead. I don't know whose side they were on, but there were heaps of them. They were big and fairly slow, so I think they were bombers, which made me hope they were from New Zealand. It reminded me of that time up in the mountains when we were camping in Hell and we'd heard the first wave of invasion planes, without realising what they were. Maybe these were the first wave of the re-invasion planes. I know the New Zealanders had been lobbying for new planes from the USA.

Stratton didn't get bombed again but I think that was because there wasn't much left to bomb. The city seemed almost demolished, and down along Melaleuca Drive, the main factory area, you'd be lucky to find one brick that was still full-size.

So our "blear," as Fi called it — where we just went "bleary," doing nothing but sleeping and talking and scavenging food and scouting around — lasted a week, and then some. We didn't see any soldiers, and we made certain we didn't get in a position where the kids could ambush us again. We caught glimpses of them from time to time but when I say glimpses, it was usually the sense at nighttime that we weren't alone, that someone was following or watching. I only got a good look at them twice.

The first time was one afternoon when I saw a boy climbing out of a window of a smart-looking white house halfway up the hill in Winchester Heights. He saw me, but he was at the point where he couldn't go back; he was too far out of the window already. He hesitated for a moment then jumped. When he did, three other kids came out of the garden and they ran off together. I guess they'd been waiting for him. They ran like they were scared of me though, like they thought I'd shoot them, because they spread out and zig-zagged, the way we did sometimes.

None of them looked back.

I thought they were pretty crazy to break into houses in Winchester Heights, because there were always people around there.

The other time I saw them was kind of the opposite — they were going into a building, not coming out. It was an old milk bar on Railway Road, which had long since been looted of everything. But right on dusk I saw what looked like a tall skinny person going in there. When I looked harder I realised it was a boy with a little kid riding on his shoulders. This time they didn't see me.

I waited a while but they didn't come out, so I sneaked a bit closer, watching carefully for trip-wires. There was something about the way they went in that made it look like they were going home: just the relaxed way the boy walked I suppose, even with a kid on his shoulders. From time to time I heard voices, at one point a laugh, and much later the world's most aggravating noise: a young child crying on and on, like there's no particular reason but it's not going to shut up anyway. I don't know if it was the same child I'd heard before, near the old stables, but I was convinced I'd found their new hiding place.

For an experiment I tried leaving out some food, like I'd discussed with Fi. I didn't put it too close to the shop, because I thought it might freak them out if I made it obvious that I knew where they were, but I left it at the other end of the block, in the middle of the footpath, where they could hardly miss it. I had to protect it from possums, so I put it in a big yellow Tupperware container from Grandma's kitchen, with a sign saying FOOD — HELP YOURSELF.

It was nothing much, just potatoes and grilled lamb and some beans I'd boiled a little the night before, to make them crunchy. To my great disappointment, when I went back the next morning, it hadn't been touched. And the same thing that night. I gave up then and took it away. I couldn't understand why they wouldn't eat it.

18

THAT WEEK PASSED, AND MOST OF ANOTHER — altogether, twelve days in limbo. Stratton seemed peaceful enough. The Kiwis finally bombed again one day, late in the afternoon, but on the other side of town. We didn't know what the targets were.

West Stratton stayed dark at night and quiet in the day, unlike the closer-in suburbs. Occasionally a vehicle raced past, but we hardly ever saw foot patrols. I should have liked the silence of the streets. Somehow though, I developed a hatred of them. Hatred and fear. They were so still, so dark at nights. It was a ghost town. Normally there's a background of noise that you don't even notice; the hum of traffic, the buzz of lawnmowers, the giggling of kids, the chatter of neighbours, the feet of pedestrians. People calling to each other. TVs muttering, CDs humming, phones screaming. Even a rural like me knew what suburbs sounded like.

But now there was nothing. Most of the time anyway. There were the noises we made of course: that was OK. Apart from them the whole suburb seemed closed off from the world, sealed in a time capsule.

I quite like solitude in some ways, at some times. Solitude and silence. But this was different. It was such an empty silence. Like the end of the world. It wasn't of course, just the end of our world. Sometimes I thought it would go on forever. Sometimes I stood on the back steps listening, kind of begging for a noise, a sign of life.

I don't know how those kids had stood it for so long without going mad. Maybe they were mad. Or maybe they hadn't been in West Stratton for long.

We saw no sign of any other squatters, so in the end I assumed that it was the kids who'd camped in Grandma's house, and thrown the poker. They were certainly capable of that. Sometimes it made me angry that we had to be scared of the little mongrels. I felt insulted that we worried about being attacked by kids of that age. But when I wasn't angry I felt desperately sorry for them, and worried about them. If adults were here I'm sure they wouldn't have let them run around wild. I was worried about the kind of people they would grow up to be. How would they ever get used to normal life again? How would they learn to live peacefully, go to school, be friendly? If I was honest I'd have to say that most of what I'd learnt about life had been from my parents. It's not like they sit you down and give you big talks. Some families might do that, have family meetings or whatever, but that was hardly our style. I learnt by watching and listening. You drink it in with your mother's milk, with your first baby's bottle of OJ, with your homemade lemon cordial and your water full of wrigglers from the tank, and the little sips of beer that your father jokingly gives you and little sips of wine that your mother lets you have, and the cups of tea around the kitchen table where you relax and talk about the day, and how you have to move the small mob from One Tree tomorrow and why Mr Rodd's wife has left him and how at the age of seventeen Dad got his driving licence by taking Sergeant Braithwaite to the pub so he could collect a slab after work and whether Roundup's a better herbicide than Sprayseed.

All that stuff. You just pick it up.

But these kids, how would they pick it up? Not by running wild around the streets of Stratton, smelling of months of living wild; snot hanging from their noses, and faces unwashed. Not from attacking the people who could have been their friends, who could have helped them. Not from stealing. Not from knowing that death could be waiting through the next doorway or just across the street.

I began to think the damage to our country, to us even, went so deep now that it would never fully be repaired. I realised the worst damage wasn't the bombed buildings, the burnt-out cars, the shattered windows. It wasn't even the neglected farms and the holes in the fences and the crops gone to seed. It was the damage deep inside us. Words like spirit and soul started to mean more to me now. I felt closer than ever to Robyn, if that were possible. She understood that there are some things worse than physical injury and physical death. If your spirit and soul are damaged beyond repair, then what does it matter that you can still react to stimuli, respire and excrete, and do all the other functions of living creatures described in Chapter Four of our Year 9 Science textbook?

We had to start healing some of the damage. Maybe we couldn't do much about the kids, but I had to try not to let myself get too damaged by the awful things that had happened. What I'd done with Adam, in New Zealand, or what he'd done to me, that was the kind of thing I could control, should have controlled. I had to try harder with that kind of stuff in future. I wished I knew more about religion and church. It meant so much to Robyn, gave her so much strength. I envied her that.

As I thought about all of this, I decided it was time I

started to take more care of Lee. I'd never looked at Lee from that point of view. Perhaps I should have. "Take care of," that sounded funny applied to Lee, but I suppose in some ways that's what we'd been doing all this time. Taking care of each other. Not always taking enough care of ourselves though. Lee definitely didn't look after himself, and, I must admit, I neglected myself a bit sometimes.

So I started doing a few things to improve the atmosphere. I chucked a few flowers in vases and put them through the house. I raided some neighbourhood fruit trees, and made a fruit salad. Just stuff like that. It felt very weird in one way, to be doing these things in the middle of a war zone. But in this war there were no rules. We made it up as we went along. The whole thing was surreal, and you had to accept that as early as possible, or you were in trouble.

I also started talking more, which probably sounds weird, but with the pressure of Kevin's problems, and the terror and wild thrills of the airfield attack, we'd all done much less talking. Now, in the relative safety of Grandma's, we were having more conversations, but not enough. Fi and I had always talked, though still not much lately, and Homer and Lee talked a bit. They had a lot of respect for each other these days. No one really talked to Kevin.

So I tried to be more outgoing. I remember Robyn saying once "Talking about yourself can be selfish or generous." When I asked what she meant, she said: "If you never talk about yourself, about your problems and stuff, that's selfish, because you're not giving your friends a chance to help you. And if you talk about yourself all the time, you're selfish and boring."

I was still conscious though of the way Lee attacked

me over my comment to Kevin. “Ellie, why do you use that primary-school-teacher voice,” or whatever he’d said. Ouch. Robyn had been good without making a big thing of it. I mean she wasn’t good all the time — hardly — but when she was nice to people, it seemed natural. With me it didn’t always come out that way. Maybe because I wasn’t naturally nice. I hoped that wasn’t the reason.

What I’m saying is, I didn’t go around being Pollyanna, or a refugee from the Brady Bunch. I wasn’t, like, “Hi everybody, how are we today, isn’t it great to be alive?” I’m not that stupid. But I did try to be not quite so into myself. And that’s all I want to say about that.

SUDDENLY, ONE DAY, THE MOTORBIKE SOLDIERS appeared. They were scary. They hunted in packs of four at a time, and they threatened us in ways that jeep patrols and foot patrols never could. For one thing, they were so quick, suddenly appearing at the end of the street. For another, they were very mobile, able to go up and down driveways and across lawns and gardens. For a third, they were professionals.

They came through West Stratton every two or three days, and we learnt to fear them. Luckily the fence around the back garden was high and solid, so from the front, or the driveway, no one could see the work we'd done cleaning up the place. But it'd be a dead giveaway if they ever got off the bikes and came in. All Kevin's spadework looked highly suspicious. So we rushed to disguise the work, covering the soil with leaf litter as though it had been blowing down for months, sticking dead things back in the earth to hide the new growth, unstaking the vegetables and letting them sprawl again. And we put in a homemade alarm system, a string trailing from the peppercorn to the kitchen window, so the person on sentry could alert the others. Each time a patrol appeared we only had about thirty seconds to shut down — that's how quick they were.

I felt the war was closing in on us again. We made the decision to stop calling Colonel Finley. We tried four nights in a row, then skipped two, then tried for another two, then quit. It spooked us all to stop, but it would have spooked us more to keep going. All we ever got was the static, the funny static, not normal at all. It sounded just too electronic for me. It made me even more paranoid than normal.

My efforts to be more involved, more outgoing, improved some things I think. Homer said I was easier to get on with. Maybe everyone was trying harder. Despite the new tensions there were more jokes than we'd had for a while, more conversation about stuff other than the war. It sure was a relief to hear that.

But one thing didn't change. Lee still went wandering at night. I didn't like it at all. I didn't like my fears about what might be happening, what he might be doing. Some instinct told me he was getting into danger, going too close to the edge, taking physical risks, and maybe other risks as well.

He didn't go every night, only every second or third night. Sometimes he came home exhausted, sometimes grim and tensed up, sometimes pleased with himself. But always there was that sense of alertness, something powerful being suppressed. Whichever mood he was in made me edgy. I had a dream where he was a panther leaping out of trees and grabbing babies and swinging them onto his back, then streaking away. When I woke up and lay there remembering it, I couldn't work out if he was saving the babies or taking them away to eat.

Of course my real fear was that he was staging one-man raids, launching attacks on enemy soldiers. At some dark level I imagined him as a silent killer, stalking the streets, savagely striking people down from behind: a dangerous panther.

So I started following him. Not like a detective. I don't

think I'm being dishonest when I say that: I wasn't trying to stick my nose into his business. It was more what I said before: he didn't have parents anymore and it made me more — I don't want to say the word but I will — more protective.

I followed him three times. The first two were a wipe-out. I lost him badly; once when I let him get too far ahead, and once when a small convoy of trucks cut between us, and I had to wait for them to pass. By the time they'd gone Lee was nowhere to be seen.

The third time was different. It was a cool clear night, refreshing after a long hot day. No sign of the storm I was walking into. A light breeze tickled my face, whispered against it, except I didn't hear its message. Lee was a shadow in the distance, a movement between buildings, somehow not a person anymore, certainly not the person I'd come to know so well during this long year. I couldn't think where he might be going. I couldn't work it out. The night before, when the first rumbles of the convoy came down the street, Lee seemed disinterested. He didn't even look around, just increased his speed and faded into a dark patch at the end of the block. I don't know where he went after that, but if he was staging a private guerilla war surely he would have taken a good look at the trucks of the convoy.

Nothing though. Nothing at all.

On this night there was no convoy. We followed a different route from the other two nights but after half a dozen blocks I realised we were heading in the same general direction. At Halliday Road, which is one of the main exits from Stratton, he swung right and went straight on out of town. By then we'd covered a couple of kilometres already and I began wondering how long this trip would be. Whatever, it was obvious he had a definite purpose. This wasn't just a vague wander around.

We walked another two kilometres. I was getting worried that out here, where it was flat, he might hear me, or even see me if he looked around. On the other hand, I could now afford to drop back farther, which made it easier. All I needed was a glimmer of him, a tiny human smudge on the pupils of my eyes. Once in a while a noise came, a slither of a foot on a wet slope or a rattle of loose gravel. I hoped I wasn't making any noise he could hear, and I hoped no one else heard the sounds he made.

When he did change direction, my ears gave me the clue. I heard the softer sound of his boots on bitumen and I stopped and looked up quickly. I was closer to him than I'd realised and I had to duck down again in case he noticed. But he crossed the road swiftly, walked another ten metres, then opened a gate and went into a paddock.

He closed the gate behind him. He seemed to know his way so surely. He'd obviously been here a few times before. Why? If he was haunting the countryside, attacking and killing, he would hardly keep coming back to the same place. And he would take much more care, looking around more often, stopping and waiting every once in a while. He seemed dangerously overconfident.

I eased myself through the gate. There was a name on it, "Karen Downs," so it was obviously a property. It gave me a shock because there was a girl called Karen Downs at school. She always beat me at Computer Scrabble. The coincidence between the names distracted me for a moment and when I looked up I realised I'd lost Lee again. It was so frustrating. Seconds ago he'd been moving towards a gap in a long row of pines — a windbreak — and now he'd disappeared among the shadows. I couldn't tell if he was standing in the gap or if he'd gone right or left. Or, in fact, gone straight through the trees and was now well on his way across the second paddock.

I stopped for a minute, watching and waiting. When I couldn't see any movement I moved closer, walking slowly and carefully, crouching to keep my profile as low as possible. I stopped every few metres, scanning the treeline with my ears. There was nothing, just the constant hissing of the leaves, and, back towards the road, the purring of a boobook owl.

I dropped even lower. I'd almost forgotten I was stalking Lee. It was getting more and more like an operation against the enemy. I was as nervous as if I were spying on them. For those last ten metres into the treeline I was pretty much on my belly, wriggling though the grass like a tiger snake. I just hoped I didn't find a big wet fresh cowpat with my bare hands. The grass was wet with dew already.

Once in the treeline I stopped again and listened. A car went past on the road, at high speed. In this silence you could hear it from ages away, both coming — and going. It was using headlights, but I was too far from the road to be threatened by them.

After its noise faded at last I stood and listened again. There was nothing. If stars made a noise then I would have been deafened by their singing, because the heavens were lit from one end to the other, crammed with stars. There were some parts where you couldn't imagine how another star could squeeze in. But unless the wind was the voice of the stars I had to assume they were silent, because the wind was all I could hear.

I started getting angry. Had I come all this way for nothing? Why was I here anyway? What the hell was Lee doing, running some kind of private war? He had no right. And was I doing something sneaky and horrible, turning into a spy? Or was it something important and understandable? I knew Fi or Corrie would never do anything like this. Oddly enough, I had a feeling Robyn might; that she'd at least understand my motivation.

Well, as usual, I was just going to have to make my own judgements.

I stood up, very cautiously, and looked around. As I did, the faintest movement caught my eye and I thought I saw Lee's dark shape disappearing over the rise in the next paddock. An instant later and it was gone. I threw caution away, went over the fence, and ran like crazy. I realised fairly quickly that he must be on the driveway, a well-made dirt road going into the property, not overgrown at all. I figured from its smoothness that it was getting a fair bit of use, which of course made me all the more curious and worried.

But I kept running, till I got near the top of the rise. Then I hurried on crouched over, my heart accelerating with every step, my eyes trying to search ahead in the darkness, with only the starlight to help.

The next paddock was the home paddock: you entered it either by a gate, for stock, or, next to it, a cattle grid, for vehicles. Beyond those were the buildings. You've seen one farm, you've seen them all, and yet every farm's different. This one had a modern brick veneer-type farmhouse that would have looked more at home in the suburbs. To the left the blue water of a swimming pool caught the reflection of the stars. There were quite a few bushes and shrubs, but I couldn't see any garden.

Farther to the left were the sheds and silos and kennels

and chook yards. That's where Lee was heading. I could see him more clearly now. He went quickly and confidently along the southern side of a big machinery shed. He was easily visible against the silvery galvanised wall. I kept parallel with him, but a long way apart, staying in the shadows of the treeline that bordered the paddock. When he reached the end of the shed he set out towards a big wooden building, that was dark and old, and pretty dilapidated.

Lee was halfway to it when something happened that caused every hair on my body to stand in its follicle. My scalp felt like someone had run 240 volts through it. My mouth opened so wide I didn't seem able to shut it again. I just could not believe what I was seeing.

From out of the old barn someone was walking towards Lee. They met in the clear ground between the barn and the galvanised shed. She was tall with long flowing black hair and she moved like a snake, like she was all muscle and no bone. They met. They put their arms around each other. They kissed.

After a few minutes they separated and walked towards the barn, not holding hands, but staying close to each other. The blood came back into my body. I watched every move they made. As they merged into the shadows of the building the girl paused and looked around, quite searchingly. She hesitated for several moments, then I think Lee, who was already inside, must have called her, because she turned suddenly as though answering someone, and went on into the darkness of the doorway.

I was in shock. It was like someone had come up behind me and hit me over the head with a baseball bat. And I was outraged. Outraged by everything, including the fact that Lee hadn't even bothered to look around, to check the area. He'd grown as careless as that. The girl was more careful than him.

The blood was running through my veins again but I had no idea what to do. Or if I should do anything. I couldn't move. My mouth was still open but I don't think any air came in. I was mesmerised, like a hypnotised chook.

And it was that which saved my life. My stillness meant that the men converging on the barn didn't see me.

I don't know what I first noticed. A twitch out of the corner of my eye. I remember frowning and turning my head slowly, suddenly feeling I was going to see more than a falling twig or a hungry owl. And I was right about that. In the next three seconds I saw four men. They were moving very slowly and carefully towards the barn. I looked to the other side, but thankfully, saw no one. This was a frontal attack, it seemed. Maybe there wasn't even a door at the back of the barn.

I looked at the men again. They were closing in steadily. I don't think they were soldiers: they looked more like farmers. They were carrying farmers' weapons, shotguns, not automatic rifles. But for all that they knew what they were doing. They looked more than a match for Lee. They looked more than a match for me.

At least I still hadn't been seen. That was because I hadn't yet moved. On the other hand, I couldn't just stand there and watch them go in and catch Lee. Would they kill him on the spot or take him into Stratton Prison? That was the only question I had time for, and it was only in my mind for a moment. The next second I picked up my left foot and moved it across in front of me, to the right. I watched the men as I did it, terrified I'd see a head turn. My leg was shaking and I hardly dared put my foot down, because I was so scared it would crackle on the bark and sticks.

I put it down, then moved the other foot. I was just as scared, but at least the first movement had unparalysed me a bit, got me going. I took eight more steps, each as nerve-racking as the first. It was so hard, because I knew I couldn't go too slowly; although these guys were moving slowly themselves. I'd have to cover three times the ground they did. With each step I tried to see where my foot landed, making sure there was no bark underneath, but it was difficult among the trees, where even the starlight didn't reach.

I still had no idea what to do. If I went round the back and there were no doors and no windows, I was sunk. I could bang on the wall but Lee would probably respond by running straight out the front, into the arms of the enemy. I couldn't tackle four armed men on my own. All I could think was that if I got around behind them maybe I could distract them in some way, or perhaps even find a weapon. So I kept heading to the right. When I'd withdrawn far enough into the darkness I ran swiftly down the treeline, keeping behind the trees, hoping they'd think I was a fox or a possum, if they heard me at all.

By the time I came into the open again I had the makings of a plan. I'd only thought it through as far as stage one, but that was an improvement on what I'd had before. I felt in my pockets as I ran along and confirmed that I had a light. Not a packet of matches but a cigarette lighter. One of those little disposable things. I couldn't even remember where I'd picked it up, at Grandma's probably.

I'd seen three big haystacks, one under a roof but the other two out in the open. I ran as fast as I could to the first. It was a hundred metres from the barn. How badly would these people want to kill Lee? So badly that they'd ignore their haystacks burning? With my hand trembling I pulled out the lighter and flicked the little roller. I held the flame to the hay. My God, I've had trouble lighting some fires in my life, but I'd never tried setting fire to a haystack before. It went up so fast I nearly singed my eyebrows. Unbelievable. Now it was a race between me and the flames, to get the other two stacks going before the men realised what was happening behind them.

I ran to the second one. As I lit it I glanced back at the first. There was only one flame so far, but it was already two metres high. I lit the next fire, and ran to the third stack, the one under a roof. But as I headed towards it I had a better idea. Just to the left was a truck loaded with hay. It was facing the barn, and the driver's window was open. I swerved and raced across to it. As quietly as I could, I opened the door and leaned in. By stretching I managed to reach the gearstick, and shove it into neutral without even using the clutch. Then I released the handbrake.

I didn't bother shutting the door, just ran around to the back. There was no time now to look for the men, but I heard a little crackling noise behind me, which meant the fire was gaining hold fast.

There was quite a steep slope running down to the barn. I realised that the truck was almost perfectly placed. I gave it a huge push. I felt like one of those mothers who find the strength to lift cars when their babies are underneath. Lee wasn't my baby, but maybe my strength came from wanting to save my own life. Whatever, the truck got rolling. I was surprised by how fast it accelerated. I trotted behind, lighting the load as I did. With the moving air to help, the flames caught even more successfully.

By the time we travelled fifty metres the hay was burning quite freely.

I still couldn't see the men, because the truck shielded them, but I got plenty of evidence now that they'd noticed what was happening. There were shouts, followed by several shots. I think they were firing at the cab of the truck, assuming someone was in there, driving. I heard one bullet go over my head with that now-familiar sound, like a high-pitched cicada. It didn't say much for their accuracy that they couldn't hit a truck. I wondered if they'd be able to hit the side of the barn.

I ran after the truck, which was gathering speed at quite a rate. The faster it went the more fiercely the fire burned. I had to drop back again, because the flames were blowing in my face. I had one hand over my eyes, shielding them, only able to look down at the ground. But within, I'd say, seventy-five metres of the truck starting its little journey it was an inferno. Flames on wheels. The wildest sight, if anyone had time to stop and look. A travelling bonfire.

Normally, if you send a vehicle rolling away on its own it doesn't go straight. I knew that from mucking around with the Landie, letting it drive itself when I was hand-feeding stock. This truck went straight because the gully leading down to the barn formed a natural funnel and kept the truck aimed at the door. I didn't know that though until I felt the shadow of the roof and looked up and saw I'd followed the rolling bonfire right into the barn. It accelerated through the big open doors and hit the far wall with a grinding thumping noise. But I hardly heard that above the roar and crackle of the flames. In the still dry air of the barn they took on a new life.

Realising I was now silhouetted against the light, I

threw myself to the left, rolling across a long row of bales of hay until I thought I was out of sight. I glanced at the truck. The flames were already touching the roof of the building. They seemed twice as high as they had been outside. The barn was full of hay and horse feed — there were bags of it right beside me, and a row of pegs for bridles and stuff. Through the flames, on the other side of the barn, I could hear the proof that there were horses: a frantic fanfare of whinnies and screams. The air was full of burning bits of straw, some black and dead already before they hit the ground, some still red with fire. Little spirals of smoke from spots all over the floor told me that this place was going to be blazing from top to bottom in a matter of moments.

I couldn't bear the shrieks of the horses. The knowledge that I caused this, that they would die horribly in flames lit by my hand, was too much. I looked around, desperate to reach them. The fire from the truck had spread across the entrance. No one from outside could get in now. But there was an upstairs, a kind of loft running the full width of the building. To my left was a stepladder. I ran to it and shinned up the thing so fast my hands barely touched the sides. I got to the top, turned right and ran full speed across the boards. The heat up here was dreadful and I felt myself gasping for breath before I'd gone ten metres. They'd always told us in Science that heat rises, and here was the proof. As I crossed the truck itself I got a blast of heat that scorched my jeans, my hair, and my face. It was like someone held a huge hair dryer a couple of centimetres from me and turned it on full blast.

At the other end I was shocked to find no ladder. Below me were three horses kicking wildly in their stalls. Farther along were two more and a small group out of their stalls, milling together in a frantic terrified squealing mob. I went back a few metres until I was standing over a small heap of loose straw, said, "God help me," which was the quickest prayer I could think of, and jumped into it.

The pile was as small as it looked and I hit the floor under it pretty hard. My bad knee jarred. It always let me down when I needed it. But there was no time for a medical examination. I hobbled over to the first of the closed stalls. A big chestnut mare was charging backwards and forwards in the narrow space, like she wanted to smash through the gate but didn't quite have the courage. She was swinging her head: the whites of her terrified eyes reflecting the red of the flames. I pulled out the peg that held the gate and went sideways fast: this mare had lost all sense and one blow from her hoofs would kill me. As I pulled out the peg from the second pen I glanced to my right and to my astonishment saw Lee. I'd almost forgotten that he was the reason I was there. He was doing the same as me, freeing trapped horses, and I realised then how the other horses had got out of their stalls.

He glanced at me at the same time as I looked at him. For a moment our eyes met. He showed no reaction. He must have seen me first; he would have got the shock of his life when he did.

I released the last horse, a black colt, then asked myself the big question, the biggest of all: How are we going to get out? The entrance to the barn was completely blocked by fire and I couldn't see any other exit. Although it was a big building we didn't have much time now: the other side, where I'd gone up the ladder, was engulfed by flames already. The reason we hadn't been fried alive so far was that the fire favoured that direction, for some reason.

Maybe the breeze from the entrance was blowing over there. But the air was so hot and I knew we were fast running out of oxygen: my lungs were hurting, and no matter how much I sucked in air it wasn't enough.

I looked wildly at the wall. Somehow we had to get through there, preferably taking the horses with us. The side wall, that I was looking at, seemed pretty solid. Up the back, where it was only planks instead of logs, might be a chance. Between me and the wall was a tractor, a grey Fergie, with a shovel out the front. I wished it was bigger but it was all we had. I clambered over the big rear wheel and onto the seat. I pressed the ignition button and the engine turned over. But it didn't start. I stabbed the button again, sweating and swearing out loud in my frustration. Not that anyone would have heard: the noise was enormous now. The tractor still wouldn't start. "Oh God, please," I cried, and stabbed it a third time. It caught, coughed, spluttered, paused a long moment while my heart paused with it, then finally caught and ran. I've never heard a sound as sweet as the pulse of that engine. The gearstick was between my legs. I chose low second, pushed the lever to maximum revs and charged straight at the wall. There was no rollcage on the damn thing and I knew the risk I was running, but what choice was there? Better a beam of wood on the head than burning alive in this hell. My lungs were scorching and I didn't feel like I was getting any oxygen at all. The shovel hit the wall and the shock of the impact ran all the way through the tractor and all the way through me. For a moment I thought we were through. The wall seemed to go out of kilter and I saw the loft sway as though it was about to fall. Straw rained down and I hunched my shoulders waiting for the heavy beams to thump onto my head. But nothing else happened. I began to think the tractor wouldn't do it after all. The shovel and the arms that held it seemed badly out of shape now, not surprisingly, but as I backed up I used the lever to raise the shovel a bit, hoping that might help.

I reversed as far as I could and slammed my foot on the brake. As I did Lee leapt up behind me, and gave me a pat on the shoulder. It helped somehow, in a weird way. I accelerated again, going even faster this time. I think the previous time I had actually slowed a little as I approached the wall, not consciously, just the unconscious fear of running into something solid at absolute full-on speed. This time I didn't hesitate. We hit so hard that Lee fell right off the back. I heard a kind of screaming noise that for a horrible unforgettable moment I thought was Lee. But it was the galvanised iron roof ripping away from the wall. The wall leaned out from the top, away from us. It was something but it was not enough. I flung a desperate glance behind me. I didn't want to run over Lee, although he probably deserved it. But he was crawling away from the wheels. He knew I had to go again. The big rear wheels spun as I pushed the throttle to maximum again. The tractor lurched backwards.

That brief glimpse I'd had behind was truly a scene from hell. The horses, silent now, huddled into the farthest corner they could reach, almost suffocating each other as they leaned away from the flames their desperate terror outlined in every trembling muscle, every drop of sweat on their shining coats, every gasping rasping breath. My own breath was gone. I was coughing like crazy and the coughs were agony. I had my left arm over my mouth as I reversed, to filter out the smoke. I went back as far as I could, as far as I dared. Then, head down, trying to escape the heat and the smoke, trying to protect myself from the building that I was expecting to collapse onto me, I charged again.

I knew this was the last time. If I had to go back for a fourth attempt, it would be too late. I'd die in that furnace. Already the chances of the horses escaping were next to none. They were too scared now. They'd be too hard to move. Luckily I was thinking about them and not about the wall as I hit. Otherwise I don't know whether I would have had the courage to hit it quite as hard as I did. The wall seemed to pause, to wait, maybe hoping something would come along and save it at the last minute. The wheels of the tractor spun madly. The wall began to sway outward, from the top. Crossbars popped and fell. I looked up. Sure enough the beams were sagging, and as I gasped the first one dropped. I screamed, even though it missed me by two metres, landing to my left with a huge dead thump. Ahead of me the wall at last went down, hitting the ground outside. I didn't hear the impact, but I felt the bellow of air that rocked the tractor, blowing a storm of dust into my face. At least oxygen came with it and I got something into my lungs, but behind me I heard the whoosh of the fire, its excitement as new ammunition arrived.

The front wheels of the tractor now had something to grip. They bit in and the tractor lurched forward. I still had the throttle-lever pushed to the limit, so I took off suddenly. Another beam came at me, but this one wasn't falling flat like the last one. It was swinging sideways as it fell. I guess one end broke off before the other one. The bottom half was coming right at my face. Half a tonne of falling timber. I threw myself sideways, at the same time scared I'd go under the wheels. The beam crashed into the back of the tractor as I went sprawling to the ground. Somehow I landed on hands and knees. I staggered up.

The tractor was pinned by its rear and was now up on its hind legs, the engine racing and the front wheels spinning furiously. Above me the roof was sagging but had not fallen. I heard a wild whinny and spun around. The horses, all heads and legs and tails, were stampeding. I went down again, huddling into the smallest ball I could make. I think one of them might have actually leapt over me. The edge of a hoof struck me on my side, half its weight on me and half on the ground, a painful blow but at least only there for a second. It felt like someone had hit me in the ribs with an iron bar. Then Lee grabbed me and hauled me to my feet.

We ran. I was holding my side where the horse kicked me, and limping on my jarred knee. One glimpse back showed a terrible sight: a horse pinned under a beam, kicking and twisting. Then, with a roar and a gush of wind, half the roof fell on it. There was an instant wall of flames and I couldn't see anymore.

20

If the men were fighting the fires they must have been doing it from the front. That made sense, because they wouldn't have known we were breaking out from the rear. They'd probably think we died in the flames. It wouldn't be until they found the burned-out tractor halfway through the wall that they'd figure out what had happened.

So we stumbled away into the night, without any opposition. We were both shivering and shaking like the temperature was five below zero. We climbed through a fence — that was the only time Lee let go of me — but we scratched ourselves bloody doing it. The cruel thing about this war was that after anything dangerous there were no adults to wrap blankets round us and give us hot cups of tea. There was nothing but more darkness, more danger, more fear.

Then Lee took me by the shoulder and we trekked across a ploughed field. In the next paddock there were sheep, and I was very pleased to see them, because I knew it meant we'd find water somewhere. I followed the lie of the land until we came to a small dam with stagnant greeny water. I wouldn't let Lee drink it, but we splashed it all over us, and it helped.

Looking back at the farm I saw four distinct towers of flame, like four fiery rockets each standing on a base waiting to take off. I've seen a few fires in my life but never one like that. Those guys would have their hands full for a while yet. I wondered why there were four towers. I was only responsible for three.

As we approached the road, across another ploughed paddock, two fire engines from Stratton rushed past, not using their sirens or red lights, but flat out nonetheless.

The walk back to Stratton took forever. I couldn't believe we weren't getting there. I mean, a dozen times I'd think, "We must be there, we must!" and I'd look up and we were still surrounded by farmland. Maybe we took smaller steps than normal, maybe we were just moving more slowly, maybe we'd lost our sense of time or direction, I don't know. I know the last couple of kilometres I was completely out of it: my head and legs were numb — except for my knee, which was killing me — and my side felt like it was on fire. Tears kept running down my face and after a while I gave up trying to wipe them away. Lee was good, I've got to say that for him. He kept talking, telling me there wasn't much farther to go, and not to give up.

Once we got clear of the farm I wouldn't let him touch me again though.

When we got to the house Kevin was on sentry. He started to say: "Where the hell have you been?" but one look at me and the words died in his throat. He jumped down and ran into the house. I stopped and leaned against a wall, thinking, "It's all right now, I don't have to do anything. Fi'll be here in a moment." Then she was there and she took me inside, and in one way everything was OK: I was lying on a sofa and getting wiped down and they were trickling water into my mouth and tucking rugs around my feet. Homer was there too, but I didn't want him; it was only Fi I wanted. And she was fantastic. She sent Homer away quick smart and she found some burn cream and some stuff for my bruised ribs from deep inside one of Grandma's cupboards. She supported my head with a pillow and she stayed there holding my hand until I fell asleep.

But of course that wasn't enough. When I woke up the next morning, my ribs ached, my knee throbbed and the side of my face burned like I was too close to a radiator, but I knew I'd get over all of that.

The real hurt was somewhere in my stomach. People talk about heartache and broken hearts and all that stuff, but I don't think I feel things in my heart so much. More in my stomach. Right in the middle of it. And God I felt it that morning. It seemed to me that Lee had betrayed us in every way possible. I didn't know any details, but I didn't feel like there was much worth knowing. A relationship with a girl who had to be our enemy, a relationship that risked all our lives, a relationship that was a big ugly slap right in the faces of his friends.

It was love and loyalty that had kept us together all this time. It held us together through experiences that would have destroyed most groups. I suspected not many adult groups — maybe none — would have survived the way we had. Seemed like adults let their egos get in the way too much. Of course we've got egos too, but when it came to the crunch we listened to each other and took each other seriously. We didn't often shout anyone down or tell them to shut up. But here was Lee saying that a bit of sex with some slut was more important to him than nearly a year of the most powerful experiences of our lives.

In particular, I felt that Lee had spat right in my face. First spat and then slapped me. I could almost feel the sting where his open hand had left its mark. I don't think

I've ever felt more rejected. I didn't know if I could ever trust anyone again.

I was scared about something else too. I try not to be scared but I think I'm really more scared about emotional stuff than physical stuff. What I was scared of now as I lay on the couch, with my face and arm and leg throbbing and burning, was that Lee might try to blame me for what had happened. That he'd say: "Well, you wouldn't let me touch you, so that's why I went off with her."

Would he do that? Would he sink so low? I didn't know anymore. I felt kind of guilty sometimes, when he tried to crack onto me and I wasn't in the mood, wasn't ready for it. It didn't happen every day, but he'd been angry each time. I know they taught us at school that girls shouldn't feel under pressure from guys, and guys won't die if they don't get what they want, but in real life it's not that easy.

The funny thing was that in the old days I wasn't exactly backwards in coming forwards. I don't think Steve would have complained. I don't know what had changed, or why it had. Oh, the war of course, that was our excuse for everything. But maybe it was only vanity. If I could have a long hot shower and some new clothes, if I could put on some of that moisturiser stuff from the Body Shop, I know I would have felt better about myself.

But it was inside too. Just like I didn't feel too gorgeous on the outside, I didn't feel too gorgeous on the inside. That terrible party in New Zealand: the further I got away from it the worse it became. It should be the other way round.

There was something else I was scared of, and that was how I could explain to Lee why I was following him. I don't know why I always end up putting myself in the wrong — after all, I hadn't done anything wrong — but I thought it would look awfully bad. It had never crossed my mind that he was meeting a girl. I wasn't spying on his love life; I was trying to make sure he wasn't risking our survival by taking on an enemy army single-handedly.

Maybe it would have been better if he had.

It was a few hours before I saw him. He came into the room so quietly that I didn't know he was there. I'd had my eyes shut for a minute and when I opened them again he was standing next to me. We just looked at each other for quite a long time. I'm pretty sure neither of us blinked.

"Are you OK?" he asked.

I didn't say anything.

He sat on the end of the couch. I pulled my legs away, just a reflex, to give him more room, but he noticed and I could tell he thought I'd done it deliberately. He stood again. His head was down. He didn't seem to know where to begin, and I wasn't going to help him. With the room so dark I couldn't see his face very well. Eventually he cleared his throat and said: "I didn't mean this to happen."

"How'd you meet her?" I knew there was no expression in my voice. I didn't do it deliberately, but I knew my voice sounded dead.

After a while he shrugged.

"By a fluke. I saved her life." He grinned, very briefly, like he realised straightaway that he shouldn't be grinning.

"Excuse me?"

"I saved her life. I was in a paddock picking mushrooms. You remember, ages ago, I was bringing in mushrooms every night?"

I didn't say anything.

"Well, it was a really hot night. I was out there, half looking for mushrooms, half sitting around thinking. And I heard a scream. A serious kind of scream, where you know it's big trouble. I didn't even think about the war. I just bolted over there. I got to the top of this hill and there was a dam and I could see someone splashing around wildly, on the far side. So I ran on down there."

He seemed like he was happy to stop the story there, but I sure wasn't.

After a while, when he hadn't said anything, I said: "Well?"

He sighed. "She'd snuck out of the house and gone for a swim. And there was a big deep dark section and it was a lot colder than she'd expected. She got a cramp."

"I didn't know you were such a swim star."

"Oh I can swim. I'm just not as good as you or Homer. I'm OK over a short distance."

"So she fell into your arms and violins started playing?"

He shrugged again. "Did I mention she was naked?"

"No, you didn't actually."

"Oh. Well she was."

He was so nervous it would have been funny in a different situation. But I was furiously and bitterly jealous. I didn't want to hear any more about the meeting at the dam. I pushed on.

"Then you met her again?"

"Yep."

"And again and again?"

"I really liked her, Ellie. I knew it was wrong, I knew it was dangerous, I knew I was cheating on you, even if we haven't been so . . . you know, lately, but I couldn't stop myself. I couldn't stop seeing her."

"So what happened tonight? Last night, I mean."

"You probably know more about that than I do."

"She sold you out?"

"I don't know. What did happen out there? Where did you come from? The first I knew anything was going on, I heard this crackling noise and I said, 'What's that?' and she just bolted out the door and I went and looked and there's this bloody truck on fire coming straight at me. Then I heard shooting so I ducked back inside. The truck came rolling in and I thought, 'I've made a bad move here.' But I realised the place was going to go up like a volcano. I thought I'd better at least get the horses out."

"When did you see me?"

"When you were coming across that walkway thing. To be honest, I thought you were Robyn for a second. I totally freaked. Then I saw it was you. I freaked just as much. But I had to keep working on the horses, so I concentrated on them."

I knew what happened after that. I went back to the other question.

"So do you think she sold you out?"

He hunched right over, his hands under his armpits. I realised he didn't want to answer. But that itself was an answer. After a while he did actually say: "I hope not. But she sure got out of there fast."

He looked at me and I realised how much it was hurting him. That was when I was at my most jealous of her, I think, and at my most angry. He'd been incredibly stupid, but she had no right to treat him like that, not after all he'd been through. If she'd walked into the room right then I would have ripped her apart.

"What's her name?" I asked.

"Reni."

"I wasn't following you to spy on you," I said.

He looked relieved, like he'd wanted to ask, but hadn't been game.

"I thought you were running your own private war," I said. "I was scared you were attacking them on your own."

He didn't say anything. I think he wanted to hear more, but that was all I was going to give him.

"But I still don't understand," he said. "I mean, were there soldiers outside that barn, or what?"

"Four guys with guns."

He nodded. "She did seem nervous," he admitted. "And the way she bolted . . ." To himself he muttered, "One day I'll find her again. I'll find out what happened."

Now I could have ripped him apart. Would he never learn? Somehow though, I bit my tongue. I don't even know why. Sooner or later someone'd have to tell him to stop being so stupid, so selfish, so suicidal. I just didn't want to be the someone.

"How much did you tell her about us?"

"Nothing. She assumed I was like those street kids. I never told her any different. I didn't want her to connect me with the jail break for instance. Or the Wirrawee Airfield. I thought that'd strain the friendship a bit."

He tried to say it lightly but I'd never seen him so unhappy, not even when he was talking about his parents.

"It's the not knowing, that's the worst thing."

I didn't comment. I didn't touch him either. I think he wanted me to, but I couldn't. I didn't know if I'd ever touch him again.

After a long time he said: "Would it help if I said I was sorry?"

"No."

After an even longer time I said: "Can you go now? I want to get some sleep."

He got up and went out. He hadn't looked at me for ages, and that was fine by me.

EPILOGUE

THERE'S ONLY FIVE OF US, SO HOW CAN RELATIONSHIPS get so complicated? Homer and Fi, Lee and me, and Kevin on his own, now that Corrie's gone. That's how it should have been. That's how it looked at one stage. But life never seems to go according to plan. As I lay on the couch I ended up feeling more sorry for Lee than I did for myself. Later that day I backtracked and decided he didn't deserve any sympathy. The argument raged backwards and forwards inside me. "On the one hand," I'd say to myself, "we weren't actually on together at this exact time in our lives."

It was a funny sort of relationship; it went on pause for long periods of time, but to me it was always there in the background.

But, on the other hand, Lee betrayed more than whatever relationship we might have had. He betrayed us in almost every way possible. He betrayed us in more ways than I could count. We were putting our lives on the line every minute of every day, just to get these people out of our country. So what does Lee do? Get on with one of them. I thought Lee had more brains than most guys but it seemed that when it really counted his brains were in the same place as theirs.

Our relationship became one of embarrassed silences, avoiding each other, being uncomfortable together. That's the worst relationship of all, I reckon. It's the one thing

I've never been able to stand. I like things to be out there, open and direct.

Despite the tension between us, we never told the others what had happened. They gave up asking in the end. I didn't even tell Fi. Homer was actually the most persistent. He couldn't get a word out of Lee so he concentrated on me.

To distract him one day I asked him how he felt about Fi. It sure distracted him. He stopped mid-sentence and gaped at me. "Why . . . why do you ask?" he stammered. "Has she said something?" Then he looked suspicious. "Has Lee said something? Did Lee say something about me?"

I felt a great secret delight when he said that. It could only mean one thing. He had talked to Lee about Fi. And he must have said something about liking her, or he wouldn't have reacted that way. Somehow I kept the smile off my face, but it wasn't easy.

"You still like her, don't you?" I teased him.

Now it was his turn to block the questions. I couldn't get any more from him, but I was convinced Fi needn't give up yet. He had strong feelings about her. I just couldn't figure out what the feelings were.

Physically I eventually got better. I moved upstairs to a bedroom and convalesced there. My ribs were the colours of a Pizza Cappricciosa and they kept aching for a long time. My knee was always going to be a problem, but I'd learnt to live with that. The burn on the side of my face stung and itched and blistered a bit, then it healed. I'd thought I might end up with a scar like Fi's, but I was lucky.

I hated the lying around though. I just naturally like to

get stuck in and do things. I'm not very patient. The only times I enjoyed were when Homer came upstairs and lay on the other bed and we talked about things we could do, attacks we could make, targets to hit.

Perhaps it was because of those conversations that Homer answered Colonel Finley the way he did. We were out in the paddocks one night, about three kilometres from Stratton. All five of us were there, partly to get another lamb, partly just to have a walk, and get away from the dead weight of the city. Stratton was suffocating sometimes: the awful silence, the fear, the knowledge we were living in an enemy environment. The strains between us.

We really shouldn't have still been in Stratton. My injuries kept us there a bit longer, sure, but no one seemed to have the energy or motivation to start the long walk to Hell. It was dumb, because we could never feel as safe in Stratton as we did in Hell. We weren't even safe from our own people — the feral kids were as much a threat as the soldiers, and none of us had made another move to help them.

On this night Homer, unbeknown to all of us, brought the radio. We had a new system now when we caught a lamb. While Homer and I killed, skinned and gutted it, and then cut it up, Lee, Kevin and Fi would dig a hole and light a fire. When it was down to coals we wrapped the bits of lamb in wet paper. We did the same with the vegetables we'd brought. If we couldn't find any other paper we used old newspaper, although it made the food taste a bit funny.

Then we covered the pit and went back to Stratton. The next night we came out again and dug it up. It was a great system. We didn't need any special tools, the food never got overcooked, and it was safer than any other method we'd tried. The fire in the pit was invisible from a distance, because it was below ground level, and once we'd covered it there was no sign of it. Plus the flies couldn't get in.

The only problem came one time when we couldn't find the pit again. We had to prod around in the ground with sticks, each of us certain we knew where it was, each of us telling the others they were looking in the wrong places. Kevin eventually found it.

This particular night, after we'd buried the food we were lying around trying to find the energy to go back to town. And Homer pulled out the radio. "Thought we should have another go," he explained. "We've given it a good break now. Time to try again."

No one said anything. We were all too surprised, I think. We watched as he pulled up the aerial. Then he began the ritual of making the call.

It was obvious from the start that things were different. There was none of the whistling or buzzing or weird stuff we'd heard the other times, just normal static. We sat up and took more interest.

And within a few minutes there was an answer. A woman's voice, with her unmistakable New Zealand accent, responding with "Lomu." She knew who we were, which was always reassuring: that we hadn't been completely forgotten.

"Colonel Finley's orders are that he be woken at any time if we make contact with you," she said. "Do you want to go off the air for fifteen, then call me again? Over."

We sat grinning at each other. I felt very warm, and it

wasn't from my burnt face. It made us feel important, having Colonel Finley woken up to talk to us.

When Homer called back we got the Colonel. It was nice to hear him again. He absolutely raved about the Wirrawee Airfield. He didn't mention it by name — it was safer not to — but he said it was one of the defining moments of the war, that it had come at the perfect time, that we'd be recognised "in the appropriate way" when we got back to New Zealand. Even when he was raving he talked in a formal military way. But it was wonderful to hear it. We thought we'd done all right, but we hadn't been sure what it all meant.

Then, out of the blue, came the offer none of us expected. Colonel Finley was going on in his usual dry way, never changing tone even when he was excited. But suddenly I realised where he was heading. ". . . and that's freed us up a little in some of those critical areas like transportation. Even civilian transportation, and strictly speaking you still come under that classification. Over."

I grabbed Homer's arm and leaned over to ask him the question. "Are you saying what I think you're saying? Over."

He confirmed it. "I'm saying we feel we can probably bring you home. Over."

I stared at the others, in shock. They looked at me, at Homer. No one spoke for what seemed like half an hour. The only sound was the busy static of the radio. I thought of my parents and realised what my answer had to be. Then Lee said, very quietly: "There's still heaps to do."

Homer nodded, like it was the answer he wanted. Kevin stirred, as if to say something, then stopped again, and sat leaning forward, gazing anxiously at Homer like a little kid. Fi put her hand to her face. She looked at Homer too for a moment, then looked away at the dark paddocks.

Homer cleared his throat and spoke. As he did, the words seemed to hang in the air as though they were engraved there. Like they were written in rock.

"We're home already."

ABOUT THE AUTHOR

John Marsden is the author of many acclaimed international bestsellers, including *Letters from the Inside* and *Winter*. He has won numerous awards, including the Christopher Medal and Australia's Children's Book of the Year Award. The first book in the Tomorrow Series, *Tomorrow, When the War Began,* was named an ALA Best Book of the last half-century. He lives in Australia. Visit him online at www.johnmarsden.com.